KNOWING IS NOT ENOUGH

Patricia Walker Chatman

Knowing Is Not Enough
© 2012 by Patricia A. Walker Chatman
www.patriciachatman.com

Published By

Walker Chatman Publishing

Scripture taken from The Student Bible, New International Version®
Copyright © 1986, 1992, 1996 by The Zondervan Corporation
All rights reserved

This book is a work of fiction. Names, characters, places and incidents are the product of the author's imagination or are used fictitiously. Any resemblance to actual events, locales, or persons, living or dead is coincidental.

Library of Congress Control Number:
ISBN 978-0988622708
Printed in the United States of America

To Bryce . . . From your first cry, I heard a song. Everything is for you. I love you.

Search me, O God, and know my heart,
test me and know my anxious thoughts.
See if there is any offensive way in me,
and lead me in the way everlasting.

Psalm 139: 23

What does it mean to be blessed . . . it means you have the following people in your life . . .

Henry and Virgie Walker
Charlynn Walker
Henry and Jeanette Walker
Jomo and Kuda Walker
Kevin and Sherie Shank
Sharon Gordon
Sherrhonda Denice
Regina Reed
Rotesa Baker
Lisa Hokes
Nicole Spencer
Nicole Jones
and Blu

Your patience, guidance, support, dedication and LOVE have allowed me to live out loud in a place where dreams come true . . . thank you.

The Hapkido Philosophy has a theory about water. They believe that water provides clarity of thought and purpose. Water gives you clearness of mind, intentions, and motivation. It is inspirational. Water can take the shape of whatever holds it. Water is powerful, unstoppable and it doesn't resist any object in front of it. Despite what lies in water's path, water always finds a way. Much like the Hapkido Philosophy, I have a theory about love. Love can take the shape of whoever holds it. Love has its own path. It is relentless, unyielding only adhering to its own set of rules. Love is powerful, unstoppable and it doesn't resist any object or person in front of it. Love can provide clarity of mind, purify intention, and it is the source of endless motivation.

Love finds a way.

Great Britain Hapkido Association (1971)
Hapkido Philosophy
Water Theory(Yu)

Prologue

Happily-ever-after ended sooner than I'd expected.

Women are the only people who can find truth in a lie. Especially when it comes to the men in our lives. I conned myself into believing our lies were true. To the outside world we had the perfect marriage, but all houses look good from the curb. Our marriage, not unlike any other, lived amid accusations and disappointments. Then it hits you, somewhere between washing dishes and folding clothes—*is this all there is for me?*

I didn't know the answer to that. Wish I did. What I did know was happiness would never exist for me in this union.

It was time. Neither one of us would get what we needed to stay in this marriage from words alone. I didn't have the passion or the energy to do anything about us. Not anymore. It was time to let go of the lie and embrace reality. I was writing Jake out of my story. Now all there was left to do was tell him.

I invited him back to our, soon to be my house. I sat down at the kitchen table, reflecting about how we'd argued over which table to buy; ultimately I won. Dressed in a suit I'd picked out for his birthday, Jake pulled out a chair and joined me.

I examined his eyes in search of the love I knew a century ago. Initially, separating for a while seemed to be a good idea. Looking at him, I'm not so sure anymore. He appeared to be a new person, different, from the man I'd known. We both have lived six months of life apart. Considering all he achieved with other women living in the same house, I could only imagine what or whom he'd gotten into without me. Starting over would mean getting to know *this* man, accept *his* lies, and his mistakes. I had absolutely no desire to do that.

I started things off. "Our lives are such a mess. Let's just get this over with."

"I'm not going to argue with you. I know it's a mess, but I don't think divorce is the answer. You need to try to forgive me."

"For what?" I got up and poured myself a cup of coffee. "Why would I do that with someone who doesn't love me?" I returned to my seat next to him.

He frowned. "You misinterpreted what I said. I didn't mean I don't love you at all."

"I'm confused. Exactly what does *not love you* mean? You either love me or you don't, and you clearly said you didn't." I took a sip. "Am I missing something?"

Jake made a dismissive gesture with his hand. "I only meant the romantic love I felt for you is gone, not that I don't love you. Of course I love you."

"Do you see," I waved my finger, "that those kind of statements only make sense to anybody with a penis? I love you enough to live in the same house with you, but not enough to touch you?"

"Don't twist my words Alex. I think marriage counseling could help us find what's missing."

I quickly lost patience with him. "Okay—again, maybe it's me, what exactly did we lose? Considering you never stopped dating." I threw my hands up in exasperation. "I'm so tired of us. You can't misplace what we never had."

"So you don't even want to try?"

I didn't meet his eyes. "Jake—you cheated on me days before our wedding. These wounds aren't healing anymore. I'm carrying them and it's causing permanent mental damage now. I can't keep doing this—I won't."

He wasn't giving up. "Alex, just think about it. I don't want to go through with this, but if it's what you want me to do—I'll sign the papers to file right now."

I stood up and walked out of the kitchen.

"Where are you going?"

"To get a pen."

Chapter One

Reflecting over the last seven years of our marriage, I've realized a few things. Jake and I were irrevocably broken. We had so many pretenses in our lives. I've replayed all of the starts and stops we made along the way. Each disagreement took us further away from each other.

This made me wonder if it is the journey or the destination that makes the inevitable outcome more heartbreaking.

I've rerun each infidelity and infectious argument in my head, trying to figure out what I could have done different. Other than the obvious, I had nothing. Maybe I should have tuned into the Lifetime channel. Our problems were portrayed there every couple of hours.

On an unusually slow day in my office, I was catching up on paperwork when she called. Karen, my friend and administrative assistant, was out, leaving me to answer the phones.

I hadn't spoken to my friend Liz in years. I was more than surprised to hear her voice. The conversation began casually enough, two old acquaintances reminiscing about our days working side by side in the hospital. Liz congratulated me on opening up my business and asked a few questions about nothing in particular. We caught each other up, but as fascinating as self-employment could be, I sensed that wasn't the reason she called me.

Finally she got to the point. "How is Jake doing?" Liz asked.

"Oh," I said, surprised she'd asked, "he's good." I sighed. "He started a business too, you know."

"No, I didn't. What's he doing?"

"Well, he's not doing it anymore. He had some of those hot-dog vending carts, sort of like what you see in New York."

Liz was surprised, "I thought Jake was a graphic designer."

"He used to be . . . well he is, that's what he's back to doing now, but he had hot-dog carts. You didn't see them outside the hospital?" I asked. Liz, silent, seemed to think about it for a minute, "Oh, my God. Those were Jake's?"

"Yes—they were all his."

"I never knew that. Why didn't we ever see him out there? It was always some young guy running it. I never saw Jake."

"Well," I sighed, "we had a lot going on at the time. It was hard for him to get out there, but the team helped him out."

"Okay," Liz said. "That's so funny: everybody wondered what happened to the guy. There one minute and gone the next. So Jake laid the people off?"

"Yeah, he didn't have a choice. Actually, if I'm not mistaken, I think the guy who worked at the cart outside the hospital works in the cafeteria now."

"Huh—all right," she said and paused. "The only reason I asked about Jake is because I saw him Friday."

"You saw Jake?" I was confused. "You couldn't have—he's out of town, won't be back until tomorrow."

"No," Liz said, "I'm pretty sure it was Jake."

"I don't think so, Liz, maybe somebody who looked like Jake."

She insisted, "Alex, I'm sorry, but I know Jake when I see him. There isn't that many men out there that look like Jake. The man I saw Friday with this tall woman was Jake."

Tall woman. "What did she look like?"

Liz hesitated for a minute, "She was pretty."

"But what did she look like, Liz?" I asked, not that I needed a description. I knew in my heart who she was talking about.

"I don't know Alex, she was tall—"

"Okay—she's tall, what else? Did she have short curly hair?" Fearing each response, I needed to know.

"I'm trying to think of who she looks like, but yes—short and curly—really light eyes. I wasn't that close to her, I really couldn't say what color but they were light. I focused on him not her. I knew she wasn't you, but—"

My pounding heart rang in my ears. "Okay, I think I know who he was with."

"I'm sorry, Alex," Liz offered. "I thought you should know."

"No, no—it's not your fault," I said. I didn't want to be short, but I literally hadn't talked to Liz in forever and out of the blue she calls me and outs my husband as an adulterer. "Did you see anything else?"

Sorrowful, she said, "No, not really."

I could hear it in her voice that wasn't true, "Liz, I can tell there's something more—please tell me. You know if I ask Jake he's not going to tell me the truth. You called me . . . tell me, what did you see?" I pleaded.

Liz hesitated, "Well—I did see them kiss—I think." Her words wrapped around my heart, squeezing every vessel bleeding inside out.

My voice cracked, "Are you sure?"

"I'm sorry, Alex. I debated whether I should call and tell you. Now I'm thinking it wasn't such a good idea after all."

There were tears streaming down my face. I ignored them. "Did you talk to him?"

"No, I stayed at my table until I saw him at the valet service."

I could feel my stomach tightening. "Did he recognize you?"

"No, I don't think so. I'm sorry Alex, I didn't want—"

"That's okay Liz, I understand. Did you see anything else?"

"Not that I recall." She paused. "Oh, wait, I saw your friend there too."

"Who? Tobey?" I responded.

"No . . . the guy, Sanford."

I grabbed a few tissues to dry my eyes. Each answer lent itself to more questions. Not all of them for Liz. I wasn't prepared in the slightest to hear that Jake lied to me about being out of town, and on top of it that he might be having yet another affair. I'd sensed something might have been going on between Jake and Taylor, but not this. I thought he was attracted to her. If I needed confirmation of anything above flirtation, Liz gifted me that.

I heard Karen enter the office. She popped her head in to announce her return just as I hung up the phone. Right about the time the tears were starting to fall yet again. Karen, apparently surprised to see me so emotional, asked what happened.

"Nothing happened," I said.

Karen seemed worried. "Then why are you crying?" she asked.

I shook my head. "I'm sorry Karen, that's not true—something did happen. I'm just finding out."

She grabbed more tissues from the box on my desk and handed them to me. "Alex, tell me what's going on."

I took them and wiped my eyes, "Liz—you remember Liz?"

Karen tried to soothe me by rubbing my back. "No, not really, who is she?"

"An old friend from the hospital, she was at my wedding. You probably wouldn't remember her." I was talking through my sobs.

"Liz? Is that who you just hung up with? What about her?"

"Yeah well, she saw Jake and Taylor at dinner Friday."

Karen looked confused. "They work together—that's not a big deal."

I pulled the tissue away from my eyes. "Karen," I said, "think."

Karen seemed to realize the implication. "What? I thought you said Jake was out of town?"

"I did—I thought he was, but according to her he's right here in town."

Karen looked shaken, "Is she sure?"

I blew my nose, "Yes Karen she's sure."

"Do you believe her?"

"Why would she call and lie about something like that? I haven't talked to her in six years."

"Exactly," Karen exclaimed. "Why would she call you out of the blue and tell you something like that?"

I continued to cry, "I don't know. Does it matter?"

Visibly confused, Karen said, "I'm sure it doesn't—what are you going to do? Confront him?"

I drew in a very shaky breath. "I know what Liz said, but I would think before I accuse him of anything. I need more than her word." I pulled the last tissue out of the box. My eyes were burning. I grabbed a mirror from my desk drawer, both eyes red and swollen. "I look a mess," I said.

"That's the least of your worries. What are you going to do?"

"I don't know maybe there's something at home that will tell me where he's staying."

"Then what?"

"I don't know. It's not like this has happened before."

"So, you're about to go home and look for a clue or something."

"Maybe," I said, suddenly unsure of the right thing to do. "I think that's the plan. I don't know what else to do." I took a deep breath and exhaled. "Just the thought of him being with her infuriates me."

Karen asked, "You sure you don't want to call your sister to go with you?"

"No, I'll go—maybe I can go online, check his phone records or something. I don't know this is crazy. I'm so pissed off."

"When is he supposed to be back? I mean, when is he supposed to *fake* being back?"

Holding back more tears, I said, "Tomorrow. His *fake* plane is supposed to land tomorrow," I smiled mirthlessly. "I would say you have to laugh to keep from crying, but that wouldn't exactly be accurate right now."

Karen went to her desk to get more tissue while I grabbed my keys and purse. "I'll be back before my next appointment gets here."

"Okay," she said, holding a box of tissue. "Be careful."

"I will. It's not like he's there." *Or so I think . . .*

On the drive home, fueled by my conversation with Liz, I drifted in and out daydreaming of Taylor and Jake kissing. I parked on the street. Having no recollection of how I got there to conduct the shortest investigation in history. Jake's car was parked down the street from our house. *Why would he lie about being out of town then come back to the house? Maybe he forgot something. He would have to know I'd figure out somebody was in the house? Or, perhaps thought I was just that stupid!* The noise on the street drowned out the sound of anyone entering or leaving our house, I counted on that to be the case. Undetected by Jake, I entered the house. Unbeknownst to me, he wasn't alone. My foot hit the sixth or seventh stair that's when I heard it. Granted a long time ago, but I remember what *it* sounded like. Quietly, I crept up a few more steps. Faint at first, clearer at the top definite down the hall a rhythmic purr of a woman being made love too became painfully clear. Lifting my heart with my feet made it hard to move. I didn't want Jake to have the luxury of deniability, not about this. I needed to see him. As painful as the journey up the steps had been, I pushed down my internal anguish. Steadfast, inching down the hall past our bedroom, engulfed in their passion. Neither heard me outside the guest room door. Blinded by tears, aching at the sight of their naked bodies lyrically intertwined, unnoticed, I turned away, backed down the hallway toward the stairs leaving as quietly as I entered. At the foot of the stairs, I contemplated all sorts of thoughts, but when you've had as much drama as I, you become numb to it all. Another crushing scene was not going to change what I'd seen or known all along.

Knowledge is a blessing and a curse. In my car, I cried and contemplated what exactly was supposed to come next. If it was just the cheating that would be one thing, but it's the judgmental eyes of your family and friends when the decision you make is contrary to the one they would make for you. This was not my first time at the rodeo, but it doesn't make it any less painful or difficult to bear.

There was no way I could return to work. I called Karen and asked her to reschedule my appointment. Then considered my next move, obviously I couldn't go back inside. Jake knew my normal pattern of behavior. I shouldn't be home till seven o'clock. It was only a little after three. A nearby park afforded me the solitude I needed to think, cry, and contemplate what I wanted.

As time ticked away, I realized it was ridiculous to figure all this out in my car, so I decided to let the humiliation of the day pour out of me. I didn't want to plan anymore, I just wanted to cry and get it all out. If, and that was a big if, I confronted Jake I wanted my words soiled with anger not tears. Whatever the manner of our confrontation, life as I knew it was over. Be it not for this, I probably would have remained unhappily married. I didn't dare allow myself the dream of living another life, one that didn't include Jake. If I had, Jake and I would've been over a long time ago. I have given unhappy seven years and then some. That's long enough. I intended to make the mental transition away from him. The rest, well, that's just geography.

Chapter Two

From my line of sight, just above the steering wheel, the reticent brilliance of the sun began to set. It would be nightfall soon, signifying my time to commence the drive home. I raised my seat then leaned forward, gripping the steering wheel with both hands to rest my head upon. The display of my cell phone was visible from the passenger seat. A missed call showed up on the screen, presumably from Karen.

I closed my lids, rolling my eyes inside, took in a deep breath to fill my lungs and exhaled. The release felt soothing. It helped, if only a little, to ease the pressure in my head and heart. I picked up my cell phone and contemplated for a split second returning Karen's call. *Not yet.* I placed the phone back on the car seat where it originally lay.

I drove home, accompanied by the slideshow that played over and over inside my head. I parked directly in front of our house. I felt safe at a distance looking on from the curb. Watching the front porch, I mulled over getting out the car or driving away, back to the peaceful mind-numbing tranquility of the park. Jake's car wasn't down the street anymore. My mind, once again, flashed glimpses of them in bed.

I sat hoping as time passed those reoccurring pictures wouldn't continue to appear, but it was too soon to hope and sitting in the car wasn't going to make my obsessive thoughts or heartache go away. I needed to go inside sometime, and there was no time like the present. I exited the car, walked up the porch stairs, opened the front door and entered.

Inside the foyer, I closed the door, clinching the knob from behind me. The house looked and smelled uninterrupted. No outward signs of the day's betrayal. I checked the kitchen, office, and downstairs bathroom, searching for clues of unwelcomed guests. There wasn't anything, not even a glass in the sink, which made me wonder how many times they'd been inside the house without my knowledge. Jake was getting better at this. He'd learned to pick up after himself.

I made it up the stairs to what would become an oversized closet. I surveyed the bedroom from the doorway until I'd mustered up the courage to put my head in. The room smelled of peaches from way too much air freshener.

I pulled back the comforter from the bed. *Huh—new sheets.* Well, that's a slip-up. Surely I'd notice this. Maybe that's my silver lining—*my freedom and linen.* I rarely went into the guest room: now I'd do it even less. I exited and closed the door behind me. If I had yellow caution tape I would have put that up too.

Safely seated in my room on the edge of the bed, I contemplated the present and the past. Jake would be home tomorrow night—unless he extended his stay, wherever that is. My shoes were still on with my purse and phone in hand from when I'd entered the house. I wasn't moving any further than my bedroom. I didn't have the mental or physical energy to do any more than lying down. I took off everything but my underwear and laid the clothes on Jake's side of the bed.

The next day started much differently than I'd imagined.

I awoke to the sound of a man's snoring. Which meant one of two things: either Jake's fake flight landed early or a burglar was in my bed stealing a nap. The alarm clock on the nightstand was positioned away from immediate view so I had no idea of the time. Without disturbing the person next to me, I cracked open my eyes to see 11:00 a.m. displayed in red. I've never slept this late, time to figure out if I should be scared or angry. My body remained still. Moving only my head, I turned to face the invader. *If only I could be so lucky.* It's Jake and my arousal awakened him. He faced me eyes wide open. "Good morning," he said. "I'm surprised you're not at work."

Jake reached over to rub my back. Avoiding his hand, I rolled out of bed, landing on my feet. "What's the matter with you?" he asked.

I surprised myself at how instinctively I got out of the path of his touch, "Nothing's the matter. What time did you get home?"

Jake rose up in bed, fully dressed. "Around seven o'clock."

"Oh—I didn't hear you come in."

"You were knocked out," he said.

18

Realizing I only had on panties and bra, I reached over for a blanket to cover my body. Jake seemed taken by surprise. "What are you doing?"

Fixing the blanket to cover all the important parts I said, "Nothing, just covering up. I forgot I didn't put on my pajamas."

"Since when do you care about that?"

I fanned his words off with my free hand. "Since now."

Jake shook his head. "So, what are you doing today? Why did you stay home?"

The blanket dragged the floor behind me as I walked to the closet to put something on. Jake, sitting up, leaned against the headboard his eyes following me to the closet. "No reason, I'm staying home today."

"What for?"

"I need a reason to stay home?" I asked.

"You usually have one." *That's true I usually do.* I found a robe in the back of my closet, a gift from Jake's mother. Thank goodness I still had it. Being exposed in front of Jake in any way made me feel vulnerable. My emotions were raw enough with clothes on. I responded back to him, "You're right I usually do."

"So, what's the reason?" he said.

"I wanted to talk to you."

Jake examined my face. He looked confused. "Oh boy, this can't be good. What you want to talk to me about?" He got up and looked out the bedroom window.

"How was the conference?"

"The conference?" he echoed.

"Yes, Jake," I said. "The conference—how was it?"

With a puzzled look, he said, "You've never cared about my conferences before."

"You're right I didn't. I probably wouldn't care now if I didn't know you weren't actually at the conference," I snarled.

Jake stood up to face me. "Let me explain," he said.

I folded my arms, shifting my weight in anguish. "What do you need to explain, Jake?"

He took a breath. "Whatever you think you know, it isn't true."

"What do I think I know, Jake?"

Jake said firmly, "Whatever your friends told you."

"Well, let's talk about that for a minute, because my friends didn't tell me anything."

"Good, because there's nothing to tell." Jake stepped into my physical space. I circled around him and walked toward the bedroom door. At a comfortable distance, I asked, "How's Taylor doing? Did she enjoy the conference?"

"How should I know, Alex? I haven't seen Taylor."

Lie Number One. I walked back to Jake and looked him in the eyes, "Well, based on what I heard from the hallway, and saw in the guest room, I would say she *really* enjoyed the conference. You and I haven't had a *conference* like that in months."

"I . . ."

My words fell flat. "Don't bother, Jake, there's nothing you can say."

Jake sat back on the bed, apparently searching for words. "Alex, I'm sorry—I'm so sorry. I swear to you that was the only time." His eyes filled with tears. "You have to believe me."

I pulled a chair over from the corner of the room. "You mean with her. Yesterday I was ready to start our dance again, but I'm all cried out. If she wants you—she can have you. All I want is to be free of you." I got out of my chair and knelt in front of him. "I don't want to know anything. I want you to take whatever you need and leave. Permanently, this time."

Jake looked down at me and whispered, "You got to give me a chance to explain."

My eyes welled up with tears. "Jake, you brought her to my house—made love to her. It's unforgivable."

"I know—I know what I did is outside of the limits of wrong, but you're not even letting me explain—"

"Jake, how can you explain what I saw? What I've been putting up with the last seven years? Please understand, this isn't anger—its exhaustion."

Jake searched my face for a sign of hope. There wasn't one. After a long silence, he said, "I'll call my mother and see if I can move in with her for a while until we sort this out." He rubbed his hands across his face to wipe the sweat off his brow, and I saw tears spilling from his eyes.

Drained of all my senses I stood up. Jake reached out and inserted his hands inside mine, then pulled me down beside him. We sat silent for a few minutes. "It won't be for a while, Jake," I finally said. I felt rampant emotions beneath my calm exterior. I wanted to hate him. Hatred would be an easier emotion to express. My stomach was in a knot. What emotions I couldn't unravel or deal with I cut out. Normally, it would have killed me to see him cry, but as much as I loved Jake—I loved myself more.

Jake raised his head and asked, "What does that mean, Alex?"

"I'm not a perfect person and we are far from a perfect couple. I don't know how I am going to live with what I saw, let alone live with you. This is it for me."

"You got to know, the sex meant nothing and it's done . . . over. It was over before it even started," he said.

I shook my head. "It doesn't matter, Jake."

He went on. "I love you. Please don't do this."

His voice scratched my heart. It felt like teeny paper cuts on my nerve endings. "Jake, you have to go. If I could have told you last night I would have—I don't want you here."

He didn't answer.

"Call your mom," I said.

"I don't want to call my mom, Alex. I love you, please—just slow down. We can fix this."

I snapped, "Why do you love me? Because, I'm convinced you never even liked me. So, why—why do you love me?"

Jake blankly stared back at me. "Why do I love you?"

"It's an easy question Jake—why?" I paused. "Just tell me why?"

Jake looked around the room as if he searching for the right words. I didn't want to give him any more time to come up with the wrong ones.

Finally I broke the silence. "It's okay, Jake. I didn't really think you would be able to tell me. Please call your mother and explain it to her—she'll understand."

Jake picked up his cell phone and called his mother. I walked out the room, closed the door behind me to allow him time to talk with his mother and work it out. Downstairs, I made myself a cup of coffee and waited. Jake entered the kitchen with the same overnight bag with which he'd returned home.

Over the years our families had grown close. Knowledge of yet another affair had to remain between us. Friends might be aware of my suspicions, but I would never validate them. Jake, yet again, pleaded to stay and fix our broken marriage. He was willing to do anything to make it work. I knew he meant it, but it'd been less than twenty-four hours: I wasn't being impulsive. Jake was seated right in front of me, and while it sounds like a cliché, the reality was I couldn't see him. Jake's eyes reflected my inner torment.

Seven years of my life fighting for this marriage: gone.

Chapter Three

We should reverse the order of things. Marriages should be held in a courthouse, and divorces should be in a church.

Meeting in front of a judge for the dissolution of a marriage is one of the most depressing things I've ever done. The courthouse itself made the proceedings more miserable than they already were. Linda and I arrived at nine o'clock, walked up to the entrance, and waited under a wide awning with everyone else.

The morning air was clear and crisp. The fresh smells reminding me of mama's line dried sheets. A nice memory to hold onto before what came next. Security, positioned to our immediate right, stood guard as we entered the building.

Linda and I emptied our pockets into the plastic bins. Kenneth, my attorney, pre-advised us not to bring in cell phones, others were not, which resulted in us moving through the security checkpoint faster. I wondered if the heightened degree of security was to prevent us from bringing anything in or keep someone from getting out.

Kenneth greeted us outside Courtroom A. Until then, I'd never been inside a courtroom, and it was surprisingly busy and not as *civil* as one would expect. The American flag was on one side and the Michigan seal proudly displayed above the judge's head. Every available space inside and outside the courtroom was taken.

I'd have preferred no one heard us arguing about a kitchen table. I had the uncanny ability to recall every argument we'd had over furniture and who gave us what gift. *That's what sums up divorce. It's not that you want the stuff. You just don't want the other person to have it.* And you question the other's motivation in wanting it…is it to spite you? Or do you really love that vase my mother gave us?

Linda, Kenneth and I sat a few rows from the back pew. I leaned over, turned my head, and whispered into Linda's ear, "I'm ready to get this over with."

Linda, fixated on the theatrics playing out before us with the current case, said, "Oh yeah, lots of angry people in here."

From the corner of my eye, through a sea of heads, I spotted Jake with his attorney. Jake's head was slightly bent, nodding at whatever his attorney whispered in his ear. I leaned my shoulders back in my seat trying to figure out what his attorney said, but I couldn't see his lips only Jake's frequent nodding and seldom glances up at his attorney.

Linda turned her head to face me, "What are you looking at?"

"Jake and his attorney," I answered. Linda turned her head. "No, don't look," I spoke through my teeth.

She turned her head back facing forward, "All right. So what do they look like they're talking about?"

"Beats me, I can only see Jake."

"They're probably not talking about anything. Lean forward before he sees you."

I took her advice and rose back to my original position. Kenneth read legal papers. At the risk of violating confidentiality, I glanced down. They didn't appear to be mine. "Kenneth, should we be talking about anything?"

He said we didn't and reassured me this was only a formality.

The wedding took hours and the divorce took minutes. *"What — therefore — God has joined together — let no man put asunder."*

A man in a black robe behind an awkwardly high bench did exactly that.

Jake and I were officially no longer married. Linda wanted to talk to Jake to check on him. I didn't need to know his emotional status. I wanted to leave. *Knowing is not enough.*

Linda needed to do what she believed to be the right thing. Despite my need to get out of there as fast as possible, Linda asked if I would mind if she went over to him. I did mind, but my caring ended up immaterial, Linda didn't have the script I was acting from. *I wonder if she would be so nice to him if she knew about the affair. Well, the latest affair.* "Go ahead," I said. "I'll wait in the car." I wanted no part in the rolling credits: Jake was officially history.

It didn't take Linda long to catch up with me. As it turned out, a change of scenery was all I'd needed. The coffee shop in the lobby did the trick in the short run. Still in the courthouse, but out of the courtroom. We were getting closer to leaving. Linda caught up with me there. "Don't sit . . . let's go," I told her.

Out of curiosity I wanted to know what Jake said to her.

"Not much," Linda said. "Jake's upset over the whole thing."

"Everything isn't always what it appears to be Linda. He'll be all right."

"How do you know that, Alex? He's hurting, just like you.'"

"Linda, I'm concerned about me right now. You're supposed to be here supporting me."

"I *am* supporting you, but I can't help but feel bad for Jake. You didn't want to try counseling? Maybe it could have helped you work it out."

"Okay, Linda, did you miss the whole courthouse thing? We're divorced now. I hardly think it matters. But to answer your question, no, I know it doesn't make sense to you, but it's not that simple–we couldn't work it out."

"You just seem so calm to me. What are you feeling?" she asked.

"I don't' know what I'm feeling."

"You should have tried the counseling," she persisted. "Jake wanted to try."

"Why don't you and Jake go to counseling? I just want to go home."

"All right, smart ass, but let's get something to eat first. Are you hungry?"

"Not really, but I can sit with you if you want."

"All right, I'll take you home."

I shook my head. "No, that's okay, we can go. I need to call Tobey and let her know what's up, though."

"Okay, call her while I get the car."

"Don't pull around. I can walk with you. The lot's not that far."

I started with Tobey. She had fifty million questions that I wasn't up to answering. "It went as well as could be expected," I said. Tobey sensing I wasn't in the mood to talk cut the conversation short. I wasn't in the mood to go to eat, either. I shouldn't have said I would go.

Linda talked nonstop as we drove. I didn't know what she was talking about. I think she believed she was taking my mind off things—it actually made me feel worse. The only saving grace was they actually had tables available when normally there's a wait. Breakfast was no different: she kept talking and talking. The hostess grabbed two menus and escorted us to a booth in the back of the restaurant. From my window seat I had a clear view of the street outside. I was unbelievably thirsty. The server brought over two glasses of water while Linda and I perused the menus. Normally, a picture of eggs, pancakes, and waffles would make my mouth water. Today, I felt nauseated at the sight of it. I put my menu down when the server returned, "Just coffee for me," I said.

"I'll have the breakfast sampler, wheat toast with mixed fruit jelly."

The server retrieved both our menus and returned with a cup of coffee and creamer.

Sanford knew today was D-day. I thought he would've called me. I poured creamer in my coffee and grabbed a few sugar packets, "I forgot to call Sanford." I told Linda. "Did you hear from him?"

"No, he didn't call me," she responded.

"That's strange, right?" I opened the sugar and poured it in my coffee, grabbed a spoon and stirred.

"He probably waited for you to call him," she said comfortingly. "You'll talk later."

Taking a sip of coffee I shrugged. She's probably right . . . we would talk later. I just thought it was kind of odd that he hadn't called me by now.

Linda's breakfast arrived at the table. She spread jelly on her toast and between chews and swallows continued chattering about everything from the kids to Jake for the next thirty minutes. The noise made me think too much. Two cups of coffee later I was all caught up on the kids' soccer games and dance, along with the error of my inability to reconcile with Jake. Finally, Linda was done eating, time to head home. "Let's get outta here," I told her.

"Okay, we don't have to stay. We can talk more in the car."

Talk more? "Linda, I'm so tired. I just want to go home."

She seemed unperturbed. "Okay, I'm taking you home."

"I'm just not feeling up to talking anymore."

"I'm talking. You're listening. Are you sure you don't want me to stay with you?"

"Linda, you're killing me. I'm sure. Please—just drop me off."

I barely managed a wave bye to her. It felt so good to be in what was officially my house. No Jake anymore. Jake moved out a long time ago, but it felt like he'd just left. I felt that hurdle should have been conquered by now. The images in my mind of Jake and Taylor were fading.

My thoughts were clear. I'm going to put on my pajamas, climb into bed and pull the cover over my head, and I'm never coming out.

Chapter Four

Along with the mental and physical deportation of Jake, I shut out all the external noise filling my head concerning him. This meant no more incessant thinking about him and unrelenting conversations featuring him. I desperately needed a timeout, distancing myself from friends and family, no returning calls to well intentioned, but inquisitive friends, declining party invitations and happy hour with the girls, and stopping all posts to Facebook.

All except for Sanford, I wanted to talk to him. Although disappointed, I accepted acquaintances whys and lies for not telling what they heard or saw regarding Jake and Taylor. Sanford, that's a different story. We were friends—I trusted him. I wanted to know why he didn't tell me what he witnessed. I didn't necessarily need to agree with his reason. Perhaps I just wanted to understand.

Sanford and I had a long history. We met in 1995, my sophomore year in college. Carla, my roommate, and I walked across campus to what Greeks hyped up to be the party of the year. The fraternity house would've been an enviable residence if it were located anywhere else. On campus, the most popular social gathering place, stocked to the rafters with liquor, boys, and of course girls . . . lots of girls. We could hear the music thumping a quarter mile from the house. Campus police had already made a preemptive strike to ensure the party didn't overflow on the main campus. The plantation style mansion wrap around porch filled with overly spirited party goers' uncharacteristically relaxed swaggers, dangling from the balcony railings, cuddling on the porch swings and cups filled with liquor. Carla and I took in all the sights outside, spoke to a few party goers before navigating our way up the steps, through the grand entrance where we were greeted by a crowd of boys proudly displaying their fraternity hype. Neither one of us possessed boyfriends, so a group of cute boys was a welcome reception.

Standing under the archway to the smoke filled living room we scanned the area in search of our friends. In a field of infamous campus stallions it was going to be tricky to find a unicorn. House was the music of choice and every dorm was represented, including fraternities from other universities. We made our way through the living room familiarizing ourselves with the lay of the land: living room is for sitting and talking, dining room for dancing, and the bathrooms were down the hall. Searching for a seat we joined in with another group of girls standing, eagerly awaiting someone to vacate their seat. I nudged Carla with my elbow,

"Do you see that guy with all that food?" Carla moved her body to and fro. Through the sea of Greeks she spotted a guy eating what appeared to be a mountain of food. "Oh my God! Is he going to eat all that?" Carla shouted above the music.

"I don't know," I giggled. "He has it on his plate . . . what else would he do with it?"

"Wow, that's all I can say is . . . wow."

"I didn't realize they served food at these things."

"Maybe he brought it with him."

I said, "How tall do you think he is?"

"I really can't tell with him sitting down . . . 6'4 or 5, maybe?"

"At least."

"Probably about three hundred pounds? I'm guessing." Carla faced me, "Give or take."

I continued to stare at him. "Hopefully its take, he could use a little less give."

Carla and I continued to stand in the living room staring at this guy. We locked eyes for a split second. "I've got to stop staring at this guy. He's going to think I like him," I said.

Too late. After devouring his food, he stood up and walked over to me. "Hey."

I looked at him like he'd attacked a small village and eaten all the people. "Hey." I didn't know what to say beyond "*hey*." He was even bigger standing up. The music blared. Everyone headed to the makeshift dance floor in the dining room. He got to me just before it reached capacity.

Leaning into my ear in a soft whisper, he said, "You dance?" I wanted to, but I said, "No."

"But you're dancing now?"

Whoops! I was twisting from side to side, "Yeah, but I really don't want to dance . . . dance. I'm just enjoying listening to the music."

He raised his head, shifted his body to stand directly in front of me. He looked at me "You think one of your girls want to dance?"

"I don't know. You have to ask them."

He turned to my roommate who stood next to me. She also said no. As did all the girls standing in our group. Clearly this guy didn't know the rules of engagement. If you ask one girl in a group to dance and she says no, you're pretty much guaranteed a '*no*' from all the girls standing there. Defeated, he walked away. I watched him as he headed back to the living room. He grabbed another slice of pizza and walked toward the front door.

The only way to describe him would be to say he looked a lot like Grizzly Adams, except he looked more like the bear than the man.

After our brief meeting at the frat house, we met again in the student-learning center. He didn't attend our school . . . only came up for the party. A math exam forced him into the lab in search of a computer.

And I camped there looking for my math tutor.

I didn't want to take Math 102, not one more quarter. The large computer lab, with about twenty-five different systems in it granted students plenty of room to spread out. It was barely anyone in there. I always sat in the back of the lab, that way I could run my computerized math problems, and meet with my tutor.

That day, my tutor didn't show up.

I wasn't there to socialize like other students, I failed math once, and I had no intention of doing it again. I needed to study. Then into the lab walked the guy from the party, standing near the entrance, scanning the room through his thick glasses looking for a seat.

The room was empty. No need to sit next to me. He slowly moved beyond the front door toward my computer.

"Is anybody sitting here?" he asked.

I tried to pretend like I didn't hear him, but he said it again: "Excuse me, is anybody sitting here?"

I turned my head slightly to the left, looked down into the seat next to me, then back up to him, "No."

He took his book bag off his back and placed it next to the chair he intended on sitting in. I remember thinking . . . *this is a big guy. I felt unexplainably nervous.* He must have sensed it. He pulled the chair out to the side just a little before he sat down. Then I felt bad, I didn't want to hurt his feelings. Everything irritated me: my tutor not showing, and the thought of taking math class again. *I shouldn't have even been at that party last night. I needed to study.*

We continued working quietly until he broke the silence. He turned and looked at me. "Weren't you at that party last night?"

"What party?" I knew what party. He knew I did too. *I can't even believe I said that. Why would I say that after the way I looked at him last night, how could he forget me?*

"The party last night?" He wasn't giving up.

I kept looking at my computer screen. "Oh, were you there?" I don't know why I'm being such a bitch. He finally turned his head back toward his computer screen and said, "Oh, all right, never mind, you didn't see me." *Okay, not only am I acting like a bitch, now he thinks I'm a bitch.*

"Oh, yeah, the party last night. You were there too?"

He smiled. "Yeah, I was there. I thought I saw you come into the living room. My name is Sanford by the way."

I finally turned toward him, deciding to have a conversation like a real person. "Yeah, I came into the living room looking for my friends. It's Alex—my name is Alex." *Hopefully he won't bring up asking me to dance. He asked a lot of girls to dance—maybe he won't remember me.*

"Alex, that's a nice name. You go to school here?"

"Yes, sure do—sophomore year," I said. "What about you? I've never seen you on campus."

"Ohio."

"What about it?"

"That's where I go to school."

Sanford told me about his school, the fraternity and how he came up with his fraternity brothers. I'd gotten the feeling that Sanford was *king* of the nerds. We continued to talk. I discovered we both had so much in common. He was also from a big family and didn't have many friends. We both shared a love for music, books, museums and art history. Once I put my bitch in my bag, we connected. He'd been all over campus and contemplated transferring (and in fact he ended up doing so for his junior year to be closer to home).

Trite, but true, what happens in the dark invariably comes to the light, and I'll be damned, Liz would be the one to tell me about seeing Jake and Taylor– and Sanford, in the same restaurant at the same time. He couldn't have missed seeing Jake and Taylor together. *So, why didn't he tell me? It bugged me. I couldn't let it go.*

I decided to set aside my reservations and just ask him. I don't know what I expected him to say or not say. My greatest fear was Sanford adding new information to what Liz told me that would make my peaceful resolution with the divorce short lived. One of the many good things about Sanford is that he doesn't lie. Or perhaps he does. Omission, in my book, is a lie, so I think this qualified as a lie. I'm confident this qualified as one, because it felt like a lie, and I didn't like feeling like I'd been deceived. So, yeah . . . it's time to talk.

I asked Sanford to come over to the house. Sanford loved soul food, so I cooked (okay, I didn't cook, but I bought all his favorite foods): fried chicken, macaroni and cheese, candied yams, dressing, fried corn, collard greens, and chocolate cake, admittedly a lot of food for only two people. I approached this conversation being uncharacteristically deceptive. Since he didn't just tell me, I thought maybe I would have to pull it out of him. I'm upset, but I don't want to argue about this.

Sanford arrived still carrying that God-awful backpack he had since college. He worked as a policy analyst and did a considerable amount of research, so he had tons of books that he carried around with him all the time. I hugged him after he sat his backpack down on the floor, before heading into the kitchen. I grabbed the packs shoulder strap, barely lifting it onto a chair in the foyer.

From inside the kitchen, Sanford said "Still can't take stuff out of place huh?" I walked into the kitchen, and acknowledged his observation with a smile.

"No, that's not it I just don't want to kill myself tripping over all your books. Isn't that bag about twenty years old? What do you have in there, anyway? That thing is heavy as hell."

Sanford sniffed around the stove, systematically picked up pot tops looking to see what simmered inside. He ignored my question. "So what's up, Alex? Why are you cooking dinner for me? You haven't done this since—" Sanford stopped mid-sentence, and looked up at me.

I took a deep breath. "Yes, I'll say it for you: since before Jake left. But, I'm not actually cooking I'm warming. I decided it's time to get some normalcy back in my life." I started setting the dinner table. I wanted to keep the conversation moving. In hindsight I shouldn't have cared: Jake and I were already divorced, but this wasn't about Jake as much as it was about Sanford and my friendship.

"What you got to drink? I'm thirsty."

"I've got some wine if you want some. Just grab a glass from the cabinet."

"So cooking—I mean warming for me is helping you?" Sanford looked amused by this. Sanford reached for a glass, his gesture flashed me back to the last time we were all together in the kitchen, Jake and I, during happier times. I stood there, frozen in a daze before I said for him to get any glass, and he got an actual wine glass. I don't know why I thought he would get a water goblet. Not Sanford, he got a wine glass.

I pulled myself back to the conversation. "Well, to be honest, when Jake first left, continuing to *breathe* meant moving on."

"Breathing, Alex? Isn't that a little dramatic for you?"

"Yes, I'll admit to having a cold hearted snake phase. Doesn't mean I wasn't hurting—and yes, breathing, wanting to re-emerge from it all took some effort."

Sanford shook his head. "That doesn't sound like you."

"Sound like what?" I risked glancing his way, he'd opened the refrigerator to look for a white wine.

"You know, like you let him break you down or something."

"Okay, let's not forget, he used to be my husband. I did love the man."

All I needed to do was put the food on the table and we were ready to get down and eat. Sanford found an unopened bottle of wine, grabbed a corkscrew from a kitchen drawer, and popped the cork. I set the food on the table, retrieved a couple of plates from the kitchen cabinet and utensils while he poured the wine.

"I know. I just never heard you talk like that before. I thought you wanted the divorce."

I completed the table set up. Sanford joined me, pulling out my chair before his own and we both sat down. "Well, I did. But I'm not going to act as if I wanted it like that. I wanted it because I felt he left me no choice. I mean, he was the one who continued dating after we got married, not me."

He smiled, "Well, I guess you got a point there."

We put food on our plates in silence. "So, Sanford— what happened to you at the courthouse?"

He took a first bite of corn and chewed it before answering. "Oh, I wasn't supposed to be at the courthouse was I?"

"No, but I thought we were going to talk."

"I'm sorry, I got caught up and couldn't call, but you know how it is at work."

Not really, I thought. "Liz said she saw you at dinner one night."

"She did?"

"Yup, sure did." I sipped my wine. "So who did you go out with?"

He put down his fork. "Look, no offense, but this is new. I need to keep this one to myself for a minute."

"Okay, that's cool. You don't have to tell me."

"Thank you."

"You're welcome, Sanford, enough said. So other than this mystery person did anything else interesting happen that night?"

We were both talking around our food. Sanford's plate was piled high. He still had issues with his eating. Tonight we weren't counting calories.

"No, just the same old, same old. Why?"

"Well, I heard Jake ate there that night."

Sanford looked down at his plate. "Oh, really?"

"Yeah, really."

"Oh, wow. Was he alone?"

"Actually, I thought you could tell me, since you were there, too." I felt my heart beat faster.

Sanford stopped eating, put his fork down, and raised his head. "Don't do this, Alex, what did you ask me over here for? Why you playing games all of a sudden? If you want to know something ask. If you got something to say spit it out."

I don't know if it's what he said or his tone but I got upset, "Why the hell didn't you tell me you saw Jake with that woman? You knew I invested more time trying to work it out with him. I blamed myself! I can't believe you didn't tell me, what kind of friend does that make you?"

"Your marriage hit the skids long before I saw him at dinner. You're pissed off at yourself, not me." The lack of empathy in his words brought on the water works. Sanford appeared to be a little rattled, but in true to form, not by much.

I grabbed a napkin from the table, still crying, I wiped my nose. I raised my voice. "You're missing the point. I'm having a hard time understanding how you could know everything I'm dealing with, to feel someone slipping away from you and not know why, and you see him with another woman and don't tell me. That's more months of time and energy I would've spent getting my shit in order. But thanks to you, I spent it kissing his ass!"

Sanford pushed his chair away from the table: he'd had enough. He walked toward the foyer to retrieve his book bag. I rose from the table, and followed behind him. Sanford arrived at the door, picked up his backpack, and then swiveled around to face me. He searched my eyes for forgiveness, then extended his hand and wiped away a tear moving slowly down my face. With a note of concern in his voice, he said, "I'm sorry I hurt you Alex, but you have to realize you're not the only person who's got things going on."

I stood there, mounted in place, staring back at him baffled as to what to think, say or do. Then it finally occurred to me—Sanford choosing not tell me wasn't as simple or insensitive as I originally assumed it or him to be.

Sanford opened the front door and walked out.

Chapter Five

It'd been nearly a year since my divorce. I hadn't spoken to Jake or Sanford. Neither of our paths ever crossed, for which I remained thankful. Early Wednesday morning and after a considerable amount of time soul searching, I longed to jump back into the social life I reveled in, before Jake and the divorce. Presuming it still endured without me. A few trepidations swirled in my head about calling my sister and Tobey, considering my unexplained self-imposed exile from all socialization. I hoped, in spite of my lack of candidness, reasoning or warning they would ultimately understand why I needed to take a step back. Maybe—just maybe, Linda and Tobey would be willing to forgive and forget and agree to have dinner with me this Friday.

I called out to Karen seated in the front office. "Can you get Linda on the phone for me?"

A few moments later Karen said, "Linda is on line one for you."

"Thank you, Karen."

I picked up the phone, "Hey, Linda."

There's a trace of laughter in her voice. "Boy, this is a surprise. You're not dying, are you?"

"Ha, ha," I said. "Very funny, and no, I'm not dying, at least not yet. I do want to get out this Friday. You game?"

"Oh good, we're done with the mourning period over Jake."

I relaxed back in my chair, "Yeah, I think I've turned a corner. I just want to get something to eat and listen to some good music. I need to do something other than work every day."

"Okay, I hear you. Who did you invite? Is Sanford coming?"

"Sanford? No, just you . . . so far and Tobey."

A brief pause, "Is that because he wasn't invited?"

I shook my head, then it dawned on me *she couldn't see me through the phone.* "No, we're still not talking, and I don't see that changing, at least not by Friday."

A clear noticeable irritation in Linda's voice. "Okay, so you know this has been going on long enough, right?"

"Yes Linda, of course I know it has."

"Well?"

I said, "Well what?"

"Alex?"

"Linda? Can we just focus on Friday?"

Linda, silent, discharged an exasperated groan through the receiver evidencing her struggle to pursue the subject or let it go. Ultimately she regained her calm resolve. "Yeah, count me in."

I felt relieved she conceded and moved off the subject of Sanford. "Okay, good. You think Tobey will come?"

"I don't know. When's the last time you talked to her?"

I evaded her question. "Ah, it's been a while."

"Um—how much of a while, Alex?"

"A long while." I detected by the tone of Linda's questions this conversation wasn't going to be quick. In hindsight unrealistic on my part to expect it would be. I put the phone down and placed the call on speaker. "And now I know why I haven't called."

"What are you talking about?"

"I didn't want to have this conversation. That's what I'm talking about."

"There may have been a time when you were the victim in your life, but that phase passed a *long* time ago. Why haven't we heard from you?"

"Haven't you ever needed to take a step back and reevaluate your life?"

"No—not really. What needs reevaluating?"

"Linda, not your life, my life."

"Look, it's not that I don't get it, I do. You needed space to get your head together, but what you did was something different. We haven't heard from you. You haven't talked to mama and daddy lately either. Then—after months of silence, you call out of the blue." Linda paused, "Oh, I'm sorry, that's not right is it: after months of silence, Karen calls out of the blue."

I said, "Okay, I deserved that. This idea may have been a mistake."

Linda's laughter came through the phone. "No, no, no, this wasn't a mistake. Why would you think that?

"Besides the obvious?"

"I'm sure we would all love to tell you how we felt about your little disappearing act face-to-face."

Laugher oozed through my weighted sigh. "Okay, well, you're lucky—I want this drink really bad, or I'd retreat back into my hole."

Good news for Linda. "Very good, little girl. So does this mean you're willing to invite Sanford and put *that* behind you too?"

"One firing squad at a time, Linda, I'm not ready to go that far . . . and don't you think about inviting him either."

"Okay, okay, no Sanford."

"You know what? To be honest with you, at first I thought I wasn't talking to Sanford, but I think he's not talking to me."

"Oh, that's funny."

"I know, right?"

She laughed. "So where do you want to go?"

"Let's go to The Boulevard."

"Okay," she said, "But you have to call Tobey."

"Not a problem, I'll call her," I said.

"—I mean *you* have to call her, as in not having Karen call her, like you did with me."

"You act like—"

"Like what?"

"Never mind," I said quickly. "I promise. I will call her myself as soon as we hang up."

Linda's laughter filled the room. "Okay, well, I'm hanging up now."

"I'll call you Thursday to let you know what time."

"Okay, talk to you then."

I pushed the end-call button on my phone then I contemplated some, not all, of what Linda said concerning me dropping out of sight and Sanford. She's probably right—no, undoubtedly right. I needed to call Sanford and at a minimum break the silence.

"Hey, Karen, has my last appointment arrived yet?"

Karen yelled from the other room. "Not yet. Do you need something?"

"No, I'm going to call Tobey to see if she wanted to go out this Friday." An idea occurred to me. "Hey, Karen, speaking of which, do you want to hang with us Friday? You think Keith and the kids can go it alone for a few hours?"

Karen appeared in the arched doorway. "Well, I could ask him. I haven't been out in a long time." She thought about it. "Okay, I'm in!"

"All right, I'm holding you to it, so call Keith, but don't ask him. *Tell* him you're hanging with the girls." I laughed. "Asking might be a guaranteed no."

She grinned. "Okay, let me get myself back out there before Mr. Johnson comes in. Where are you planning to go?"

"The Boulevard. That used to be our spot, I'm anxious to see if anybody still hangs out there."

"Oh, okay, well The Boulevard it is. I'll make a quick call to Keith." She went back to the front desk.

I punched in the numbers to Tobey's mobile phone, but she didn't pick up. I left a message. "Hey, Tobey, it's me. I know it's been a little while. Just wanted to touch base and see if you're free this Friday, so call me back, okay? Bye."

Just as I hung up the phone, Karen walked in. She had spoken with Keith. "I'm good for Friday," she reported, "and your five o'clock is here."

I'm happy this is starting to feel like old times. I put a few things away before heading into the lobby.

"Hello, Mr. Johnson, would you like to come in now?"

"Thank you, Dr. Nichols." He followed me past Karen's desk, down the short hallway into my office.

I directed Mr. Johnson toward the couch. "Please have a seat. How has your week been?"

Seated, Mr. Johnson wrung his hands while shifting in his seat. "I'm still having a hard time sleeping. I've been talking with my attorney about the case."

"When is the case going to trial?"

"Soon, I think. After the arraignment, things were supposed to go pretty quickly. The trial date is set. My attorney said it's pretty much an open-and-shut case from the prosecution's perspective. I'm just working with my attorney to sue the company the guy worked for. I may sue him, too, I don't know yet."

I nodded. "So beyond the obvious, is there any other reason why you are having difficulty sleeping?"

"I'm having a hard time shutting my brain down at night. I keep having these dreams about Michelle being hit. I can't get it out of my head."

That's worth exploring, I thought. "Can you remember anything specific about the dream?"

"Yeah, I can, but it's just bits and pieces. Glimpses—snapshots, maybe—of what I imagine happened at the time of her death. Dr. Nichols, it's been almost a year, and I can't seem to take a step forward."

I nodded again. "There are five steps in the grief process and depression is normal. There isn't a timeline of when you will start to live with the loss of a loved one. I believe your dreams are a manifestation of your fighting the grieving process."

He thought about it for a moment. "I know that whenever I feel happy, I feel like it's taking a step away from Michelle. I don't think these sessions are working. Suing the company the guy works for, and if he gets time for what he did—that's what'll make me feel better. I think only then will I have some closure. I need closure."

"Let's be mindful not to confuse closure with revenge or retaliation," I reminded him. "I know you're seeking healing.

However, I don't believe the outcome of the trial and suing the company is going to give you that. Coming to the sessions has helped you with the various stages of grief. Ultimately, you have to decide if you want to continue."

He thought about it. "Maybe if I could just get some sleep I would feel better."

"Okay," I said thoughtfully. "Are you eating?"

"Yes. Well, I'm probably overeating at this point. Eating is not a problem."

I noted his response on my tablet. "When was your last physical?"

"It's been a while. Why?"

"Well, I'm concerned that your lack of sleep and overeating may cause other health issues—specifically with your immune system. Call your primary physician and schedule a physical. Also, please let him or her—I'm sorry, what's your doctor's name?"

"Dr. Smith."

I wrote down his physician's name. "Okay, tell Dr. Smith about your difficulty sleeping. I'm not typically in support of sleeping pills, but in this case I want to see what your doctor recommends."

He nodded. "I'm tired. I think I'm willing to try just about anything."

"Well, let's not go to extremes," I said. "I think having a candid conversation with your general practitioner will alleviate some of what you're describing, but we need to continue talking and working through your grief. If I heard you correctly, you believe the therapy sessions aren't helping. How would you like to proceed after today?"

"I'm tired, Dr. Nichols, and honestly, I do believe the therapy sessions are working. It just doesn't always feel like I am getting somewhere. Not that I have unrealistic expectations, it's just that it feels like she died just yesterday when it's been many yesterday's ago."

"How long have you been feeling this way?" I asked.

"Every time I speak to the prosecutor about the case or remember what we used to do together—even go in our closet."

"Can you describe what you're feeling during one of those instances?"

"I think so, talking to the prosecutor, that's the whole thing, her death, the funeral. I feel like I can't breathe, and my heart is breaking into pieces."

"Are all of Michelle's clothes still in your home?"

"Yeah, it's all still there."

I continued to write. Michelle's clothes still being in the home was of concern to me. "What do you mean by its all still there?"

"Her clothes, shoes, jewelry—everything, it's all still in the house."

"You mentioned earlier you feel as if you're not moving forward. Do you think keeping Michelle's personal belongings in the home may be preventing you from moving forward?"

He said, "It could be—I hadn't thought about it to be honest with you. The idea of removing her stuff—Dr. Nichols, that's something I can't do."

Calmly, I said, "I'm not suggesting you remove *all* Michelle's personal belongings from your home. I'm trying to get a better sense of what triggers how you're feeling." I read from my notes. "Specifically around what you described as an inability to shut down your brain, sleep, and take a step forward."

Mr. Johnson looked relieved. "I'm just not ready. I know I may not be handling this the right way, but I'm just not ready."

"Try not to think in terms of right and wrong. Cleaning out a loved one's personal belongings can present a great deal of anxiety for the surviving spouse. It's a personal decision based upon what works best for you."

"I have thought about it, more than once. It just doesn't feel right."

"Okay. So, let's discuss your dreams a little more and what you described as an inability to shut down your brain. Besides the bits and pieces regarding the accident, can you tell me what else you're thinking about right before you go to bed?"

"Dr. Nichols, can we talk about this next week? I'm beginning to feel sleepy."

"Sure, we can pick this up next week. See Karen to confirm your next appointment."

Mr. Johnson rose slowly and left the office. I stared after him. Maybe suing the shit out of that driver's company would give him closure. Who the hell knows? At this point it had been a year and he really wasn't further along. *Well I guess that's not true, I thought he was further along, now he's stuck in one place. I'd better type these notes up while the session is fresh in my head.*

While reviewing my notes I heard the faint sound of a phone ringing. I was in such a hurry I had to search around my desk until I found it. "Hello?"

"Hey, this is my second time calling you back."

"Tobey?"

She laughed. "Yeah, who else?"

I smiled. "Okay, now I recognize the voice. It's been a while but that's you, all right. What's up, girl?"

"Nothing's up with me, what's up with you? I haven't talked to you in months."

I sighed. "I know. I'm sorry. Linda already chewed me out, so hopefully you'll cut me some slack."

She didn't sound upset. "Yeah, I'm good, believe me, I understand. Now, that doesn't mean I agree with how you handled all this, but I do get it."

"I know it's crazy, but I really did shut down. Between Jake and Sanford, I just didn't know who to trust."

"Now, don't get mad, but I think you blew that out of proportion."

"Oh, really? Why do you say that?"

"I mean, so what, Alex, he didn't tell you he saw them out. Liz did. Would it really have made that much of a difference? I could have saw them fucking on a corner and I wouldn't have told you."

"What? Why?"

"The way you were tripping about Jake, there is no way I would have told you anything other than I saw them. Anyway you wouldn't have believed us if we did."

"You seriously can't believe that, Tobey. If you'd told me I would've believed you."

"Believing us and doing something about it is two different things. But if we're going to talk about this, then let's talk, we've been through this before . . . haven't we. You saw it yourself and didn't do or say anything to him. So, don't tell me that you're mad at Sanford because he didn't tell you. You're mad at yourself."

"So . . . who told you?" I asked.

"I figured it out on my own."

I felt wounded and couldn't fight back. I'd called Tobey to hang out with me, not to give me a lecture about someone I'm not even married to anymore. I knew I had issues when it came to Jake. Trust and believe, I knew. I felt my blood pressure starting to rise.

Only the truth can affect you this much.

I didn't have a reason to be mad at Sanford, and she was right. I sort of suspected Jake might have been doing something he shouldn't. I didn't need Sanford or anyone else to affirm it for me.

That being said, knowing all this didn't make me any less upset. "Tobey, are you driving? I can hear the wind in the background."

"What's that got to do with anything?"

"I think you need to focus on driving, not arguing about old news with me."

"I'm not arguing. I'm fine."

"Well, I'm not. I'm tired. It's been a long day already. I want you to come and hang out with us on Friday, but honestly, Tobey, I'm moving on, so I don't want to talk about this anymore."

"Well, okay, count me in." I could almost detect a halfhearted smile. "I promise to behave."

"Okay, I really want you to come, but I just can't handle any more than I am dealing with right now, so I'm going to hold you to that. I know I'm not moving as fast as you guys would like, but this is going to have to be good enough for now."

"I got you."

"So, okay, girl, Friday night at The Boulevard around five or six. I want to get there for happy hour."

"Okay, cool. See you then." She hung up.

Boy, what an exhausting conversation. She really wore me out.

Right on cue, in walked Karen. "Are you okay?" I imagined she'd heard the entire conversation.

"Yes, I'm okay. Don't worry. Okay, Karen, that's enough for one day. Let's shut it down."

Chapter Six

The gradual disintegration of my marriage stretched out over years.

My focal point was Jake and our marriage, not myself. There wasn't time or room for me, and any physical trace of the person I'd been before I met and married Jake had all but evaporated. Consequently, ending the relationship ignited the initial catalyst for my goal of rejuvenation. I felt good about my circumstances and myself. I liked the uncertainty of not knowing what could or would come next, which proved to be considerably more invigorating than predictability.

I'd forgotten how much preparation went into going out. Seems like we'd made these plans weeks ago, but Friday night arrived on time and despite all my efforts to the contrary, I still didn't have a clue what to wear. My intention to buy something new hadn't panned out. Life, in spite of me not having much of one slowed me down this week. I'd have to figure something out from what I had in my closet, because I'd officially run out of time. We'd all agreed to meet at The Boulevard around five or six, and it was already four o'clock. I felt like this might possibly be my rebirth onto the singles scene.

I wanted to look special–well, that's not true I wanted to look good. But, admittedly, if there is such a thing as natural sexiness, I didn't have that gene. But, in the right dress, I could get there. Hopefully, where I couldn't manage extra time, I could ensnare a little luck. There had to be something to help me amp up my sex appeal lying in wait in the back of my closet.

I'd coordinated this little outing because I missed my friends, but I had to admit–I missed male companionship more. I hadn't engaged in anything sexual in a couple of years, and sex made it pretty high up on my list of things to do by the end of the year. So the outfit I chose to wear had to accomplish a couple of things: not to look like I was trying too hard to meet a man (even though decidedly I was), and not to look like the lone slut amongst a group of schoolteachers.

A quick search through my closet produced one out-of-date pantsuit and a couple of matronly dresses. Cute, but too conservative. Not quite hitting the sexy feeling I'm after. I laid them out on my bed, looked each one over front and back, but couldn't decide. One of the dresses could work.

I needed reinforcements. I called Linda from inside my closet to get a second opinion while I continued to search for the right outfit. "Hey, Linda?" Linda's house was incessantly noisy, my nieces' and nephew's elevated voices in the background.

"Hey, what's up?"

"What is going on at your house? It always sounds like you have a whole elementary school in there."

Linda said, "I feel like I have a whole elementary school in my house. But it's just these three little monsters of mine."

"It's just a matter of time before we find you and Mitch tied up and the kids are gone on a joy ride."

"Well, if they do, I hope they run errands to give me a break."

"Yeah, that's probably not going to happen–the errands. Okay, I'm having trouble deciding what to wear. What are you putting on tonight?"

"Oh, I haven't had a chance to even think about that yet." Then she yelled at the kids. "James, get off that computer and help your sister with the dishes!" In the same breath, she managed to yell, "Tracy, come here!"

I riffled through more clothes. "Haven't you started getting ready yet?"

"No, I'm waiting for Mitch to get home. He's running late."

"I thought he would've been home by now."

Linda continued talking to Tracy. "Hey, babe, can you call your father for me and see what is taking him so long? Tell him don't forget I'm going out with Auntie Alex. Now scoot, hurry up." In search of another cell phone, Tracy's footsteps faded from earshot, presumably to call her father. Linda yelled again, "Tell him Auntie Alex is getting antsy."

I tried to interject something. "You know we're supposed to meet Tobey and Karen there by six, and—" I looked down at my watch, "It's after five."

"Yes, Alex, I may not be able to *stay* on time but I can *tell* time." There was a break in the conversation again, most likely Tracy returning with information. "What did your father say?"

I overheard my niece's sweet voice laced with giggles. "He's on his way and said to tell Auntie Alex to keep her pants on he's moving as fast as he can."

Linda cried with laughter. "Okay, you hear that? Mitch is on his way, so as soon as he gets here, I'll be heading out. It should only take me about fifteen minutes."

"Did you say what you are wearing? I have two dresses that are 'might's' and a pantsuit. What do you think?"

The weight of Linda's footsteps could be heard through the phone. A high-pitched animated voice pierced through the phone: Linda had to be in the family room. The kids were interacting with whatever they were watching, laughing and yelling back and forth. "Wear a dress for a change, I'll probably wear something black. I haven't been working out lately so I'm feeling a little fat." Linda paused. "Why do you care what I wear?"

"Because I have lost about ten pounds and I want to wear something fitted to show off my body, but I don't want to be the only one."

"Who are you, and what did you do with my sister?"

"I know–it's time to try something different. I'm feeling good, so why not?" I reiterated my question. "A dress or pants?"

"I think the dress is good, go for it, but you're on your own, I'll probably wear one too." She paused. "So answer me this, Alex, what is the whole goal of tonight?"

"What do you mean, the whole goal?"

"You know what I'm talking about. What's the purpose of all of this? If you wanted to see us we could've just met up at your house."

"Busted–"

"Yeah, sister—busted big time. Spill it, what gives?"

"Okay, this is the longest I've gone without being in a relationship–" Linda tried to interject, but I stopped her, "—

and that's cool. I needed that time alone. But now I feel confident enough to get back out there."

"So, again, what's the purpose of tonight?"

I laughed. "You always bring me right back. I want to meet someone and I can't do that unless I start inching my way back into the game . . . so to speak."

"And that's okay Alex. It's just that if I'm a wingman, I want to know up front."

"A wingman? Yeah, okay . . . whatever," I said.

I laughed as we hung up.

A dress would be the glamour-girl outfit of the evening for me. Neither one of the dresses on my bed would add the right *ump* I searched for. My last night on the town as a single person was over ten years ago, but I did seem to recall having more clothes to dress up in than this. Then it dawned on me: *I moved those clothes to the guest bedroom.* Down the hall, in the guest bedroom, I found a timeless little black dress, and thanks to the running workouts, it still fit. If a woman's best revenge is looking good, I'm completely vindicated.

Baby's officially out of the corner.

Chapter Seven

The valet attendant opened my car door and extended his hand, a small yet meaningful gesture. I hadn't felt the touch of another person in a long time. I'm back on memorable ground. The splendor of the hotel personified with every step I took down the red carpet headed for the grand entrance. I marveled at the exterior stone archways and glass entrance, adorned with brass fixtures that glimmered in the glow of the moonlight. The Boulevard, off from the main lobby, patiently awaited the city's elite.

The dim lighting illuminated the restaurant's mixture of sophistication and comfort. Groups of beautiful people, seated in chocolate lounge chairs with silver pillows, and fresh flowers sipped cocktails while waiting for their tables. During dinner, a live jazz band entertained restaurant guests.

On the lower level a DJ played the latest dance music: rap, rhythm and blues, and pop.

I entered the restaurant and walked up to the reservation desk. The host occupied assisting other guests, gave me a chance to scan the room. I drew in the sights, and sounds of the restaurant. Despite the length of time, the vibrations and aroma of The Boulevard were just as I remembered. Contemporary art ornamented the walls. My eyes landed on one remarkable drawing of Miles Davis. It was still there. The charcoal sketch reminded me of the time Jake and I celebrated our one-year anniversary at the restaurant. A slice of chocolate cake drizzled with fudge, and a blanket of fresh strawberries. One fork, and a love for Miles. The host researched the name of the artist for us, and after a few more visits he presented it to us. We reveled in the thought of hanging a piece of our romantic history in our new house. I kept the name and number in my purse for what seems like our entire marriage. In my daze, I made it up to year four of our marriage when the abrupt um-hum from the host brought me back to reality. Our group was on the reservation list for a table in the lower level. A hostess dressed in black escorted me toward the winding staircase to the nightclub. Before heading down I took another glimpse at the drawing of Miles. *It's a beautiful portrait.*

The décor downstairs was much different from the upper level. The rosewood room and sparkling black floor glistened under the blue recessed lights. Through a collage of tables, the hostess walked me over to where Tobey and Karen were seated.

I said, "Hey, ladies!"

"Hey, Alex, long time no see!" Tobey stood to give me a hug. "You look great!"

I smiled as we embraced. "Thank you! I feel pretty good, and I am so ready to get back out here and have some fun for a change!"

Tobey broke away and returned to her chair. I sat in the chair directly across from her.

"I feel you."

"So, what's going on?"

"Karen and I were just talking about Keith and the kids—but, never mind all that, let's get you a drink." Out of my peripheral vision, I spotted an old friend of Tobey's at the bar. I thought his name might be Glen or something close to that. I hadn't seen him in a long time, but he looked familiar.

Karen pointed in the direction of the bar, leaned over the table to me and said, "Do you see that guy looking at Tobey? Tobey do you know him?"

The server arrived at our table. I ordered appetizers for the group and a glass of wine. In the short time it took for the server to take my order the gentleman at the bar curiosity appeared to intensify. "You know what, Karen? I think I do know him. Tobey, is that Glen over there at the bar?"

"Where?"

"Sitting right there." I pointed in his direction. "At the bar." Tobey turned around to look but there were too many people obstructing her view.

Tobey said, "I can't see. Let me get up."

"Girl, don't get up! I don't want him thinking we're talking about him."

Karen said, "But we *are* talking about him."

I tilted my head and with a hint of sarcasm I said, "Thank you, Karen."

Tobey cut in. "I couldn't care less if he thinks we're talking about him."

I grabbed her arm but she broke away and headed toward the bar. Karen and I looked at each other, entertained as we helplessly watched Tobey disappear into the crowd.

Tobey disappeared as Linda arrived. I hadn't seen Linda in a long time and was genuinely glad she'd come. She'd apparently changed her mind on what to wear, because she wore a flattering black pantsuit with a grey pearl choker. Even though she felt fat, she certainly didn't look it. At five-three, I'm the tall one of the two of us. Linda's petite frame flaunted her commitment to athleticism even through a pantsuit. Her usually soft curly locks were converted into straight flowing tresses that hung mid-way down her back.

Linda sat down in the vacant chair next to me. "Where's Tobey?"

"She's on a fact-finding mission."

"A fact-finding mission? What does that mean?"

"Well, see that guy at the bar—in the black shirt?" Linda turned her head but another patron obstructed her view. "I can't see anybody at the bar." Before she could finish her sentence, Tobey walked back to the table . . . with the guy in tow.

Tobey pointed to her new companion. "Hey, everybody, do you remember him?" I spoke up first while Linda and Karen looked him over.

"Yeah, I think I do remember you." I added, uncertainly, "Glen?"

He smiled. "Actually, it's Peter."

"I'm sorry! I thought I might be off a little."

Peter exchanged pleasantries with Karen and Linda, giving me a quick minute to size him up. Being tall next to all of us wasn't a hard feat to pull off, but with that being said, he was still a big guy. From my seat I guessed he stood about six feet, fair complexion, with a strong jaw line and dark features. His build reminded me of the basketball players in college. It was quite remarkable for him to be over forty and still be in great playing shape, which couldn't have gone unnoticed by Tobey.

Tobey returned to her seat and Peter pulled up a chair from a neighboring table. The server returned with appetizers and my drink.

Peter said, "Would you ladies like something to drink? I see you two have already gotten started." Tobey had a drink and the waitress patiently awaited another order. Peter asked the server to put my drink on his tab. Linda ordered something and Karen asked for water.

The server appeared irritated.

Karen said, "What's up with the waitress?"

I enlightened her. "People generally don't tip from a glass of water."

"Well I will have to give her my sincerest thank you."

I laughed. "She would probably prefer your sincerest dollar."

When the server came back she seemed to be in a better mood.

While they debated on what or what not to drink, I focused my attention toward the dance floor. "I think I want another glass of wine, if that's all right."

"Yes, of course," Peter said. "How about you, Tobey, you getting a refill?"

"You know what? I think I *will* have another."

"What were you drinking?"

"Vodka and cranberry. Hey, Alex, you need to go to the bathroom?"

I thought for a moment. "Ah, sure, I can go. You want to come, Linda?"

Linda shook her head as a guy approached the table. After a brief conversation, she stood up and followed him onto the dance floor.

I walked past the dance floor toward the bathroom. Tobey, delayed by a lingering conversation with Peter, caught up with me. Out of my peripheral vision I got a quick glimpse of Peter sitting down next to Karen. Once we cleared Peter's eyesight, I said, "Tobey didn't you and Peter used to go out or something? He seems nice."

Tobey said, "Alex, you don't remember what happened with Peter?"

"I knew I remembered him from somewhere, but I don't remember anything happening between *you* and Peter at least nothing out of the ordinary."

She gave me a puzzled look as we slipped into the ladies' room. "I can't believe you don't remember!"

"Tobey, okay," I said and raised my hands in complete befuddlement. "Why don't you just tell me what it is that I don't remember?"

"Okay, remember, I told you I met this guy, and we hit it off?"

Puzzled, I said, "Vaguely. Why would I remember that?"

She made a face. "Well, you *should* remember, because I told you how he just disappeared on me."

"What do you mean, he just disappeared? He left in the middle of your date or something?"

"No, no, no, nothing like that let me explain. We went on a few dates. The last night I saw him he came back to my place. We hooked up. In the morning he had to leave early. We were supposed to get back together later that day. Then—" she paused and threw up her hands.

I cut in. "Then what?"

Tobey put her hands down. "Then nothing—I never heard from him or saw him—well, until now."

There was a line for the stalls, but we sat in the chairs in the anteroom.

"Wait a minute," I objected. "Tobey, I don't remember you ever telling me this. How long has it been since you saw him?"

"Two years!"

"Oh, my God, are you kidding me?"

"No, I'm not kidding!"

I wasn't quite sure what all this meant. "Okay, so it's not like you've exactly been losing sleep over this man. You mean to tell me you didn't hear from him at all in a couple of years?"

"He called me one time, but I didn't answer. I was too pissed off."

I shook my head and pulled out a compact to check my lipstick. "You should've answered, Tobey, at least to find out what happened."

"I was so mad at him at the time—I couldn't think of anything left to say."

I said, "He could have explained what happened and apologized." I glanced at her. She looked miserable. "Okay, what do you want to do? Are you upset? You want to leave?"

She shook her head, but didn't say anything.

"Okay, tell me this—do you still have feelings for this guy?" I asked.

She shrugged. "Let's just say I was disappointed. I didn't expect to bump into him."

I rubbed her arm. "I don't think he remembers the situation the same as you, or he wouldn't be talking to you let alone at our table. He may be trying to make amends."

A stall opened up, and I left Tobey and went in. When I returned, Tobey looked a little better. She checked herself out in the mirror. *A good sign she's feeling better.* I washed my hands and applied some lotion from my purse. "Are you okay to head back out?"

By the time we got back to the table only Karen and Linda were there. We sat down, I gave Linda a look, and she raised her eyebrows in a mute question. I mouthed I'd tell her later. It looked like another round of drinks on the table, probably compliments of Peter. While Tobey and Karen talked, I leaned over and whispered in Linda's ear. "Where did Peter go?"

"Oh, he said he would be right back. I don't know where he went, though."

"Oh, okay. Did you know anything about him and Tobey?"

Linda looked just as confused as me. "I don't know what you talking about."

"I'll tell you later. It's too long to talk about here," I said.

Linda asked, "Is Tobey interested in him? He's cute. I actually thought he might be good for you."

I shrugged and sipped my wine. "No, no, no—Tobey used to date him."

Linda put down her drink. "I don't remember ever seeing him. When's the last time she saw him?"

"I think she said about two years ago."

Linda's eyes widened. "Two years? Well, what does she want?"

I said, "I don't even think Tobey can answer that question."

From the corner of my eye, I saw Peter walking back to the table, and when he got there he asked Tobey to dance. She got up immediately, and Linda and I resumed our conversation. "Tobey should talk to him—you never know, he could be her Prince Charming. Speaking of which, did anybody here catch your eye?"

"Nah—but, it's nice to be out."

"You think you'll come here again?"

"Yeah, I think I will. I used to really like this place."

"I think it's nice," she said, "but you need to do other stuff, too."

"I will. I actually thought about going to this poetry reading I overheard some ladies talking about in the bathroom." Well, why not? It would be something different, at least.

Linda grinned. "Oh, that sounds like fun. Let me know. If you want, Mitch and I can go with you."

"Thank you! I'd love that." It really was sounding like fun now.

"Okay, but you have to let me know so I can drop the kids at Mama and Daddy's."

"I will," I promised.

The night wound down and it appeared Tobey and Peter were getting along. I'd hoped to find my own happy ending, or at least get close to it, but that wasn't going to happen–too much to expect from one night out. Linda and Karen left soon after Tobey returned from the dance floor. Being happily married means you get bored in these places real quick.

I get bored too, but it's a different kind of bored. The kind of I'm-bored-here-but-let's-move-on-to-the-next-place. *Their* bored is let's-go-home-and-get-into-my-pajamas-and-see-what's-on-TV. I sat alone and finished nursing my drink until it was time to go.

I looked over at Tobey. "Hey, girl, I think I'm going to take off. You okay here by yourself?"

"She'll be okay," Peter answered. "I'll make sure she gets to her car."

"Aw, such a gentleman."

Tobey looked like she shouldn't have had that last drink. "Alex, I think I am going to head to the ladies room."

"All right, go ahead," I said. "I'll keep Peter company until you get back."

Tobey stood up, patted my hand and smiled. Oh, yeah, she'd had more than a few. "I think Tobey may need you to take her home," I said to Peter.

"She's still pretty upset with me, so I don't think that's going to happen," he said.

"She seemed like she was warming up."

He shrugged. "I have more explaining to do."

"Well, keep talking to her—she'll get there," I said.

He turned to look at me. "So what about you, Alex—married? Single?"

I frowned. Disappointed in my own status. "I'm newly single."

"I take it that's not a good thing," he chuckled.

My turn to shrug. "It's an okay thing."

"When's the last time you went out?"

I looked in the air, as though the answer were there. "Ah, since I got a divorce?" I raised my pointing finger. "One time."

"One time before tonight?"

"No," I laughed. "Tonight is the one time."

Tobey walked to the table and sat down next to me. I knew she was dying to know what we'd talked about . . . just as much as I wanted to know what they'd talked about earlier. Either way, it would have to wait. I wanted to get out of there.

Despite Tobey's return, Peter continued asking me questions. "Are you ready to meet someone?"

"Ahhh—"

Tobey answered for me. "Yes, she's ready!"

"Wait a minute," I said. Tobey and Peter stared patiently waiting for whatever else I had to add to the discussion. "Okay, you're right, I'm ready. It just seems a little—"

"A little what?"

I exhaled, "I don't know what I'm talking about—yes, when the time comes and I meet someone, I'm ready to start dating again."

Peter said, "Well how about I hook you up with one of my boys?"

"What? No—no—"

Tobey straightened up in her chair. "What do you mean, no! Yes, Alex."

I shook my head. "No, I don't want to be fixed up."

Tobey asked, "Why not? This is perfect."

Peter looked on as we discussed the matter back and forth. "Let me know if you change your mind," he said. "He's a nice guy. I think you would like him." And with that, he decided to call it a night. He paid his tab, said many goodbyes to Tobey with a promise to call, and left. I figured that was officially our cue. "Tobey, come on. Leave your car here, I'll take you home and we'll come pick it up in the morning."

"Oh, Alex, I'm fine."

"You're far from fine, and I'm not risking you going to jail. You'll get pulled over for DUI and with your temper—no, me taking you home is better than bailing you out of jail."

On the way home, Tobey nodded off. I couldn't help thinking about Peter's invitation for me to meet his friend. Perhaps I spoke to soon. It would be nice to meet someone.

"Tobey? What were you and Peter talking about?" I asked.

"What?"

"You and Peter, did he tell you what happened? Did he want to keep seeing you?"

"Huh." Tobey didn't bother opening her eyes. "Yeah he told me, but I don't know, Alex. He said he wasn't ready for a relationship back then—got scared—blah, blah, blah."

"You don't believe him."

"No, not really."

We both laughed. I continued driving. Listening to music blaring inside the club for hours made me appreciate the silence. We were almost at Tobey's house when she asked, "Have you thought anymore about what I said?"

"You'll have to be more specific than that."

"Sanford. Have you given any more thought about contacting Sanford?"

"No, I haven't." Tobey shifted in her seat. "Wait a minute, let me finish—but I will call him."

We made it to her house. Tobey unlatched her seat belt and turned toward me. "I'm glad, Alex. It really is time to move forward with everything."

After a moment of silence I said, "Thank you."

"Thank you for what?"

"Keeping me straight, girl—keeping me straight."

Chapter Eight

Of all things I could do on a Saturday, providing cab service to Tobey didn't make my list. I needed gas, so I called ahead from the station. After five rings a slurred voice mumbled something unintelligible. I wanted to turn around and go home, but I'd come this far. "Are you up?"

"Yeah, I'm up, just a little hung over."

"Okay. I'm around the corner, so make sure you're looking out for me, because I don't want to come up."

"Why not?"

"It's just I want to get some stuff done today. Okay, so come down, I'm here."

"All right Alex, I'm on my way." Tobey surprised me, she came down right away. Once she settled into the car I started to talk about our night out. "So did you have fun?"

Tobey nodded. "I did. It was good to see Peter and clear everything up." She gazed out the car window. "Yeah, but he didn't remember it the way I did. Go figure, most men don't remember things the way we remember them."

"The truth isn't a male or female thing, it's just the truth," I pointed out.

"Yeah, I guess you're right." She didn't appear to be interested in a philosophical discussion about truth and lying. "Anyway, he wants to be friends, and that's all we can be."

I stopped for a red light. "As long as you're okay with being his friend, then friends it is."

"I don't think I have a choice in the matter."

"Actually, you do have a choice. You could choose not to be his friend."

"Oh, yeah," she said with a laugh. "I didn't think about what was behind door number two."

"See, that's what you have me for. There's always a door number two. The good news is you don't have to decide this today. Since he's no longer on the menu, it really doesn't matter."

"You're right about that one, too."

The downtown skyline came into view. We exited the freeway onto the service drive headed toward The Boulevard. "Hey did you park in the lot or in the garage?"

"Oh, in the garage on the seventh floor. They'd have towed my car if I'd parked in the lot." I pulled into the garage and went up to her floor. Tobey pointed. "There's my car." She grabbed her purse, opened the car door and stepped out waving her hand. "Thanks for the ride."

She started her car and drove toward the exit. I followed her out of the garage when my phone rang. It was Tobey. "Hey, are you taking the freeway home?"

"Yeah, I'm going to head to the gym, then go home, but you know, I wanted to talk to you about Peter's friend. Do you think I should meet him?"

"Yeah, isn't that what I said? What can it hurt?"

I shook my head, even though she couldn't see me. "I think I want to try and meet someone on my own first."

"Either way, it won't hurt to meet him too."

I heard horns blowing through the phone. "Tobey, is that you blowing your horn like crazy?"

"Yeah, I hate driving on the freeway. They treat the lanes like they're suggestions." Tobey started yelling at the other drivers.

"You do realize they can't hear you," I pointed out.

"Yeah, I know. Now, what were you saying—oh, check that guy out."

"Do you think Peter's on the up and up?"

"I don't know, Alex." She laughed. "I haven't talked to that man in over two years, how the hell should I know? Nothing to do but to meet him."

"That's true. I'm going to a poetry reading next week and I don't want to feel like I'm rushing this—I'll hold off meeting Peter's friend."

"No holding off I'm setting it up. Have you called Sanford?"

I reached a decision. "After my workout I think I'm going to call."

"That's good," Tobey said. "Let me know how it turns out."

The short drive to the gym helped clear my head. I didn't like uncertainty and the unknown. Sanford sat firmly in both columns. It's like reading the last page of a book. I wanted to know everything would eventually turn out all right.

I arrived at the gym ahead of the Saturday morning crowd. The idea of seeing Sanford made me nostalgic. Doe Eyes from my favorite movie soundtrack blasted in my headphones. I ran to the symphonic rhythm of the violins and soft pedal of the piano.

Chapter Nine

Saturday afternoon, long after my workout, I called Sanford and got his answering machine. I contemplated hanging up, but left a message. My goal was to catch up with him for a face-to-face. A game of phone-tag didn't figure into the plans.

In the not so distant past, Sanford taught a class on Saturday mornings, and we'd meet up for brunch afterward. I hoped, all things being constant, he would be on campus. I drank the rest of my coffee, grabbed my purse, and drove to Sanford's office.

The drive to campus gave me more time than necessary to replay our last talk. With it weighing heavy on my mind, I reviewed every scenario of how this visit could play out.

Flashes of our heart-to-heart jumped out of my memory between traffic lights. I don't remember us being mad: just done. My only objective from the conservation I hoped to have with Sanford was getting my friend back into my life. That's it, nothing more.

Just as I arrived on campus, the sun peeked through the leaves overhead, an effervescent green umbrella sheltering those who sought knowledge and understanding from the rest of the world. My foot lifted from the accelerator. I drifted down the long narrow winding road, lost in the beauty of the surroundings. As angelic as the scenery on campus was, it's the last place students wanted to be on a Saturday. I parked the car and walked, navigating my way through the rich landscape to the School of Business, home to Public Policy and Administration . . . and Sanford. The building's aroma was a mixture of coffee, books, disinfectant, and dry-erase markers.

Alongside his colleagues, down the long hall of faculty offices I got to his office door and smiled. DR. CONSTANTINE SANFORD. I opened the outer door and entered a small seating area. Immediately inside were two maple office doors, but both glass panels were dark. I sat down in one of the adjacent chairs and read my way through an entire article on welfare policy in the *Journal of Poverty*, authored by Sanford. I finished the piece and was flipping through the magazine, hoping to find entertainment news, when I heard voices in the hallway.

Sanford entered the main door and stepped into the seating area with keys in hand. His head bent down, seemingly deep in thought, iPod ear buds in both ears with his right hand clutching the shoulder strap of his overused book bag. He really looked good. He looked to have lost about seventy-five pounds.

I checked him out, carefully, head to toe. He slowly raised his head and recognized me seated in the lobby. I couldn't tell by the expression on his face if he was happy or disappointed to see me.

He tugged on his earplug wire, removing both from his ears in one pull. His forehead tightened forcing his brows below the frame of his glasses. His expression made me uneasy.

"I tried to call you before I came, but I got your voicemail." I stood up and placed the magazine back on the table. "Um, not this one—I mean, your home voicemail."

Sanford released his backpack and fumbled with his keys, but his eyes were firmly affixed on mine. The walls in the tiny lobby felt as if they were starting to close in on me.

I said, "You look good." I shifted my weight back and forth, left to right. "Did I surprise you?"

He finally said something. "No, you didn't surprise me. I got your message. I figured you would catch up with me eventually. Just didn't think it would be today."

I picked up my purse from the office chair and took a step toward him. "I know showing up here may be a reach, but I really wanted to talk to you." He singled out a key and used it to open his office. Then picked up papers slid under his door. I followed him into his office. He cleared a place for me on a chair across from his desk. Sanford's office resembled the stereotypical professor's office: stacks of books, laptop, papers, old art and everything in desperate need of dusting. Sanford's tiny office and oversized desk made the room smaller there wasn't room to stand, let alone a chair. He finally sat down behind his desk and put his bag and papers on it.

A year may as well have been a hundred. He'd accomplished a lot in a short period of time. He wasn't published the last time I spoke with him. I looked about at his office walls. There were magazine articles with his name on them, recognition awards, and pictures celebrating his achievements with people I didn't know. Events I didn't participate in. Milestones I knew nothing about. This ridiculous disagreement cost me more than I initially realized. I felt he'd let me down when I needed him the most. By the looks of things, I hadn't been there for him either, *but it doesn't appear he needed me. I missed all of it.*

I sat down, took in a couple of deep breaths and made a failed attempt at relaxing. "So, how are you?"

"I'm doing good. I just had another article published in the *Journal of Poverty.*"

I nodded. "I saw that, congratulations." I pointed to a magazine cover framed on the wall. "I actually read that one." He looked at me quizzically. I added, "In the lobby. I've been waiting for a minute. It gave me time to look at the reading material."

"No *People* magazine for you to look at?"

I smiled. "No, smarty, there wasn't a *People* magazine. If there was, I didn't find it."

Sanford turned on his laptop and sifted through his mail. By accident or intentional, his grim exterior expelled a half-hearted smile. That's all I needed to feel better about my decision to come. I took a deep breath and exhaled. "I've missed you, Sanford, and I wanted to apologize and explain why I got so angry."

"You don't have to apologize. I already know why you got so angry."

I raised an eyebrow. "Oh, okay."

"Alex, I know you felt I betrayed you. I guess in some ways I did, but I didn't want to hurt you."

"But you did."

"Believe me—I'd never want to hurt you. I told Jake he needed to talk to you. Obviously he never did, but Jake should have told you, not me. I know you don't agree with that, but that's how I felt. I still feel that way."

"I understand, Sanford, I just don't agree. I don't expect Jake to be honest with me but I do expect you to. I don't know what that says about my ex and our marriage, but I trusted you with my heart and my feelings more than I did him. So, yeah, you're right, I did expect you to tell me even when he didn't."

He sighed. "Exactly, how could I tell you something like that? I don't care who it is. I don't want to be responsible for breaking up someone else's marriage—"

"Sanford, I don't mean to cut you off, but if you saw Jake out with someone else, my marriage was already over. All you would have been doing is getting me caught up on the game. That's all I expected from you. I guess what I didn't understand is why you wouldn't do that for me. I would do it for you. I would tell you if I saw your girl out with someone else."

Sanford shook his head. "First of all, you know I'm not seeing anybody. Second, you know I would have told you if I thought it was the right thing to do, but the truth is—and I hope you don't get mad at me all over again—but I didn't. You and I know what happened the last time."

"This time would have been different. I guess that's the difference between men and women. I believe telling would have been the right thing to do."

Sanford leaned back in his chair, hunched his shoulders while resting his arms. "I just don't see it that way, Alex. Not this time."

"I guess it's old news now." I wasn't feeling a whole lot better. "So are you at least going to tell me who you were there with?"

"That's a negative."

I released a deep sigh. "I'm not winning today."

"You're winning—you're always winning, you just don't know it."

I crossed my legs, readjusted my body in the chair, trying desperately to hide my blush behind my hand. Sanford's music could be heard faintly through his earplugs resting on his desk. I pointed to his iPod. "What are you listening to?"

"It's a song a good friend of mine turned me onto."

"Is this good friend me?"

"Of course it's you. When you called I thought about this one and plugged it in."

I pulled my iPod from my purse and waved it. "I listened to it in the gym."

"Huh—" Sanford rocked in his chair. "How ironic."

"Yeah, I guess some things change."

"But others remain the same."

"So what do we do now, Sanford? Friends?"

Sanford smiled and reached across the desk to take my hands. "Of course we're friends. If nothing else, I will always be your friend."

"Good. So will you hang out with me and Tobey?" Sanford released my hands and leaned back in his chair. "Where you going? The usual spot?"

"Of course." I smiled. "Please, it would mean a lot to me if you came."

He gave in easily enough. "I can meet you. I'll be there after I teach."

"That's okay. We should be there for a while."

He nodded. "That's all well and good, but when are you going to catch me up on the last year?"

"If you pick me up on Friday, I can catch you up then."

"In a bar? How are we going to talk at a bar?"

"No, we can talk a little at the house before we leave and then in the car. Trust me, there hasn't been a whole lot happening on my end. You'll be caught up in five minutes."

"All right, well, give me the five minutes you got—did you say Linda's coming?"

"Not two weekends in a row, but she and Mitch are going to go with me to this poetry reading. I forgot what night. It's on my calendar."

He looked concerned. "Did you start writing again?"

I frowned. "No, I haven't."

"So what's stopping you? You should have plenty of material from the last couple of years."

Rubbing my eyes, I leaned back and looked up at the ceiling. "I don't know." I yawned, "It was only a hobby anyway."

Sanford turned toward his computer, pulled up a document and printed it. "It was more than a hobby." He pulled a piece of paper from the printer and handed it to me, an old poem I'd written shortly after we graduated from college. "You have got to be kidding me. How long have you had this?"

"Since you wrote it—don't you remember?"

"I remember writing it." I read on, paused for a second and looked at Sanford. "I don't remember giving it to you. How did you get this?"

"I have just about all of your old poems."

I finished reading. "That is crazy—I haven't seen this in—wow, it's got to be at least ten years."

"Close to that, perhaps a little more," he said.

I handed the paper back. "So how did you get them? You said you have more?"

"Every time you emailed me one, I saved it."

Pupils dilated, I placed my hand over my open mouth. "When Jake and I moved, I lost track of them. I couldn't, and still can't remember where they are. I thought I put them all together in a binder—can't find the binder."

"It's a good thing I kept them then."

I smiled. "I'd say it is. Were they any good?"

"I think so." He smiled. "But I'm biased."

"I can't wait to read them again. Hey, can you bring some when you come Friday?"

"Yeah, I can bring all of them."

I waved my finger, "that's even better."

There was a timid knock at the door. Sanford raised his voice. "Yes?"

"Dr. Sanford?" It was a young woman's voice.

I stood up. "I guess that's my cue." He stood up as well and came over to hug me. I didn't want to let him go, but the voice outside was waiting. I pulled away from him and headed toward the door. I grabbed the door handle, stopped short, and turned back to Sanford. "Before I go, how much weight have you lost?"

"For a minute there I thought you didn't notice."

I smiled. "Of course I did."

Sanford rubbed his hands down his chest and stomach. "I thought I would have to be like a girl and ask if you noticed how much weight I lost."

Playful, I tapped his chest. "Goofy . . . you look good."

"Thank you."

I opened the door and walked into the seating area where a young lady with books in hand eagerly awaited her professor. Sanford patted me on the shoulder and whispered, "Did I mention how good it is to see you?" He walked over to the student. I turned and shot him a quick smile while I exited out of the main entrance.

Chapter Ten

Tuesday, still seated at my desk after work, I held the flyer in my hand for the poetry reading on Wednesday night. Initially, I'd asked Linda to go, but I was rethinking that invitation. Since my visit on campus I couldn't get Sanford out of my head. I really wanted to go with him instead.

Over the years there'd been times when I thought *maybe* Sanford and I could've been more than friends, but then senior year I met Jake and it didn't seem to matter anymore. We were, and only could be, friends. All notions of anything else had been pushed out of my mind a long time ago, but if my radar wasn't too far off, I could've sworn Sanford was flirting with me.

I could also confirm that I liked it.

At the risk of being over analytical, *what's really going on here with Sanford and me? I've never thought of Sanford romantically before, at least not seriously. I'm probably only entertaining this because I'm feeling a little lonesome.*

Lonely or not, I wanted to see him. I picked up the phone, punched nine for an outside line, then Linda's number. It was six o'clock and I wanted to catch her before she got too deep into her evening with the kids.

Linda picked up on the first ring. "Hey," I said. "Can you hear me?"

"Yeah, I can hear you, but barely. I'm in the grocery store. What's up?"

"I think I'm going to ask Sanford to go with me tomorrow night. Any opinion about that?"

"I think it's a great idea," she said. "Do you still want Mitch and me to go?"

I hesitated. "Umm, probably not."

She seemed fine with the change in plans. "That's good: it'll give you a chance to talk."

"I think so," I said. "He was kind of flirting with me the other day."

"How do *you* feel about that?"

"I don't know yet," I admitted. "Ask me after the poetry reading."

"You can tell me if you liked it or not."

"Okay," I said. "I liked it."

"I know you did. I could hear it through the phone. This is a change in position."

"It was just a feeling," I said. "I'm sure it will pass as quickly as it came."

"I don't know," she said. "Sanford has—"

"Has what?"

"Nothing . . . enough said. I'm almost at check-out, so-"

"I'll call you afterwards."

"Okay . . . don't forget."

I hung up the phone and shut down my work on the laptop. Before wrapping up completely, I pulled up my email account. I hadn't checked it all day, which isn't typical of me. I'm generally forced to look at it between patients to stay on top of the ridiculous number I receive. A quick glance over the slew of unopened mail determined I wasn't opening all of these. It was already after six, there was no way I intended on staying here anymore. Mouse in hand, I needed to figure out from reading each subject line, which messages should be opened now, and what could wait until the morning.

Sanford's job kept him on email more than the average person. Around nine-thirty eight he'd emailed me with *Let Me Know* in the subject line. *Let him know what?* I double-clicked to open the message. It contained the flyer from the poetry reading. The message inside read, "Is this the event you were talking about? Let me know." I hit reply and responded, "Yes, this is it. Do you want to meet up?" He should get that before I made it home.

After a full day of paperwork and patients, I wanted to take a shower and climb into bed. But my curiosity about Sanford's reply to my email took precedence. I dug out my cellphone, grabbed a bottle of water, and headed up the stairs to my bedroom. I turned the television on, and put the water bottle on the nightstand, maneuvered a pile of pillows to give myself a head rest while stroking the screen of my cell phone. Unbelievably, ten more emails just from the time it had taken me to get home and comfortably in bed. The only one I was interested in was from Sanford. I tapped to open it, "Absolutely, what time?" *That was a good question. I'll have to work tomorrow, plus we're going out on Friday. Maybe it's my body talking, but I already know I want to make an earlier evening of it.* I emailed him back, *let's meet at six o'clock.* I drank a sip of water, removed my glasses, and pulled the covers up over my head to sleep off the day.

The next day, I touched base with Sanford early to make sure he got my message and we were still on. Karen hadn't scheduled anyone until ten o'clock, which gave me the luxury of dragging my feet in the morning. I arrived at the office to the aroma of fresh brewed coffee. "Good morning," I said.

"Good morning."

I approached the front desk and picked up the mail. "Any calls?"

"Yes, I've forwarded the messages to your inbox."

"Thank you, ma'am. I'm going to call Sanford real quick before I get started."

"Sanford?" Karen swiveled around in her chair. "You didn't tell me you were talking to Sanford again."

"Oh my God, I'm so sorry, don't ask me how, but I forgot."

Karen stood up and leaned against the back counter. "How could you forget to tell me that?"

The weight of my briefcase hurt my shoulders. I backed out of the reception area and walked toward my office. Karen followed close behind. "After we went out, I talked with Tobey again about calling Sanford. That Saturday, I finally did and I went up on campus to see him." I put the mail on the side corner of my desk. Karen took a seat on the couch.

"It must have gone well if you two are going out."

"Yeah, I think it did. I wasn't sure at first," I cut my laptop on, sat in my desk chair while I waited for it to boot up. "For a second I thought showing up there was a bad idea, but he came around and now we are going out tonight."

"So, is this a date?"

"No, no—it isn't a date. It's like what we used to do, just hang out together. I probably should call him to confirm." My system came up. Karen rose and stood with her arms folded. She smiled. "If I didn't know any better I would say this is a date."

I pushed the call button on the desk phone, leaned forward and returned Karen's gaze over my glasses. "It's *not* a date."

"Of course it's not." Karen walked out the office.

Rolling my eyes, I continued to make my call. Sanford answered, "Hello."

"Hey you, did you get my email?"

"Yeah, I got it. I'll meet you there at seven o'clock."

"No, six o'clock."

"Yeah, that's what I meant, six o'clock."

"Okay, see you then."

My daily responsibilities were no longer the task of the day: keeping my focus off Sanford and our impending evening superseded everything else. Thankfully, I didn't have to struggle long, five o'clock came faster than ever before. Karen wished me good evening then left for the day. A quick trip to the kitchen to put something in my stomach, then off to the restroom to freshen up, the black pencil skirt I wore was straight, I undid two buttons on my shirt to show a hint of cleavage, freshened my lipstick and a few seconds later I grabbed my things in route to the spoken word event and Sanford.

The setting sun shone through the glass doors, illuminating the bar's entry. By the time I'd made my way to the hostess desk to ask about the poetry event, I couldn't make much out in the darkened room. She led me through chocolate leather chairs to a private area and a sound stage where the crew finished setting up for the performance. Stage left, a grand piano gleamed in silence, awaiting someone's touch. Through the house jazz, I heard my name. Sanford waved to me. The faint red glow from the table lamp added warmth to his face. He pulled my chair out and waited. Even with me in heels, he towered over me until he wrapped me up in an embrace that lifted me off the floor. His touch sent butterflies through me, ceasing when he finally let me go.

"How are you?"

"I'm good." I looked him over. In college those horn-rimmed glasses used to look geeky, but now the Afro and black frames was a really good look. "You look nice."

"Thank you." He displayed every tooth from his perfectly aligned smile. "Aren't I supposed to tell you that?"

I leaned over. "Well, you can always tell me I'm pretty."

"Pretty? Who said anything about pretty?

I playfully tapped his hand. "Ah, there he is . . . real funny."

Sanford laughed. "You're beautiful as always, and I just love that you've let your hair grow longer."

"Yeah, I know—sorry, I mean thank you." I moved my hair from one side of my body to the next and combed it with my fingers.

"You want something to drink?"

"Yes, I would love a glass of wine."

"Okay. I don't think they are completely set up, I'll go to the bar."

Sanford left the table headed toward the bar. I heard my phone vibrate inside my purse. Sanford was still at the bar retrieving drinks and I pawed through my purse. It was a message from Linda asking how it was going. *My goodness we just got here.* I texted back and told her we were fine. Sanford came back with two glasses of wine. The place started to fill up. "So tell me what you've been doing for the last year."

I sighed. "Well, at first I just wanted to get my head together, but that turned into figuring out what went wrong with me and Jake, which then lent itself to what am I looking for in a relationship."

"What did you figure out?"

"Unfortunately, not a whole lot, but one thing I figured out is that I need to make sure I don't lose myself in a relationship the way I did with Jake."

"Lose yourself how?"

"I loved Jake, so much . . . I guess I just lost sight of everything else—including me."

He changed the subject effortlessly. "So are you dating?"

"Why?" I laughed. "You going to fix me up? You just got me back, trying to get rid of me already?" We both took more sips. I put down my glass and checked out the club, it had completely filled up. The band played jazz while the poets were mingling in the crowd. Sanford leaned back in his chair. "What if I told you I did have somebody for you?"

I smiled. "I would ask you who?"

"I don't think you're ready to know."

I pulled my head back in astonishment. "What do you mean... not ready?"

Sanford smiled. "Not ready, babe, just not ready."

Sanford and I took a pause in the conversation to listen to the first poet who stepped to the mic and recited a poem to rave reviews from the audience. It was a great poem. "How about another round?"

"I have to work in the morning," I said.

"So do I. Come on just one more." Stanford called the server over to our table and ordered two more glasses. "I wonder who's up next." The lineup was on each table. I reviewed it to see if my favorite poet, Janet J, would be speaking tonight. As luck would have it she was, but not scheduled to come on until nine o'clock. I'd planned on being long gone by then. Our next round arrived to the table. I was starting to feel the effects of the wine.

Sanford read my mind. "I know you're staying to hear Janet J," he said.

"I want to, but she's not on until nine. That's late."

He caressed my arm. "Hang with me, we're going to be grown-ups tonight, which means staying out past eight."

I laughed. The movement from my head caused my hair to drape down into my face. Sanford lightly brushed it away, tucking it behind my ear. "Thank you." I smiled. "Okay, I'm yours I'll stay until Janet J goes off."

"You're mine?"

I smiled. "You know that's not what I meant."

Sanford bent forward, close to me. "That's what you said."

"Okay, I'm yours until nine o'clock. Yours, as in physically present here."

He pulled my chair even closer to him and whispered in my ear, "Well I guess I have an hour to get you to change your mind." I could feel the warmth of his body as his lips slightly grazed my cheek before he leaned back into his seat.

"I can't even believe you right now." I laughed, picked up my drink and finished it off. I motioned for the server to bring one more round for the road. More poets hit the mic until it was finally time for Janet J to take over the evening. Janet J, to the strumming of her bassist, recited a poem about love, friendship, and redemption. More truth than my three glasses of wine could handle.

We paid our bill and headed for the door. Sanford grabbed my hand and walked me to my car. I wrapped my arm under his as we made it to my car. "I had a blast. I really did," I said.

"Not as much as I did. I've wanted us to do this for a long time."

"How long?"

Sanford stepped into the open door, placed his arm around my waist and pulled me close to him. Leaning down he put his lips on top of mine, gently parting them with his tongue, interlocking his with mine, each slow loving stroke intensifying the feeling. The emerging sound of onlookers broke our embrace. We stood together, me still in his arms: we never broke our gaze. After a few brief moments, Sanford released me and tucked me safely into my car. I drove away, one eye on the mirror and Sanford. He watched me under the tranquil moonlit night as I drove away.

Chapter Eleven

I love my job, but hate working Fridays.

Linda understandably couldn't make it, but Sanford and Tobey were in. We agreed to meet at The Boulevard. The sheer thought of seeing Sanford after our date made me swoon. I'd been rather enjoying the seventh-grade crush playing out with him the last few weeks. Gazing at his picture and bursting into irrepressible laugher just recalling a statement he made, late nights talking on the phone under the cover. If my mother were at my house it really would be seventh grade. *I'm resisting the urge to excessively analyze the crap out this. I already know from past experiences if I dissect what I'm feeling I'll find some reason to walk away and there's no basis for why I should. Sanford's not Jake. I need to trust what I'm feeling, and for now, not focus on the past.*

I didn't want tonight to mirror the last time we went to The Boulevard. I got it together and found something to wear—barely. I checked my schedule to determine what time my last appointment for the day was for. Sanford coming tonight was making me take my game to another level. Not having a little pampering time for myself beforehand was not an option. According to my calendar, a nine o'clock and a ten o'clock appointment were scheduled. I yelled to Karen in the receptionist area. "Hey, Karen, do you think we can move my ten o'clock to Monday?"

Karen popped her head in my office, "No ma'am. Mr. Nelson will not be pleased if you move his appointment, but after him you're free for the day."

I sighed. "Ah, okay—you're right that shouldn't have been on the table in the first place."

"How about this," She clasped her hands together. "Why don't you tell me what you're trying to do?"

"I know this sounds terrible but I wanted to go running before I got my hair done."

Karen tilted her head turning the bottom lip downward and inside out. "Aw, you can afford to skip a workout: you'll still look cute for your date."

I placed my hands up. "Slow down, it's not a date especially since Tobey will be there. If we can just move Mr. Nelson up an hour it would give me more wiggle room in my schedule. It's seven now, but if he can get here by eight o'clock I can see him before I see Mrs. Williams."

Karen walked toward the door and headed back to the receptionist area with her back facing me. She said, "That, I may be able to do. Let me call him, but next time let's talk this through a little more before I commit you to these time slots."

91

"You took the words right out of my mouth."

While I waited to find out the verdict on Mr. Nelson I typed out my notes from yesterday's appointments.

Karen popped her head back in the doorframe. "Okay, I asked Mr. Nelson to come in earlier and he can't, so you have to see him at ten o'clock. Sorry, I know you want to go work out, but it's just not going to happen, at least not before noon."

"Okay, well, if I can't change it, I can't change it. I just feel funny when I don't work out."

Karen tilted her head and frowned at me. "You have almost zero percent body fat. Again, you'll survive."

I blushed. "Okay, let's get this day moving. Hopefully Mrs. Williams will be okay and won't need any serious intervention."

Karen left and I started back writing Mr. Thomas' plan. Time flew and before I knew it, I was halfway completed with Mr. Thomas' behavioral health plan, and I met with Mrs. Williams and Mr. Nelson. Now that the workday wound down, I needed to get out of the office and over to Stacy's to get my hair done.

"Hey, Karen, can you forward calls to my cell phone?"

There was no answer. This ghetto intercom of yelling through walls is not always an effective means of communication. "Karen, did you hear me?" *We really need an intercom.* I looked down at the desk phone. The red notch for line one was lit, but when I shifted back to my monitor the light was dark again. I was in earshot of the receptionist area and I could overhear her talking to someone in the office.

I recognize that voice.

I stepped into the doorframe and a familiar scent filled the hallway. I only knew one man who smelled of coconut oil: it could only be Jake, and the man wasn't far behind the scent. I only made it to the doorframe when I almost went head first into his chest. Karen, barely visible behind him, pointed at his back mouthing, "Jake is here." I dropped my head, raising both eyebrows over the rim of my glasses, subliminally informing her— *"Yes, I know."*

There were no words or rules in the book for this. I hadn't seen Jake in over a year.

I moved out of the doorway, allowing him to enter my office and sit down in a chair in front of my desk. He looked well—*then again, when has he not*. That didn't help. "Have you been tanning?"

"No," he responded. "You know I don't tan. The Arizona sun did this to me."

"However it happened it looks good on you."

Jake smiled. "Thank you."

I smiled and pointed to his shoulder-length hair. "You grew your hair out," I said.

"I can say the same for you. I always liked it longer. You look like you did when we were in college." He cleared his throat. "I was going to call, but I figured you'd just tell Karen to say you were out or not see me."

I nodded. "Probably."

"Which one?"

"Both . . . I was about to leave when you arrived." I was sure he could see my heart beating through the tailored shirt I unexpectedly was thankful I'd worn. I walked around in front of my desk, stood with my arms folded and said, "After a year of not talking you just drop by . . . unannounced."

"It doesn't look like you were leaving."

"Well . . . I was. So, to what do I owe this pleasure?"

"Nothing and no one," he said. "I was just up the street taking care of some business and thought I'd stop in and see if you were here."

I raised my eyebrows. "Oh, so you're by yourself?"

"Yes, I'm by myself. I wouldn't do that."

"Let's not say that, okay, because you did a whole lot of stuff I didn't think you'd do."

He sighed. "I know I'm not your favorite person. I just wanted to say hello. We haven't talked in a long time."

"There's a reason for that—remember?" My bringing up the past chilled the air. Jake appeared uncomfortable, shifting in his seat. His emerald green eyes felt like lasers. I needed to get out of the room. "Can you excuse me for a minute?" Jake leaned forward in his chair as he nodded. I rounded the desk and headed toward the restroom. Firmly bedded inside, I closed the door, leaned my entire body against it, clinching the door handle in a futile attempt to catch my breath. *A few more minutes, and I would have been out of the door.* After agonizing seconds, I released the door handle, and walked over to the sink. Two steps in, and I was surprised yet again this time by Karen charging into the restroom. I turned toward her clinching my chest, "Geez, you scared the crap out of me." I placed my free hand on the sink to settle myself, and nerves.

"I'm sorry," she said. "I heard you come in here. Are you okay?"

"Yes . . . I mean no. I just need to catch my breath and get over the shock of him being here."

"Well, he never disappoints does he . . . Jake is so—"

"You know . . . one of the bonuses of divorcing Jake is not hearing how *fine* he is every five seconds."

"I'm sorry," she said.

I waved my hand. "No, it's not you Karen . . . it's me."

Karen grabbed tissue from the dispenser. "I didn't mean to upset you more. I just wanted to make sure you were okay."

I released my grip on the sink and turned on the water. In the mirror, my reflection polarized what I was feeling. A disobedient tear made its way down my cheek. I cupped lukewarm water in my hands, and splashed it on my face.

Karen handed me tissue. I raised my face, covered with beads of water, lightly tapping each one away as not to disturb my makeup. The last thing I wanted to do was return looking worse than I did when I left. "I think it's just the emotion of it all. I didn't have this reaction before." I threw away the tissue. "Let's get back out there. I'm sure he's thinking something's up."

Karen rubbed my back. "Who cares . . . he can sit there for a minute."

I checked my eyes in the mirror. "I know . . . first things first, let's get out of here." Karen exited first with me closely behind. Jake, unmoved, remained in his seat in front of my desk looking at his cell phone.

"Checking your text messages?" I asked. Jake put away his phone as I rounded my desk to retake my seat.

I sighed. "Look—I'm having a good day. I'd like it to continue that way. So perhaps we can stick to neutral subjects. Your mother, for example. How is she?"

"She's okay," Jake responded. "She misses you, which is one of the reasons I wanted to stop by. I think she would love to hear from you–you should call her."

"*You're* the reason I stopped calling her," I pointed out.

"I know, and I was wrong. You should talk. I know my mother would really like to talk to you."

"Well, I'm glad to hear she is doing okay."

He stood up. "I don't want to keep you, just wanted to see if you were okay." I followed him to the door. He turned and put out his arms as though to hug me. I promptly took one step back. He stayed in the same position and finally I relented and walked into his open arms.

"It really is good to see you." Jake released me. "I'm glad you let me come in."

"Technically, you were already in by the time I saw you—but okay."

Karen was on the phone when he walked out. A part of me was glad to see him, but the other part wondered why he'd really stopped by. Karen hung up just as Jake turned around to wave bye. Karen and I simultaneously waved back. I threw in a smile for good measure. As soon as Jake was out of sight, Karen turned to me and asked, "Have you been talking to him?"

"No, not at all. I'm just as surprised as you to see him."

"So what did he say?"

"Nothing, really, just that he wanted me to talk to his mother again and he wanted to say hello."

"Talk to his mother?"

"Yeah, talk to his mom. I don't think he wanted anything and I need to get outta here. He's already thrown me off schedule."

She followed me back into my office. "When is the last time you talked to Jake?"

I continued to pack up my briefcase with everything I needed to work on this weekend. "Well over a year."

Arms folded, Karen watched me pack up. "He surprised me, but I'm fine now, really I am." The frown lines in Karen's forehead began to fade. I could tell she was still worried, but I wanted to focus on my evening ahead not the life I left behind. Jake has a supernatural ability to take over, even when he's not trying to.

Karen asked me to call her from the car, but I knew I would be calling Linda first. There had to be a reason that Jake had shown up out of the blue, and if anyone knew what that reason was it would be Linda. She was a vault when it came to keeping secrets.

"Hey, are you busy?" I asked.

"No, just got home. What's up?"

I was surprised. "Why are you home so early?"

"Well, nosey, if you *must* know, I went for my annual physical and decided not to go back to the office."

"Oh, good—you need to take more time off." I smiled. "I guess I shouldn't be giving that advice."

"No, you shouldn't. So what's up?"

I pulled out on the street and headed toward the hair salon. "A visitor stopped by today. I figured if anybody knew something about my visitor being in my office today that person would be you . . . Ms. Sneaky."

"Sneaky?"

"Yes, Sneaky, what have you been up to? Spill it."

There was a pause. "I don't know what you're talking about."

I started feeling impatient. "Don't play. You know Jake came to see me."

She ignored the question. "Where are you at?"

"I'm in my car, driving to the salon."

"I thought you were going out tonight," said Linda.

"We *are* going out."

"Who all's going?"

"Tobey, Sanford and me."

"Sanford? Hmm—interesting."

I hadn't told her everything about our sort-of-not date Wednesday. I left out the kiss. "We've started to get back to normal." *More or less.* "Tonight will be the first time we've seen each other since Wednesday."

"Oh, wow, then this should be good. Okay, so what is it you think I did?"

Think? "I know you talked to Jake."

"Why do you think I talked to him?"

"Because you did, and I know you did. Why else would he just pop up?"

"So what did he say?"

"He didn't say anything, just stopped to say hello, and told me to call his mother."

"Was Karen there when he stopped over?"

Her questions were getting to me. "Yeah, she works there, remember?"

"Smarty, I was just asking—but the truth is I don't know what you're talking about. It doesn't sound like you need Scooby Doo to solve this mystery. He wanted to see how you were, he did that—and now he's gone."

"The last time I saw Jake was with you in the courthouse. How's that not a big deal? He just shows up unannounced out of the blue."

"Let's not get too dramatic about this, okay? What else did he say exactly?"

I took a deep breath. "He said he was in the neighborhood doing some business and decided to stop in and see if I was there."

"Okay, so what's strange about that?"

She made it sound completely reasonable, even I had to admit to its plausibility. "Nothing, now that you put it that way."

Linda laughed. "Girl, stop bugging me about nonsense. Aren't you supposed to be meeting this new guy tonight?"

I pulled off the road into a gas station and parked. "Oh, shit, Linda! I completely forgot about that."

"Maybe I should come—you're in a pickle, my dear." She laughed. "Well, try not to get back on Sanford's naughty list. Call me tomorrow and let me know how it went."

I put the car in drive and headed back toward the gas station exit. "So, still not telling me anything?"

"Girl, bye!" There was a decisive click. It didn't matter: she had reminded me there was a bigger issue tonight than Jake.

Chapter Twelve

The conversation with Linda hadn't revealed any diabolical schemes. Perhaps, despite my suspicions to the contrary, she really didn't know anything. Until proven otherwise, the visit for now was classified as just a visit. But in the category of *what matters most*, Jake's reemergence from the depths didn't stack high on the bookshelf.

Being with Sanford and avoiding meeting Peter's friend took precedence.

A key element of my "potential new boyfriend" analytical process was defining and labeling. I was feeling a little adrift in terms of what was going on between Sanford and me. If we were just friends, then it would be fine for Sanford to be around when I met the new guy. If we were on the verge of being more… I don't want to kick the ball out of bounds with, although brief, a meeting with a potential suitor in front of him—that might not go over so well.

I managed to get in and out of the hair salon in less than two hours. We agreed to meet about six or six-thirty. It wasn't in Sanford's nature to be late: I knew he would be there right at six. Tobey—unfortunately for me—was a different story. She was always late, and not just by a few minutes. If Peter was bringing a friend to introduce me to, I wanted to make sure Tobey would be there to thwart any unintended exchanges requiring any degree of explanation later.

I called Tobey, and she'd heard from Peter. The man he wanted me to meet would be there, "So make sure you look good!" she said.

"I don't know what you mean by that. I always look good."

I called Sanford on his cell to see where he was. I was batting a hundred: he picked up right away too. "Hello?"

"Hey, there, what's up?"

"Nothing much," he replied. "Just wrapping up here. What's up with you?"

"Heading home, getting ready for tonight," I said.

"Oh, what's going on tonight?"

I frowned. "I know you playing, right?"

Sanford laughed. "Yeah, I'm messing with you. What time are we hooking up?"

"I told Tobey about six or six-thirty, but you know her, she'll be late. We can get there about seven."

"Okay, seven actually works for me, but I'll probably have to cut out early. I have to work tomorrow."

"No, that's fine," I said. "I need to finish some paperwork I didn't get done today."

"All right. So just meet you there or you want me to pick you up?"

"You know what? That sounds good. Will you pick me up?"

He chuckled. "I would love to."

"Alright, so about six-thirty?"

"What time is it now," he asked.

"Five-thirty."

"Okay, I can make it for six-thirty."

"Good . . . I have a couple more stops to make, then I'm headed home."

"Where are you now?" he asked.

"Driving to pick up my dress then to the grocery store."

I could sense the face he was making through the phone. "You can't do that tomorrow?"

I laughed. "No dear, I can't. I'm wearing the dress tonight. Don't worry it won't take me long."

"I'm not concerned. I'll wait on you."

"You don't sound convinced. I'm telling you, I'll be ready."

Sanford laughed. "Yeah, okay surprise me."

"Well, I just pulled up, so I'll see you in a little bit."

"Alright."

I'd asked the owner of a clothing boutique I frequented way more than I should to alter a dress for me. I tried the dress on just to make sure it expressed what I couldn't—or wouldn't—say. To my delight, it did.

A run through the grocery store, and no sooner than I closed my car door I felt lights on my back. I raised my right hand over my eyes so I could see. Then I heard a car door open and Sanford's voice. "Why aren't you dressed?"

I opened my door, and stepped out on the lawn. "Is it six-thirty?"

Sanford looked down at his watch. "No, but you have all of ten minutes," he said. He grabbed my bags out of the back seat. I opened the front door and entered the foyer with Sanford close behind. I tilted my head back and sniffed up in the air. "You smell nice."

Sanford smiled. "Oh you like that, huh?" He turned toward me and held out his arms for a hug. "Oh, so good, these hugs of yours," I said. Sanford swayed me in his enormous arms. I peeled away and he pulled me back into him. I pulled away, and looked up at him. "You want me to get dressed?"

"I guess I can let you get dressed."

I smiled. "Wise decision my good man."

I went around the table and grabbed my things. Sanford walked to the refrigerator, opened the door, and grabbed a bottle of wine. "What's this?"

I leaned back into the kitchen and turned my head toward the refrigerator. Squinting my eyes, I looked at the bottle. "Oh, its wine, drink some."

Sanford continued to hold the bottle up. "I know that, but isn't this the same bottle from the last time I was here?" Sanford stopped and thought about it for minute then asked, "How old is this bottle?"

I leaned back up and headed out of the kitchen. "I honestly don't know. It should be okay. There's plenty of other stuff to drink." I left Sanford in the kitchen trying to decide if he was going to risk drinking some year-old wine.

I walked into the bathroom and turned on the water. I glanced at the clock. It was six-thirty. If I hurried we could be out of the house by seven. I took off my clothes, tossed them in a pile on the floor and stepped into the shower. I hit the hot spots and stepped back out. *No towel.* My skin dripping with water, I ran into the bedroom to get my towel, and nearly ran into Sanford, standing there with two glasses of wine. Like Venus de Milo minus the towel, I froze, my mouth wide open. "I thought you were downstairs!" I stated.

Sanford's eyes filled every corner of his lenses. He stepped closer to me. "Um," he said. "Your body is unbelievable."

I went for my towel to cover myself. Sanford stood so close, staring at me. I probably should've felt uncomfortable . . . but I wasn't. I was actually turned on by it. "Amazing," he said.

I grabbed one of the glasses of wine and drank it straight down. I knew I should hide my naked body, but I didn't want to.

Sanford lifted his drink up to his lips and drank it in two gulps while I looked on. He threw the glasses on the bed and grabbed my head in his massive hands, placing each thumb at my ears, pulled me in and kissed me full on.

The warmth of Sanford's tongue emanated through my veins. My breath labored, body pulsated from his touch. Standing on the tips of my toes, I raised my body just enough for Sanford to grab hold and lift me to his waist where I eagerly wrapped my legs. He glided the tips of his fingers on my skin while circulating his tongue in and around mine. Hungry for his touch, I awaited every sensation delivered from the gradual descent of his hands down my back cupping my behind as he slid them beneath me refraining to liberate his tongue from mine. Sanford carried me toward the bed gently resting me on top.

On my back I felt the strength of Sanford on top of me, my hand navigated down his back and around to the front of his pants. I wasn't thinking anymore. Celibacy and emotions aside, I wasn't about to make love to just anyone . . . this was Sanford.

I unzipped his pants with deliberate intent unleashing what enthusiastically awaited inside pleased by the realization he was a big man in every way. Sanford's penis was wet with the anticipation and his uninterrupted kisses sustained my humidity outside and in. Between my parted legs I lowered my hand filling it with him, caressing and guiding him inside of me. The tip of his penis, lured by the touch of my vaginal walls, he smoothly worked his way inside me thrusting in and out, hitting my clitoris with every stroke. I was wetter than I'd ever been before. Sanford awakened every cell in my body in each single uninterrupted stroke.

No foreplay, no oral, just him inside of me, pulling me closer and closer to him over and over, throbbing with every touch.

I couldn't hold my excitement anymore. Every nerve ending in my body cried out, expelling itself through my lungs. Tears streamed down my face as I choked down each thunderous orgasmic eruption. With other men, I could only come once, if at all. This was new. Sanford was new and two was the magic number.

I knew eventually we would have to figure this out, but for now, after a quick trip to the restroom, I was preparing myself for round two. Sanford repositioned me at the top of the bed. I felt his head between my legs and his warm tender immense tongue.

My eyes rolled back into my head as he spread my legs toward both ends of the earth.

Chapter Thirteen

Snuggled under the cover, I rested my leg across Sanford's warm naked body sketching his facial features with my index finger—across his eyebrows, around the eyes, down his nose followed by the outline of his lips. His lips were soft. I grazed my finger across them parting the edges with my finger until Sanford playfully bit the tip of my fingernail. "What are you doing?" he asked, pulling me close, kissing my forehead.

I raised my head to kiss his cheek. "Enjoying you."

"I'm enjoying you, too. I don't want to go out anymore."

I gasped. "Oh, God, I forgot about Tobey. What time is it?"

We both sat up in bed. Sanford put his glasses back on and checked his cell. "Eight o'clock."

"Tobey is going to kill us," I said.

He laughed. "Kill you, you mean—she don't care whether I come or not."

"I should call her."

"Tell her you're not coming . . . you're staying here with me."

I looked over to the nightstand—no phone. It was still in my purse in the kitchen. Staying home in bed with Sanford was more appealing than going to a club. "Okay, I'll call her." I removed the comforter from my legs. Sanford reached for my hand. "Where are you going," he whispered.

"Remember," I kissed his hand. "To tell Tobey I'm staying home."

I slipped out of bed downstairs. My screen flashed two missed calls from Tobey. I called voicemail. In the first message she sound worried, the second informed me if I wasn't dead I better get my butt over there now. I contemplated a few seconds before giving her a call. Ditching her would be easier if we didn't talk. Erring on the path of least resistance, I decided to call. To my great relief, Tobey didn't answer. I left a message ending with a sincere heartfelt apology, before turning to head back upstairs into bed when the phone rang. *Ugh*, Tobey. I sat down on a stair. "I'm still at home," I said.

"Are you on your way?"

"Actually, that's why I called I was—"

"Don't even think about staying home," she threatened.

"I'm leaving in a minute."

"Okay, hurry up." The phone disconnected. I would be foolish to assume the call dropped . . . she'd hung up on me. As much as I hated to leave Sanford, I needed to show my face, even if only for a little minute. I got up from the chair, and walked back into the bedroom where Sanford was now sitting up watching television.

"Did you hear?"

"Yeah I heard," Sanford said, "but that's okay. I have to go to work in the morning anyway."

"Are you sure?"

"No, but I don't have any clothes here."

I walked over and sat on his lap. Lower lip fully extended. I was pouting. Sanford tugged at my bottom lip. "Don't give me the sad face. I'll be back tomorrow."

I stood up and gave him a peck on the lips, cupping his face with my hands I said, "You promise?"

"I promise."

"Okay, you can go."

Sanford brushed my hair from in front of my eyes. He stood up, grabbed his clothes, and walked into the bathroom. I heard water running, and the sound of him clearing his throat. He returned to the room dressed to leave. Wrapped in a towel, I kissed him goodbye and watched him through the window to his car.

After an unexpected evening saturated with love and lust, I pushed on to hang out with Tobey. It didn't take long for me to get dressed and head her way. I navigated my way through a sea of faces, waving my hand in the air at the sight of Tobey signaling my arrival.

"Girl!" exclaimed Tobey. "Where have you been? You're three hours late!"

I tilted my head at the chair next to her, "Is anybody sitting here?"

"Peter." She pointed to the other side of the room. "But he's over there." She took a sip of her drink. "Sit down."

I caught the eye of the bartender and ordered a glass of water.

"Okay, you ask us out for a drink, and you're not drinking?"

"I'll order one in a bit. I'm making it an early evening."

Her eyebrows rushed to meet each other, with her hand firmly planted on her hip. Pointing at my throat she said, "You just got here. What's early? We wouldn't be here at all if you hadn't organized this little soirée. Something's up with you."

I clasped her free hand and pointed finger, lowering them to a respectable level. I shook my head. "Nothing is up with me: I'm fine. I only said that because I wanted to turn in early, but I can stay, that's not a problem."

"I was just about to say—"

"Let's switch subjects . . . where is Peter at?"

She shrugged and pointed again at the bar. "You want to go over there?"

"Not really."

"Isn't that why we came?"

I shook my head. "It's crowded in here. I don't want to lose our seats."

"Okay, I'll just go back there and let him know you're here. Watch my purse, okay?" Tobey walked over to the crowd of guys near and around Peter. She whispered to him and pulled him back to our table.

Peter didn't waste any time. "About time you got here. What—or who—made you late?"

Before I could say anything, Tobey responded for me. "She wasn't with anybody."

Peter turned to me for confirmation: I obliged. "Just running late," I agreed. The truth would only be the prequel to an interrogation, which I, unequivocally, refused to take part in.

"Okay, I want you to come over here and meet my friend." Peter turned toward a group of guys. Tobey, to my surprise, followed along. "Where is Sanford?" She asked me. "I expected to see him."

"He couldn't make it." I felt my cheeks flush.

"What's wrong with you? Did you talk to him?"

"Yeah, he had something else to do."

"Oh, that's too bad." Tobey exclaimed. "I was looking forward to hanging out with him."

The music helped me pretend I didn't hear her. I wanted to push fast-forward on this night.

Peter turned back to us. "You ready?" He reached over and tapped the shoulder of one of the guys standing with the group by the bar. *What a difference a couple of weeks make.* He turned around, "Alex, this is Easton. Easton . . . Alex."

We shook hands. "Nice to meet you, Alex."

"Same here." I turned and tapped Tobey's shoulder. "This is my friend Tobey."

Unlike Sanford, Easton and I faced each other eye to eye. I figured without my heels, he might have three inches on me. Easton was every bit the opposite of Sanford from his height, dress and demeanor.

Tobey continued to check out the scenery while Easton engaged me in small talk. "How do you know Peter?" he asked.

"Through Tobey, we usually talk to each other here."

"Do you come here a lot?"

"Not really. I was here in the last week or so, but before that not in about a year."

He smiled. *Really good teeth.* "Why so long?" he asked.

"Well, let's see . . . how about I give you the Reader's Digest version. I didn't hang out much while I was married. After my divorce it took some time, but I'm starting to get out. Work keeps me busy, too."

Easton nodded his head in agreement. "Yeah, work keeps me busy. What do you do?"

"I'm a therapist. You?"

He grinned. "Take a guess?"

I smiled. "I would say a preacher, but that would make your presence here completely inappropriate."

We laughed at the thought. He leaned over, whispering in my ear, "I'm an attorney."

"Oh, what do you practice?"

"Injury."

"Oh, okay. So, if I slip and fall, you're my guy?"

"Yeah . . . well, yes, I could be."

I smiled at his subtlety. "Do you have kids?"

"Yes, I have two boys."

I smiled. "How old are they?"

"Five and eight."

"You have *little* kids," I exclaimed.

He grinned. "No—well, I guess you could say that. I don't think of them as little anymore."

On to the next obvious question. "Where there are kids, there are mothers. Where is your children's mother?"

Easton appeared uncomfortable. "She's around."

"Around where?" His gesture prompted me to scan the room. "Is she here?"

Easton clearly didn't want to talk about his wife. I had no plans to use this information for anything other than satisfying my curiosity.

"It's complicated."

Unfortunately my curiosity wasn't doused by his response. "How complicated can it be? You're either married, or you aren't, and I'll be real honest with you—I think you already answered the question."

My body language said it all: I didn't want to continue our conversation. He lingered next to me, eventually coming to the foregone conclusion the conversation was beyond resurrection.

I turned away and saw a familiar face. Hunter. I didn't think he'd remember me, but I wanted to move away from where I stood. Maneuvering my way through the crowd I tapped him on the shoulder, "Hi, I don't know if you remember me? My name is Alex. I think we met here before. Do I look familiar?"

"Yeah, I remember you. How have you been?"

I smiled. "I've been good, real good. How have *you* been?"

"I'm doing okay."

He wasn't helping much with the small talk. "Didn't you tell me you worked at the college?"

"I work with your friend Sanford," he said.

I nodded. "Oh, okay, maybe that's where I remember you from."

Hunter looked around. "Is he here tonight?"

"No, he didn't come," I said. I still felt a shiver of excitement up my spine just from saying his name.

"Oh, okay," Hunter said. "So, what's been up with you?"

"Not a whole lot," I replied.

Hunter nodded his head in Easton's direction. "Your boy misses you. I didn't pull you away from something did I?"

I looked over in Easton's direction. "Not at all. I just met him . . . he's a friend of a friend."

"You might want to tell him that . . . he was giving me a serious look for a minute there."

"Well, maybe this is the perfect time for us to sit down."

Hunter and I found a couple of seats at a nearby table. We ordered drinks and I motioned to Tobey to join us. She handed me a card. "Easton left this for you."

Easton himself was already by the door, but turned to beckon me to join him. Tobey was already sitting down with Hunter, so I headed over to Easton. He pressed a second card into my palm. "Just in case you didn't get this."

"I did," I replied.

"I wanted to answer your question before I left. Yes, I'm married, but separated. Like I said . . . complicated."

I searched his face. "Let me ask you this. Why are you out here meeting people—and you're married?" I wanted to know, but I knew from his face that if I would get an answer, it wouldn't be tonight.

He patted my arm. "It was nice meeting you."

Hunter, Tobey and I had a couple more drinks before calling it a night.

At home I emptied my pockets and placed Easton's card on the nightstand. I squeezed the pillow where Sanford had lain, inhaling his lingering cologne. Shifting, folding and repositioning my head until his aroma faded.

My mind replayed the night's events too many times. I couldn't fall asleep. I figured I might as well do something to pass the time, and went downstairs and grabbed a photo album from the bookcase. I poured a glass of wine, snatched an oversized blanket from the linen closet, curled up on the couch and went over every photo of Sanford with newly acquired rose-colored glasses.

Chapter Fourteen

I rolled over in bed, grabbed my cell phone, and looked at the time. Seven o'clock. I rubbed my palm across my forehead, attempting to push back the effects of wine and exhaustion. My attempt to lull my headache into submission without medication lasted five seconds before the phone rang.

It was Linda. "Wake up, sleepyhead, this is my second time calling you. How did it go last night?"

"Why are you calling me so early?"

"I'm dying to know! How was he?"

I rolled over onto my back. "How was who?" I questioned.

"The guy?"

I felt foggy. "What guy?"

"Are you still asleep?"

"Yes, Linda."

"Call me once you wake up. Don't forget."

"Okay."

I'd barely hung up the phone before it rang again. *What is up this morning?* "Hello?"

"Good morning!" Sanford. Another person brimming with sunshine.

"Good morning."

"How did it go last night?"

I licked my lips. "It went okay. Tobey kept asking about you. She thought you were coming."

"Well, I *was* coming, remember?"

I smiled. "Yes, I remember."

"You completely missed that."

I looked around the room. "Oh, I get it . . . *coming*," I laughed. "You missed your calling."

"Ordinarily you would've gotten that joke. You must still be asleep."

"Yeah, I am. Couldn't sleep when I got home, so I went through some old photos. I drank more wine too. That was a mistake."

"Why were you going through those old pictures?" he asked.

"I don't know . . . feeling a little sentimental. I wish you would've come with me last night."

"I didn't think you cared if I went or not."

"I know—it wasn't until I got home. Looking through those pictures, I started to wish you were with me. At the Boulevard too, but more then."

"That's nice," he said. "Next time I'll come. And how about today?"

I shifted on my pillow. "I really want to see you, but first I want to go back to sleep."

He was instantly apologetic. "Oh, I'm sorry. You were asleep."

I sighed. "No, don't apologize. You didn't wake me up, Linda did."

"Checking on your night?"

"More or less."

"Did you tell her anything about us?"

"That would be a negative. I think the mere fact I'm not still on the phone with her means I didn't."

Amused, he said, "You have a point. Well, call me when you wake up? I really want to see you. I have something to tell you."

I pulled back the bed sheets. The fog of wine and exhaustion dissipated. "Oh you got to be kidding me. You can't leave me hanging with that ending."

"Don't panic. I need to tell you something and I want to tell you in person."

"Sanford?"

"Alex?"

My heart rested comfortably in my big toe. "There is no way I'm going back to sleep now, so you may as well tell me."

"I want to tell you when I see you. How about dinner and a movie?"

"Fine—dinner and a movie. What time will you be here?"

"What do you want to see?"

"I really don't care." My mind raced with nervous energy. I didn't know what to think or feel. I'd made love to him last night and today he was telling me he wanted to talk. Even with my limited dating experience, I knew *wanting to talk* doesn't work out well for the receiver.

Sanford picked up on it. "I can tell you're upset, so here goes. There's an opportunity for me to teach in D.C. and I want to talk to you about it."

"D.C.?"

"Yeah, D.C. I've been working on it for a while, and I want to get you up to speed on where I am with this."

My head worked overtime to remain unswerving, open to the mounting feelings I had for Sanford, but the heart was already feeling the significance of his potential departure. "When are you leaving?"

"I'm not going anywhere yet. What time do you want me to pick you up?"

"Let's do the matinee, about two o'clock."

"All right I'll be there in a few hours. You okay?"

"I'm okay."

Disappointed about the contents of our impending conversation, I got off the phone, lay back and marinated in the thought of Sanford leaving for any period of time. I would find out soon enough what this meant. Unable to return to sleep, I got up and made myself a pot of coffee.

May as well get this day rolling.

Sanford picked me up exactly three hours later. It was too early to go inside the theatre, so we went into the ice cream parlor next door, bought a couple of shakes and sat down.

Sanford, being his normal wonderful self, appeared to delight in the moment. I, on the other hand, wanted to get this conversation started. All of this self-talk I had going on inside my head—at least he would be present for this half of the conversation. Sanford raised my chin. "You sure you're okay?"

"I'm ready to talk about you leaving."

"I'm not leaving right now, but I've been trying to get on board with a project at the Research Institute. It's only for a few months."

I circled my straw inside my cup. "When will you know?"

"It could be a few days or weeks. I don't know, but whenever they do tell me, I'll have to go."

I looked at him. "Why didn't you mention this before?"

"Honest—I forgot about it."

"So what brought it back up?"

Sanford took a sip of his shake. "An email," he said and swallowed. "I read it last night—now I'm telling you."

I twirled my straw in the shake a few more times before taking another sip. Sanford finished his drink, got up and threw the cup in the trash. The drama queen in me struggled to enjoy the moment. I hadn't gotten a chance to settle into our new status of *More Than Friends* before it was over with. Sanford returned to the table and checked his watch. Rearing back in his chair, he rubbed his hands across the top of his jeans. "You think you're about ready to go?"

"Yeah, I'm finished."

"You sure? I'm not trying to rush you," he said.

"No, I don't have much of an appetite anymore."

Sanford took off his glasses and rubbed his eyes. "I'm not leaving the planet."

"I know, but I think I'm allowed to be disappointed."

"Disappointed I get, but you don't think you're getting too worked up?"

This is silly. "You know me—*the sky is falling.* I'm okay."

Sanford put his glasses back on and grabbed my hand as we walked our green mile back in the direction of the theatre. My excitement over the newness of this relationship just got a strong shot of reality. Sanford's absence would be physical and temporary, but I couldn't shake or define what I was experiencing. What I did know was that it didn't feel like we were at the beginning of something—not anymore.

I liked where we were, just wished it could have lasted a little longer.

Chapter Fifteen

I watched Sanford sleep, and worried about the time when he wouldn't be in bed beside me. I should savor this moment, but I can't stop thinking of when we stopped talking last year, presumably forever, only to return for a reconciliation, friendship, and then romance. Life should be lived in the moment, not in my head, but I don't know how to turn it off.

Sunday afternoon, Sanford headed home to grade papers. I needed to get some work done, too. In his absence I kept thinking about when he was leaving. *What will I do while he's gone? Perhaps we should put things on hold until he returns? My adult self realizes any sort of label is juvenile, but the girl inside knows they serve a distinct purpose. Absent the definition, I don't know who I am or what, if anything I should do.*

Finally, a few cups of coffee helped me settle into a groove dictating notes from the last session with a patient when my cell phone rang. The caller ID showed Sanford's face. I hesitated then answered. "Hey is everything okay?"

"Yeah, it's fine. I'm outside. Can you open the door?" His words didn't match his tone. *The Research Institute got back in touch with him.*

"All right."

I rushed downstairs to open the door. Sanford stood on the porch with a printout of an email. He silently stepped inside and handed it to me. Sanford's achieving his dream meant moving farther away from me. I handed it back to him. "So, what does this mean?"

"You just read the email. It's all spelled out."

I stroked my fingers across my forehead to smooth out the worry lines. "I know—I'm sorry, it was a silly question." I wrapped my arms around Sanford and squeezed him. "Congratulations, honey. I'm happy for you."

He leaned away, looked into my eyes seeming to search for sincerity.

"For real, I am."

He leaned back into the embrace. "Thank you."

I released my grip and stepped away to face him, "You have a week? That's all . . . kind of soon, isn't it?"

"Not really—considering we wrote the grant six months ago."

Sanford followed me up the stairs to my bedroom. Inside, I felt an overwhelming urge to get back into bed and pull the covers over my head. Sanford took a seat at the foot of my bed awaiting my next response.

"Hit me with the headliner. You said a week, but what day are you leaving?"

"Wednesday."

"What about your classes?"

"They'll get a replacement for the rest of the year. I'll return in six months."

"Six months?" I pulled my legs from underneath him into my chest. Sanford took in a deep breath, and exhaled as he sat back up.

"Seriously—are you that worried about this?"

"I am. I think us, you and me, as a couple, we're new—Sanford, you don't think six months is a long time?" Sanford hung his head, but didn't offer a response. "I think we should put things on hold," I said without thinking.

"Where did that come from?"

"I know I'm making a bigger deal out this than it needs to be, but I can't help it." Sanford's eyes narrowed as he glared at me looking befuddled from my unraveling. "This is too much to undertake all at once," I said.

A noise from the street broke the tension. Sanford stood up to investigate from the window to the street below. "For you or me?" he asked.

"Both of us."

Sanford sat back down at the foot of the bed.

"I want a relationship," I explained, "but not long distance."

"This is starting to sound like an ultimatum. You want *a relationship* or you want me?"

"Believe me," I said, "I want you, but six months is a long time."

Sanford stood up and walked to the door. "I don't want to talk about this anymore. I have a lot to do before Wednesday."

"Okay."

Sanford walked out the room tapping the doorframe with his hand as he went through it. "You don't have to get up. I'll let myself out."

I heard his footsteps rush down the stairs, the lock twist and door close. I don't remember Prince Charming running away from Cinderella. *Any romantic notion I had for a fairytale ending was over.*

Chapter Sixteen

"At least I know why we're watching this stupid movie again." Linda scooped up another cup of popcorn. "So what did you expect? He was going to look longingly in your eyes and say, Alex, my darling—I love you and ain't no mountain high enough to keep me from getting to you, baby."

"I'm glad I'm your entertainment for today. If you going to be sarcastic, at least you could get the song right."

"That's how it goes?"

"It's babe, not baby. I came over here to watch my depressing movie in peace."

She laughed. "It's baby, and if you wanted peace, you should've stayed home."

I rolled my eyes. "Ha, ha, ha. You're so funny."

Linda laughed, nodding her head. "I have my moments of comedic genius."

"They're rare . . . "

"Rare, but funny. So let's get into it. What did you expect him to say . . . no, better yet, do?"

Linda stared appearing to await my response. I grabbed another handful of popcorn and pointed at the television screen. "You see there . . . that's what *I* expected."

Linda raised an eyebrow. "I could've told you that wasn't going to happen."

I said, "Next time I'll have to consult you first. I don't think my expectations could have gotten any lower." I sat silently for a second. "At the risk of putting this out there—"

"What?"

I sighed. "Okay: it did occur to me if Jake couldn't be faithful here, how do I know Sanford will be in D.C.?"

Linda jumped out of her seat with the speed of light. "Now we're getting somewhere. First of all, Sanford's not Jake, and if memory serves me correct, you and Sanford are just friends . . . right?"

"Right . . . well, sort of right."

She reached over and gave me a flick to the shoulder. She picked up the controller from the coffee table and muted the television. "Right?"

"Okay," I said. "I may have left some parts out."

"What parts?"

"Sanford and I have been dating for about a month now—maybe a little longer."

"You got to be kidding me!" Linda's mouth was wide enough for me to throw a few puffed kernels in.

"Yeah and it was great until he dropped his little bomb about leaving for D.C."

"Oh, Alex, you could have worked through that."

I sighed. "I know. Believe me I knew I messed up the second he left."

She flicked her fingers against my arm. "Call him—you can fix this."

"Nope, I'm going to let this one play out."

"That's a mistake."

I nodded in agreement. "Probably, I'm getting pretty good at making mistakes."

I scratched my head as we both turned to watch the ending of the movie. Linda said, "See, even Meg Ryan had to leave Seattle to get her man. You could do that."

"Do what? Go get him?"

"Yeah, go out there."

I tilted my head staring at the television. "You crazy—I'm not doing that." I took a sip of wine. "Tom kind of looks like Sanford—with the fro. You notice that?"

Linda grabbed my arm and shook it. "It's a sign . . . you need to go to D.C. and get your man."

"Oh that's going to happen—oh in—Nevuary."

"No, I'm serious," she laughed.

"I don't think so. I'm not trying to get frequent flyer miles on my broken heart."

Linda silently turned back to the television. "Think positive," she said. "You never know what life has in store for you."

We swapped glances as Meg, Tom and Jonah entered the elevator. The elevator doors close to what we assume would be the beginning of their new lives. "One door closes, and another one opens," I said.

"See," Linda said, pointing. "You never know—that could be you."

"It's what happens after the doors close that's got me worried."

"What do you think—Tom is beating the shit out of her in front of the kid in the elevator?" Linda stood up from the couch and cut the television off. "Go get your man, Alex, and stop watching these stupid movies."

Chapter Seventeen

I'm characteristically bound by my error in judgment.

It's been a month, feels like a year, and any respectful timeframe I had to throw myself on the sword of mistakes begging his forgiveness has passed. He's there and I'm here.

We've managed to come full circle yet again, not talking. It was five o'clock, not long after Tobey's shift started. I needed to get out from inside my own head. I sent a text telling her I wanted to get together. She agreed.

The drive to the hospital gifted me with more unwanted thinking time: unnecessary thinking time. In between music, announcements and station breaks I realized something about myself. *I know how to get married (and divorced, for that matter). What I don't know is how to sustain a relationship beyond euphoria through the impending unavoidable emotional mine fields to a cohabitation that's calm. It's the middle . . . always difficult to make it through the middle, and this time around the "feel better" is taking longer. I'm a silhouette of my old self, but doing what's needed to feel connected again isn't appealing to me.*

Unbeknownst to Tobey she would be my latest diversion from my thoughts. From across the valet, through two glass doors, I saw Tobey waiting in the main lobby, dressed in scrubs and thinner since the last time we were together. She waved me over. "This is a nice unexpected surprise," Tobey said. "What's up with you?"

"Nothing." I embraced her. "Just in the neighborhood, decided to check out my long-lost friend."

Tobey and I walked inside the cafeteria and grabbed a table in the back. "How long do you have?"

"Ten minutes or so," she said. "I'm not officially on break. I told 'em I'd be back in a few minutes."

"What area are you working in today?"

"Pediatrics."

"Oh, girl." I placed my hand on my chest. "I don't see how you do it."

"Everybody says that," she said. "Babies get sick, too."

"I know, but it's so heartbreaking to see a baby sick. Let's change subjects. Tell me about you and Hunter."

She smiled. "I never dreamed we would hit it off. He didn't seem like my type."

"Type? I didn't know you had one." I grinned at her.

"I'm just saying he's not like the guys I usually go for," she said.

"Maybe that's why we're still single."

Tobey crossed her arms and sat back in her chair. "You know what, please don't take this the wrong way, but why are you here?"

A little taken aback, I asked, "How could I possibly take that the wrong way?"

"No, I don't mean it like that, but you've never come to see me at work before." Her voice was filled with concern. "Is everything okay? Are you missing your friend?"

Her concern for me was enough to open the floodgates. I didn't dare give myself permission to act on the impulse. Even I was sick of playing the role of the victim. *Time to board a new train.*

"More than I'm willing to admit, but I'm fine—I *will* be fine," I said, tapping her arm. "Don't worry so much."

"Okay, then. For a second there I thought you wanted to tell me you'd slept with him."

I thought I was going to choke. "Oh, you got to be kidding me? Who told you?"

"Don't be mad. It was Hunter."

"How did *Hunter* find out?"

"Sanford told him you've been hanging out. They're friends, remember?"

I sat back. "How is this ring of gossipers expanding?"

"I already knew something was going on when he didn't come out with us. You are so sneaky—you lied to me."

"I don't remember what I said, but I'm pretty sure I didn't lie."

"You did lie," she pointed out, but she was laughing. "You said he just decided not to come."

"I didn't say that. I said he had something else to do and I didn't lie he did have something else to do—go home." My laughter coincided with the sound of my cellphone ringing. I pulled it from my purse and raised my finger at Tobey to pause the conversation. Before I answered, Tobey offered, "I think Sanford really cares about you."

The voice on the other end said, "Who cares about you?"

"What?" I asked. "Who is this?"

"You never called, so I decided to call you."

"Jake?"

The announcement of his name sucked the air out of the room. Tobey grabbed her chest to delay an imaginary heart attack. I hadn't told her it wasn't our first time talking in recent weeks. I don't think I'd told anyone other than Linda.

"Yeah, who else would it be?" he asked.

Ignoring Tobey's arm-waving to get my attention, I responded to Jake. "It's not as if we talk every day."

He paused. "I guess that's true. I'm calling on official business. My mother said you never called."

I hit my forehead. "Dang it, I'm so sorry I completely forgot."

The entire time we were talking, Tobey was tapping the table, impatiently awaiting information. Jake continued rambling about me not calling his mother. "I told her you would call this week. You will, won't you?"

I put up a finger to Tobey for her to give me one minute then jumped back into the conversation with Jake. "Yes, absolutely—I promise."

"Okay—how are you?"

"I'm fine."

Tobey looked at her watch. We'd been sitting there for some time now. She pointed toward the elevators, rose from her chair and put her hand to her ear motioning for me to call her.

"Are you okay?"

"Yes, I was in the middle of something. I'm done, and fine. Thank you."

"Did you give any more thought to selling the house?"

"Not really, why?"

"You said you might sell."

"That was a long time ago. You're making an offer? It's a little late for you to get it in the divorce."

He laughed. "No—I don't even know why I brought it up. Really, I'm not interested in the house."

I got up, walked to the counter and purchased a cup of coffee while listening to Jake go on about me selling or not selling the house. With my phone firmly planted between my ear and shoulder, I walked through the main lobby past the elevators where Tobey stood. *She hadn't made it far.* I mouthed *wait a minute* to her before she got on the elevator. Tobey let the other occupants go ahead, while I caught up to her.

"So, are you going to make an offer?" I asked Jake.

"No, I think we're going to keep looking." *We're* going to keep looking?

My stomach tightened.

"What's wrong?" Tobey asked.

I mouthed the name at her. "Taylor."

We ended our adjoined disgust just in time for Tobey to catch the next elevator to her floor. I went through the revolving doors, no longer interested in a word Jake had to say. I wanted to end the conversation before Jake said something to take me over the emotional edge. "Well, I hope you find something. When are you trying to move?"

"Next spring. It's getting too much for Mama to live by herself. I promised I would find something soon."

I laughed. "Oh, you're moving in with your mother?"

"She's moving in with me," he corrected me. "She wanted to talk to you herself. She's having some health issues."

I finally reached my car through the parking garage. It was getting hard to hear Jake with the echo. "Jake, I'm sorry, but I have got to get off this phone. I'm here at the hospital and you're going in and out."

"Hospital? Who's in the hospital?"

"No, nobody's in the hospital. Remember, Tobey is a nurse? She works at St. Mary's. We just met for coffee."

"Oh, okay: you scared me for a minute."

I put the coffee cup on top of my car to unlock the door. "No need. Everybody's fine."

"Okay, well—don't forget to call Mom."

"I won't. I promise I'll call her by the end of the week."

"Okay, good enough. Hopefully I'll get a chance to see you again."

What? "Yeah, that would be nice."

"All right, I'll catch up with you later."

I got in and headed out of the garage, and my phone rang again: Tobey.

Before I answered a brown stream ran down my window. The coffee . . . I'd forgotten it on the roof. I answered the phone.

"Are you still talking to him? What did he want?"

"Well, you're going to be mad at me for not telling you, but this is the second time I've talked to him. I saw him before we went out. He wants me to go see his mother. That's another reason why I ran late: he came by the office."

"He's using his mother as an excuse."

"There's no mystery here Scooby Doo—he wants me to call his mother, and I will as soon as I get a chance."

"Oh, so you really think that's why he came over?"

"I'm not giving those seeds any water. Its why, and he called to remind me. You don't have to be concerned. Jake can't hurt me anymore."

"Yes," she said. "He can."

Chapter Eighteen

I loathe the silent treatment, especially when I'm not sure if I'm getting or giving it. I would have bet my last dollar Sanford would've called me by now.

My day is broken up into four acts—morning ritual, work, after work and bedtime. The clock of discontent ticks really slowly, particularly when it's self-inflicted. I made a snap decision that I wasn't ready to live with. I need to find out if it's retractable.

I arrived at work where a note was placed on my computer screen reminding me to call Ms. Thomas. From behind my desk, I stared blankly at my calendar desperately trying to recall the last time we talked. In the big scheme of things I guess it doesn't really matter, but I was curious. Regurgitated memory after memory yielded no rift, just disconnection. I'm sure there is a meaningful, yet complicated reason, which made perfect sense, but doesn't hold up under the lens of time. I did recollect wanting to make a clean break, not only from her, but everybody. *She was an unfortunate causality of war.*

Karen and I were humming right along with our day. There was Ms. Thomas, and then there was Sanford. The more I tried to stop thinking about him, the more I did. *This isn't me. I don't continuously fixate on anybody. Well, I guess I can't say that anymore. I'm obsessing over him, and I want to stop, but how? I guess if there is an up to my preoccupation it will end soon. It has to.*

"Alex, Mr. Johnson is here to see you."

"Okay, send him in."

Mr. Johnson walked in my office and he didn't look like the same man I'd been counseling. *Something is clearly different and I don't think it's anything to do with our sessions.*

"Hello, Dr. Nichols."

"Hello Mr. Johnson, how have you been feeling since the last time we met?"

"I've been feeling great, things are much better—much, much better."

I gestured for him to sit down. "How would you describe what you're feeling?"

Mr. Johnson settled down into the counseling chair. He smiled and said, "I would say optimistic about the future."

"Why do you feel optimistic?

"Let's start with the bad stuff first. We haven't gone to trial yet, but it's getting closer. The prosecutor is still confident they can get a conviction. It's pretty open-and-shut. I think they'll convict. It's just the time it's taking to get started that's what's killing me."

"Okay, things aren't moving as quickly as you would like, but they're moving. Is this movement what's brought on feelings of optimism?"

"I'm happy about that, but it's not the reason for the mood change."

"Okay, please explain."

Mr. Johnson leaned forward on the chair. "Remember my attorney, the one I told you about?"

"Yes, I think you said he was handling the civil suit."

"That's right, but I never said my attorney was a man."

Surprised by his revelation I said, "Oh, I'm sorry you didn't. Forgive me, I made an assumption, please continue."

"I feel like I've been able to get back into life. Sheila, my attorney—well, my former attorney—helped me see that my life doesn't have to end. I can find happiness again, because I've found happiness with her."

"Okay, so fill in the blanks for me. How did all of this happen?"

"Shelia was introduced by a mutual friend. Of course I wasn't looking for romance, just an attorney to take my case. Sheila was wonderful. She held my hand through the entire process." Mr. Johnson stopped speaking and appeared to reflect on his own thoughts and words. He continued, "This past year I leaned on Shelia for support."

"Can you describe what type of support?"

"Not legal—other stuff—emotional. I could talk to her and say what I wanted to say, feel what I wanted to feel without her judging or condemning me." Mr. Johnson appeared to be reflecting on his own words again.

I interrupted him. "You were describing your feeling of optimism."

"Yes, then one day we were out to dinner and I saw the most beautiful woman across from me."

"At the table with you or across the room?"

"With me, definitely with me." He smiled. "I don't know if it was the ambiance of the restaurant or the wine, but for the first time when the candlelight hit her hazel eyes, I felt as if I truly saw her. I know it sounds hokey, but it's true."

"So, just to make sure I understand . . . you've known each other for an extended period of time, but just recently started a romantic relationship?"

"Yes, it's been just over two weeks since we started seeing each other."

"Have you discussed your new relationship with your family?"

"It's crazy: I feel like I'm in high school, but no, I haven't. I plan to—just not yet."

"Can you describe that feeling of being in high school?"

"Well of course—in high school everything was easy, or at least as an adult you believe it to be so. Boy meets girl, girl likes boy. I met my wife in college I never dated as an adult man. I could just yell from the roof tops."

"I understand you're excited. What do you want?"

"I'm not understanding you." Mr. Johnson shifted back into the chair.

"I realize Sheila is not new to you, but in a sense she sort of is, because you have redefined your relationship. I just want you to think about keeping things at a manageable pace. Does that make sense?"

"Yeah it does, but doctor, the way I am feeling right now—I can't promise anything."

"What happened with Dr. Sorenson? Did you see him?"

"I saw him and I'm all good. Clean bill of health."

"So you're sleeping and eating well?"

"Good on both."

"Is there anything else you would like to talk about before our next meeting?"

"Oh, yeah, I need a new attorney."

"Unfortunately, I can't recommend an attorney to you. You may want to ask some of the other individuals in your circle of support."

"Yeah, but I'll figure this out. I want to keep it separate from them right now."

"Okay."

"All right, same time next week?"

"I believe so. I may go to D.C. I haven't decided yet, but Karen will tentatively put you down for next week."

"Okay, just call if anything changes."

"I will. Don't forget to see Karen."

I heard Mr. Johnson talking to Karen on his way out. Following him I met with three more clients, and finally I was free for the day. A couple of hours left in the day, plenty of time to make a phone call to Jake's mother.

"Karen?"

"Yes—"

"I know it's early, but you don't have to stay here if you don't want. I'll close up."

She grinned. "You don't have to tell me twice." I heard her shuffling papers. "So what are you going to do for the rest of the afternoon?"

"Transcribe my notes, then call Ms. Thomas."

I hoped that would slide by, but I had a feeling it wouldn't. "Call Ms. Thomas?" Her eyes narrowed. "Is that what you said?"

"Yup," I said. "I'm calling because she wants to talk to me about something. I think she's under the weather."

"Sick?"

"I don't know." Karen's mouth parted presumably with more questions. I raised my hand, "I'm sorry, but I've had this conversation with one of you inquisitive ladies already . . . please, go home. I'll let you know tomorrow."

Karen hesitated before leaving my office, got her things, then locked up and left. I wanted to go visit Sanford in D.C., hopefully rekindle our relationship, but I wasn't feeling brave enough to call him. I took the passive way out and decided to write an email. I was concerned about Sanford's reaction, so I threw Linda's name in to see if we could come and visit. I sat with my hands positioned on the keyboard, waiting for the words to come, but they didn't. I removed my hands from the keys.

I dialed Jake's mother's number instead. She answered almost immediately. "Hello?"

"Hi, Ms. Thomas, how are you?"

"I'm fine, who's this?" I remembered her being this vibrant, energetic woman. *Something's off, I feel and hear it in her voice.*

"It's Alex."

"Lawd, baby, I miss you so much. Did Jake tell you to call?"

Her voice filled my heart, pushing aside any concerns or questions I had about making this call. Love is all that remained for her, and I missed our connection and what that felt like. The feeling was overwhelming. Teary-eyed, I confessed, to my surprise, "I miss you, too."

"Did you talk to Jake? He told me he was going call you. So he called you?"

I wiped the warm taste of salt from my lips. "He sure did."

"Why haven't you called me? You divorced Jake, not me."

"I know. I'll do—be better about staying in touch—I promise. You got me worried over here."

"Honey, don't worry about me, this isn't nothing but old age. Lord willing you gone feel all these aches and pains one day. I told Jake not to worry you about this."

"Well he's just concerned about his favorite girl. So, what are your doctors saying . . . besides old age?"

She sighed. "Oh, this arthritis is acting up in my hip and I was getting a little forgetful about my medication. The doctors think I have breast cancer. But you know those doctors don't know what they talking about. I told Jake we just gone pray on this and if it's my time to go—then it's my time to go."

"Ms. Thomas! Why didn't you call me?"

She chuckled. "Alex, what is this Ms. Thomas mess? Call me Mom—this memory of mine is getting so bad. I don't know what I would do if I didn't have Jake. He said he's gone move in with me, did he tell you?"

I thought of Jake correcting me on who was moving in with whom. My words were enveloped in a smile. "Okay, yes, Mom, he told me," I said. "When is all this supposed to happen?"

"As soon as he finds a place for us. He's having a hard time. That girlfriend of his is helping. She can't find nothing, either. I don't know why he got her. I told Jake you found the last place. He should have you look."

"I'd think between the two of them they should be able to find something you'll like."

"They can't get along long enough."

My interest in their dysfunction, though inappropriate, was undeniable. I pushed the speakerphone to untether myself to get the 411 on what did *can't get long* mean. "Oh, now, it can't be that bad," I said.

"Huh, that's what you think."

"Just give it time. Now when is your next appointment with the doctor? If you don't mind, I'd like to go with you."

"I would love that—I really would. I'll have Jake call and give you the doctor's information."

"Don't forget. I want to come and find out how you're doing."

"He will, baby, I won't forget. Now I have to get off this phone. All this medication makes me sleepy."

"I'll call Jake just in case," I said.

"I'll talk to you later. Well, no, I'll see you, won't I?" There was uncertainty in her voice.

"Yes, you'll do both," I said, putting as much reassurance in my voice as possible.

We hung up and my thoughts went to Jake. He must be trying to manage what used to be my role in the relationship, that of problem-solver. I should go over there—*wait—stop it, Alex. Jake will figure this out. He doesn't need you fixing things for him.* Old habits die-hard.

The telephone interrupted my thoughts. It was Jake. "That was fast."

"How did your talk with Mother go?"

"You must be near her. I just got off the phone."

He chuckled. "I'm here, but I was trying not to eavesdrop."

"It went well—I think. She didn't remember asking you to call me. Something else strange happened—she's usually so even-tempered, but she was going on about your relationship—or lack thereof—with Taylor. Surprising she mentioned that to me."

"That's a non-issue. How much do you know about breast cancer?"

A non-issue? What does that mean? "I know enough to be concerned."

He took a deep breath. "We really don't know a whole lot right now. At her age, who knows what direction this could go in?"

"How old is your mother?"

"Seventy-three."

"What's this appointment she's got coming up for?"

"A biopsy—and other tests to see how large the tumor is. It's tomorrow. If you can't make it I'll completely understand and explain it to her."

"No, I don't want to disappoint her. What time and where?"

"St. Mary's at eleven."

"It's going to be just you and her?"

He laughed. "Yes, just us."

"I'm sorry. I just don't want to have multiple things to deal with all at once."

"No need to apologize. I told you, that's a non-issue. It's not a problem, you coming means a lot to both of us."

"Eleven, I'll be there.'

"See you then."

My thoughts switched with the click of the receiver back to Sanford. I wished he were here. I turned my chair to face the window. The days are getting shorter. No clients or Karen, only the humming of the air conditioner and me, alone with my thoughts of penitence. *If I have any hope of regaining what we started I need to admit I made a mistake, apologize, then catch the next plane out there and see him.*

I turned off my computer and lights before heading out the lobby door toward my car. The night sky was uncharacteristically clear. It reminded me of the time Sanford and I went to the poetry reading. The full moon glowed that night, just as it did now. I never felt more like myself than I did in that moment with him. *So what's the worst that could happen . . . I get my heart broken, he rejects me and I'm alone again? Well it's all happened before and I survived. You're a therapist it shouldn't take you this long to get here. I'm going to take a leap of faith, put all my cards on the table, and tell him how I've been feeling.*

Chapter Nineteen

A watched phone doesn't ring.

Then again, maybe it does. The phone started buzzing. An unknown caller. Karen, long gone for the evening, couldn't provide the desired, necessary screen. Whoever it was knew my direct number. Hesitant to answer, I continued to watch and listen until it reached its fourth ring. Then, as magically as it started, it stopped. *It couldn't have been Sanford, much as I want it to be. Maybe wishing it were him is better than knowing it wasn't.*

Making decisions was the hard part. The rest was logistics and geography. I made my decision. I didn't want to vacillate over calling Sanford anymore. I was over it, but the thought of talking to Sanford had my stomach in knots. I needed to eat. Time to pack in another days work, and head toward home. I could pick something up on the way, coffee and a muffin that I may regret buying and eating later.

Back home I dropped everything but my cup in the foyer, cut the downstairs lights on then walked in the family room to make my call. One bite of the muffin solved the cliffhanger on my purchase: bad decision. I turned on the television, muted the volume, and then flipped through my phone contacts until I saw his face. My finger was on the button. I stopped. Better rehearse the conversation in my head versus ad-libbing.

I'll call. He'll be glad I did. We'll talk about his leaving without us getting together, but it won't be awkward because he'll be so glad to hear my voice. He'll tell me what's going on with him and how much he misses me and I'll say the same. I'll explain I made a mistake we should have stayed together and worked around the distance. Then I'll mention coming to see him. He'll be happy. The End.

With any luck, the call will go exactly the way I want it to. I'll be the victor, and everything will fall back in place. I pushed the call button. The ringing reverberated throughout the room. It was unnerving. Too pronounced. I unmuted the television to get some background noise, and took a sip of coffee to ease my nerves. The phone rang twice, and then his voicemail came on. I hesitated too long to hang up. I didn't expect this and didn't have a prepared message. I groaned silently and left an uncoordinated ten-second pause before I stammered, "Hey Sanford, it's me. Give me a call when you get a chance." I checked the time to ensure I wasn't calling too late. I wasn't. A quick ring followed by voicemail only meant one thing: he'd rejected my call. All that pre-call prepping, only to be pushed into voicemail. *I didn't rehearse voicemail.* I propped up a pillow and lay across the couch resting my phone and coffee on the floor.

I felt antsy. *I can't just lie here.* I picked my phone back up and called Linda. She didn't answer either. An evening with my thoughts wasn't good for anybody—namely, me.

By design or justifiable, waiting for his returned call was nothing short of torture. It took three hellacious, analytical hours complete with multiple trips to the bathroom to expel an ill-conceived muffin before Sanford called me back. I maintained my position on the couch. He wasn't getting the full performance now. His rejection took the shine from this call. He's getting the under study now.

"Hello."

Sanford's voice, drowned out by the noise in the background, sounded—to my dismay—surprisingly cheerful. *And I don't think it's because I called.*

"Hey, how are you?" Before I could answer he asked, "Are you asleep?"

I raised my voice. "No, just resting."

"Sorry we didn't get a chance to talk before I left."

"I'm sorry too." I paused to rearrange what I'd rehearsed earlier in my head.

"Are you still there?" he asked.

"I miss you." The words just leapt out of my mouth. Five seconds passed . . . silence. I felt a twinge in my heart. My feelings were hurt. *You've come this far.* I asked, "Did you hear me?"

The joviality in his voice faded. "Yes—I heard you."

"Is this is a good time?"

"I'm sorry, I should've called you later. I can call you tomorrow after work if you have something on your mind you want to talk about."

If I want to talk? The picture is stronger now. Whatever lingering feelings I had for Sanford, he clearly didn't share. I recovered. "No, that's okay—it's nothing." I tried to save face. "Just checking on my friend. Seeing what's up."

"I'm glad you did."

"We're thinking about coming out there to see you."

"Who's we?

"Just me and Linda."

"All right—that's good. Send me an email and let me know when you want to come and I'll pick you up from the airport."

"Okay, I'll do that."

"I got to run, we're seeing a movie and—"

"Oh, sure, I—"

He interrupted before I could finish my sentence. "I'll catch up with you later."

Muffled movement, laughter then quiet: he'd hung up. *Well, that didn't exactly go as I'd rehearsed.* I stared into the television screen where the meteorologist informed me there was going to be a shift in the weather. *I'll say.*

I rose from the couch and glanced down at my coffee cup. *What I'm feeling calls for something stronger than coffee.*

In the refrigerator, the bottle of wine Sanford and I had drunk from the first night we'd slept together hid in the back. I figured the relationship is dead, so the bottle of wine should be too. Only a quarter remained. *It'll have to do.* I returned to the couch and drowned the emotions that never got the chance to escape the pit of my stomach.

In my office, recovered physically and mentally from the night before—but far from emotionally—I called Linda at her office. This time she answered.

"Where were you last night?" I demanded.

"Nowhere, here . . . what's the matter?"

"I called Sanford," I said, "and it didn't go as planned."

"Why? What did he say?

I sighed. "Not a whole lot. At least not to me. He seemed happy."

"What does that mean? Happy is good, right?"

"No. Happy isn't good."

"The nerve of him," she said. "That bastard!"

"Lovely. More sarcasm. Just what I need. Of course I want him to be happy, just not without me."

"Wow," she responded, "that doesn't sound selfish at all."

"Remember, you promised: a judgment-free zone," I reminded her. "He wasn't even talking to me half the time we were on the phone. I felt like I was bugging him."

"So he didn't say I miss you and want to see you?"

"He didn't. But I did, blurted it out right at the beginning."

She paused. "What did he say to that?"

"Nothing. Not one word."

"Oh honey—I'm sorry. I feel like I put you up to calling him," she said.

"You did, which is why I told him you were coming with me to visit him."

"You still told him you wanted to visit him?" She laughed out loud at that.

I laughed with her. "I felt as though I needed a reason for my call. That was all I could think of, and it wasn't a lie: I did call to see if we could come down."

"Either way count me in, it's the least I can do."

"You *should* feel guilty," I rejoined. "I was just fine in my misery. At least then I thought he was miserable, too."

"Well, maybe he's hurting inside," she said and paused. "Look, it may take an MRI to find it, but I'm sure he's feeling some kind of way about this too. Maybe he needs time to catch up."

"Versus him catching up with me, I'm going to catch up with him, and forget about us having a relationship just focus on us having friendship," I said sensibly. "So are you booking the tickets, or am I?"

"It should be a cheap flight, so I'll treat since this is sort of my fault—not completely, just sort of."

"Yippee! Have Grace send them to my home address."

"You mean Nancy," Linda said.

"Nancy? I thought your administrative assistant name was Grace."

"Oh, the last one. Grace has gone bye-bye, it's Nancy now."

"You know—that's not normal to go through assistants the way you do."

Singing. "I'm getting off the phone now Alex . . . bye, bye."

Chapter Twenty

Buried in the work I knew best, I heard Karen ask, "May I tell her who's calling?" She placed whoever it was on hold then my phone rang. I pushed speakerphone to answer her. "Yes?"

"Easton is on line one for you."

I picked up the receiver. "Who did you say?"

"Easton," she repeated.

"Are you sure that's what you heard."

"Yes, pretty sure . . . he said Easton."

I felt puzzled. "How did he get my number?"

"Well, let's see, we can try to figure all this out or you can just ask him," she quipped. "He's still on line one."

"Huh." I canvassed the walls and ceiling. No answers there. "Fine. I'll ask him." There was a click, and I answered the call. "Hello, this is Alex."

"Well, hello, this is Alex."

"Whom do I have the pleasure of speaking with?" I asked coldly.

"The receptionist didn't tell you?" He paused. "It's Easton. We met at The Boulevard." There was a warm undercurrent in his voice.

"Easton? Huh. I haven't been to The Boulevard in over a month. How long ago was this?"

"It's been about a month."

I paused long enough to make it seem I had no idea who he was. "Oh, I know. Peter's friend."

"Right," he agreed. "I know Peter."

"How did you get my number?"

"I'm a lawyer you know."

"Yes, I remember, you're a lawyer not a cop. The question remains . . . how did you get my number?"

"Fortunately for me you're not hard to find. Google," he said easily. "I've been wondering why you haven't called."

"Huh . . . that's concerning."

"That I contacted you?" he asked.

"No, I'm sorry not you in particular, just that anybody can find me."

"Whew," he said. "For a second there you had me going. I did wait for you to call me, but it didn't look like that was going to happen."

"Most people would've taken that as a hint."

"A hint for what?"

Laughing I said, "That I didn't want to talk to you."

"Nah—not possible. I'm not most people," he said.

I smiled as I looked at my nails that were in desperate need of a manicure. "I guess not."

"How about you give me a chance and go to lunch with me?"

"Wait a minute—aren't you married?" I felt I needed to remind him. "I know some women don't care, but I do."

"I'm separated—have been for a couple years. So yes, I'm married, but we're not together."

"Sure you're not together," I said. There was something about this guy. I was getting comfortable enough with him to say exactly what I thought, which was unusual for me. "Have you tried counseling?"

"Why? Are you offering your services?"

"Although I do counsel—No, I'm not."

"That's too bad. I would definitely get to see you then," he said.

I cleared my throat. "It would be couples counseling, and inappropriate, but I could definitely recommend someone."

"Alex I'm joking—we don't need counseling."

"Okay, that was weird."

"Weird in a cute way or don't ever call me again kind of way?"

"Really, is weird ever cute?" I laughed. "I'm sure you didn't call me to talk about my divorce or fixing your marriage. Do you want to talk about something else?"

"You're right. I didn't for either of those reasons. I know looking you up may be a little presumptuous of me, but I knew you wouldn't call me, so here I am taking a chance you'll go out with me."

"I'm sorry, but I'm a little psychic, and I don't see lunch with me in your future. I guess you have to come up with another way."

He laughed. "You got jokes. Okay, I guess I will. So are you free this weekend?"

He doesn't give up. "Oh, you know what? I might be going out of town this weekend to visit a friend of mine."

"When will you be back?"

"Sunday, we're leaving Friday. Maybe some other time."

"Can some other time be lunch tomorrow?"

"Tomorrow? I usually don't go out on weekdays."

He chuckled. "You don't have to go to school the next day, you should be fine."

I caught a reflection of myself in the computer screen and thought of the conversation I'd had with Sanford the night before. *What are you saving yourself for . . . prom?* "You know what—sure, I could get away. What about that wife of yours? How do you think she would feel about you going to lunch with another woman?"

"Alex, it's just lunch, and we're separated—remember. She might be having lunch with somebody too.

"How do you feel about that?" I asked.

"Alex, are we going to lunch?"

"Sorry, I do that sometimes . . . go back and forth. Where do you want to meet?"

"That's fine. I'll get used to it. How about Italian?"

A chill fluttered down my spine. "Yeah sure, Italian's good."

"What time?"

"Around one?"

"That works for me. So, I guess it's a date . . . until tomorrow."

"It's not a date, and yes, I'll see you then."

Easton may be just what the doctor ordered.

I tried to get a mental picture of him, but it wasn't working. I can't remember what he looks like. The alarm on my phone jerked me back to reality. Ten-thirty. I know this means something, but for the life of me I don't remember what. I checked my calendar and there it was: big as life, and I was going to be late.

"Hey, Karen! I leaped out of my chair and grabbed my purse, while heading toward the door. Karen darted right in front of me. I almost plowed her down. "Oh my God Karen, I didn't see you!"

"Where's the fire?" she said.

I squeezed around her. "I got to go. I'm supposed to meet Jake and his mom at St. Mary's at eleven. There is no way I'm going to make it."

My car was parked right out front and I couldn't open the door fast enough. Inside it occurred to me to call Jake and let him know I would be late, which I attempted, but no answer. I really should have planned this out better. I guess I couldn't have with my unexpected phone call today. *Easton's causing trouble already.*

My memory is terrible and without talking to Jake again I wasn't quite sure where I was going. I took a chance and got on the freeway headed downtown, hoping something along the way would jog my memory. I'm thinking he said St. Mary's, but that's probably because of Tobey. I tried him again. *Still nothing.* I drove toward St. Mary's Medical Center. If they weren't there I didn't know where to go.

It took fifteen minutes to make it to the hospital. I pulled into the parking lot at eleven. In the first available spot, I threw the car in park, grabbed my purse, and raced out. Speed walking through the parking lot, I heard my name. I stopped, scanned the lot to figure out what direction the voice came from.

Jake and Ms. Thomas were slowly navigating their way to the entrance. I ran over to catch up with them. The closer I got, my heart sank at the sight of her. Another mystery solved. I knew why Jake had called me. I'd only looked at her for a few minutes and even I could see the essence of her former self slipping away.

"Hi, Mom, are you okay?"

She looked up, didn't appear to recognize me at first, then slowly, her face brightened as it came back to her. "Hi, baby, I'm so glad to see you."

"It's good to see you too." Jake looked on, appearing pleased to see me as well. I wouldn't let him down—not about this. *Well, I almost let him down. Thank goodness I made it.* "So, we're going in?"

"Yeah, let's get on in here. I told you these doctors don't know anything."

I smiled. "I know, let's just see if the doctors have something new to say. All of it's new for me, so if you don't mind, we're going to sit a minute and see how we can help make you comfortable." I grabbed her free arm and smiled at Jake while his mother rested her head against my arm.

"I'm comfortable now. At my age, to relax is to die. These aches and pains let me know I'm still alive. I think it bothers Jake more than me."

Ms. Thomas took slow deliberate steps. I assisted her managing to catch Jake's eye.

After a brief wait in the lobby we were in. Ms. Thomas entered the exam room while Jake and I met with the doctor. As it turned out, this was only a physical examination, but we still needed to get some clarification on patient care. The doctor was gracious enough to take some time after her examination to go over everything one more time for me, while the nurse finished up with Ms. Thomas. The short of it, which I already knew, was breast cancer and the location of her tumor made it inoperable. Ms. Thomas refused radiation and chemotherapy.

At her advanced stage, her doctors estimated six months to a year—maybe.

Jake maintained his silence for most of the meeting. I reached over and grabbed his hand as we waited to hear other options. As soon as the doctor left to check on his mother, Jake let every emotion he stored up flow down his cheeks. I sat there holding him tight in my arms, crying and paralyzed by the knowledge of what's to come.

The walk out of the medical center felt longer than going in. Unbeknownst to Ms. Thomas, our hearts were heavy. I didn't want to go back to work. Maybe lunch would be good.

"Jake, you guys want to get some lunch? I haven't eaten and I won't have time before heading back if I don't eat here." Jake was game, but his mother was visibly wearing down. "I think I better get her home. It's been a long day."

"Okay, you're right. I understand—some other time." We reached their car and Jake carefully put his mother inside. She tried to attach the seat belt, "Oh, Mom, let me." I jumped into action, placing the seat belt around her waist and latching it. Once she was inside, I lifted my head to see Jake across from me at the driver's-side door.

"I guess we'll talk later."

He nodded. "I would like too, if that's okay."

"Of course . . . whatever you need. Call me later."

"All right. Thank you for this, Alex."

"No need to thank me, I'm happy to be here."

Jake got in the car and I headed back to mine. The emotion of everything took me over. I sat, had another watershed moment then drove back to the office.

Messages from Linda and Tobey were waiting for me. I would've thought Linda knew what was going on. Whatever burning questions or comments they had for me were going to wait. First things first, I needed to get myself together and return some phone calls. Then field the questions from the girls.

It only took an hour or so for me to take care of business. Karen set up video conferencing so I could hit them all at once. Their images barely came into focus before they were firing off questions. I could hardly keep up.

"Wait a minute. Let me tell you what's going on with his mother. Jake truly isn't the story here, it's about her," I told them. "She isn't well."

"What's wrong with her?" asked Linda.

"Breast cancer—it's advanced. She's pretty bad off, ladies."

"Oh, my God, I didn't know she was that sick." Linda gasped.

"I thought you talked to Jake?"

"Well, remember, I told you I wanted to talk to Taylor about doing some work for me."

"No, Linda, I don't remember you saying you wanted Taylor about doing anything. Why would you talk to Taylor?"

"No . . . well, I've talked to both of them, but not at the same time. Potentially business with Taylor and the usual stuff with Jake—just talking, but it was a long time ago, Alex . . . before the divorce."

Judging my reaction, both Tobey and Karen told me they would catch up on the story tomorrow. I was having a hard time understanding what exactly Linda was telling me. *Am I to understand she has struck up a friendship with the woman who slept with my husband?* "What business could you possibly have with her?"

"She owns a party planning business on the side, but Alex, I'm not doing anything with her. I just talked to her about my anniversary party."

"What? Okay, let's step back a minute, because I'm getting confused. How did you even meet Taylor?"

"Jake introduced me to her, but Alex—believe me, I didn't know they were messing around until Sanford and I saw them out."

"Oh, God, *you're* the mystery person Sanford was out with?" I couldn't breathe. The air evaporated from the room.

Still on video, Linda saw me grab my chest. "Breathe, Alex," she said.

I was beyond hearing her. I ached from distress and ended the videoconference. My cellphone rang. I knew it was Linda, but I didn't answer. Between Easton, Ms. Thomas, and this, there had been quite enough heart-stoppers for me today. Karen appeared at my door to inquire if I was okay. I didn't know. What I did know was the time: three o'clock. I wanted to get out of there and escape to the sanctuary of my house. I made desire reality, and left.

Linda continued to call. At the third stoplight I muted the volume. I knew she wanted to explain and at some point I would be ready to hear it. Just not now . . . please, not now. But in true Linda fashion, she kept calling until I reached my house to see her standing on the porch.

"Why are you here, Linda?"

"Because you wouldn't answer your phone."

I grabbed my purse and briefcase from the back seat. "I didn't answer my phone because I didn't want to talk to you."

"Exactly, that's why I'm here. I have to tell you everything."

"You didn't tell me everything when it happened. Why is it so important you tell me now?"

"I've been carrying this guilt around. I need to get it off my chest. I'll understand if you're mad at me, but you have to hear me out."

We continued up the walkway toward the porch, opened the door, and entered the house. I motioned Linda to the living room where we sat down to hash it out. "You're not here for me. You're here for you. You're feeling responsible and you want me to help relieve some of that guilt. I'm telling you it's been a long day I need a minute."

"Yes, do I feel responsible—of course I do, but not for what you think. I'm not going to give you time to make up this story. Let me tell you what actually happened, and if you're mad I'm ready to deal."

I crossed my arms and legs. "Okay, you're here, what's the story?"

"Jake did introduce me to Taylor, but that was a long time ago. I told him I was thinking about doing an anniversary party for us—Mitch and me, but nothing definite, which is why I never mentioned it. He said he knew somebody at work who does that, which is how I talked to Taylor. I never *met* her."

"I thought you said you met her."

She shook her head. "Be clear, I never met her. I saw her for the first time with Jake at the restaurant."

"So if you never met her, how did you know that was her at the restaurant?"

"I got that from you. You said that was who he was with. I put two and two together it wasn't that hard to figure out."

"Why didn't Sanford just tell me he was out to dinner with you? Why all the secrecy?"

Linda took in a deep breath. She appeared conflicted. "Sanford wanted to talk to me. I agreed to meet him, and then we saw Jake and this woman and all hell broke loose." Tears began to form in her eyes. "I'm sorry, but Sanford didn't want you to know. Your friend saw Sanford, but she didn't see me—so, I kept his confidence and didn't tell you. You got mad at Sanford—it snowballed from there."

"What were you talking about that was so serious you wouldn't tell me?"

"My God, Alex, don't you do this shit for a living? Isn't it obvious?" She walked into the kitchen and returned with tissue.

"Apparently not," I said.

"Well, I'm not here to enlighten you. The rest is not my place to tell—you have to get that from Sanford. I won't betray him." She sat back down. "I don't think it matters now, anyway."

I stood up, full of nervous energy. "What doesn't matter?"

Linda stood up and gathered her things then walked to the front door, leaving me standing alone in the living room. "I'm truly sorry if I hurt you. I'll still pay for the trip, but I'm not going. Maybe that'll give you time to figure this out."

Chapter Twenty-One

I felt Easton's eyes studying me. After what seemed like a minute or two, he said, "You're so beautiful, but you look tired. Anything I can help with?" He made me feel at ease.

"I wish you could. My life is reading like a Greek tragedy right now, with me in the lead."

He smiled. "Maybe this is the part where the hero shows up."

I smiled. "Perhaps it is."

"Let me try and take your mind off of things. First, I need to know if you absolutely have to go back to work."

I looked up in search of a reason why I did. Nothing came to mind that I couldn't reschedule. "You know what? I do, but I'll call Karen and have her reorganize everything."

I pulled out the cellular, excused myself from the table, and called Karen. She thought that after my argument with Linda taking the afternoon off would be a good idea. *Truly, how much help could I be to my clients when I'm in need of some intervention myself?* Easton was willing to provide it. *I just hope he's up for the task.* I returned to our table. "Okay, I'm all yours, but I have one request."

"For you beautiful lady, anything. What do you want?" *God, it sounds good to hear a man say, whatever I want. I don't think I've ever heard those words uttered to me. Easton is getting serious points with me already.* I smiled. "I want to get out of here and pick up something we can eat at a park. Can we do that?"

"We sure can—any park in particular?"

"We're in Mason, so I don't know where the closest park is, but I need the peace right now. I think the park can get me there."

"Let's go."

Easton got out of his chair and motioned for me to walk in front of him. We left the restaurant and submitted the valet ticket. We settled on leaving my car there, and taking his truck.

Easton pulled into the nearest convenience store. When he got back he had directions to Sullivan Park, not far from where we were. The park was perfect. He turned on some music and retrieved a blanket from the back of his truck, laying it out in the sun for me before bringing out food he'd bought at the store. We each grabbed a soda from the bag. He poured them out and refilled the bottles with wine.

The park, quiet since most people were at work, seemed a million miles away from everyone and everything. I could smell Fall approaching. It was shaping up to be a pleasant day, with good food—well, edible food—wine, and Easton.

Easton folded his jacket into a makeshift pillow for me. I listened to my song, while the warmth of the sun speckled my body through the changing leaves. I hadn't gotten a chance to really look at Easton. He looked different from when I'd first met him. He seemed taller, too. He was really cute. I hadn't seen his body before, but I could see the shape of his chest through a starched white shirt. Mama likes. *Maybe I've been putting my energy into the wrong person.*

Easton lay down beside me, and I thought, *this is really nice. It will be even nicer if I can stop staring at him.*

"You want to talk about your day?" he asked.

"Well, it wasn't my day that was bad, it was my evening—last night. I got into a disagreement with my sister."

"Is she your only sister?"

"Ah no—not hardly . . . there's seven of us. She's right above me. We are—well, we *were* extremely close." I paused. "I shouldn't say that . . . we're still close."

"Why did you say you were playing the role of the lead in a bad play?"

I'd forgotten I'd said that. "Well, you see—wait, are you sure you want to hear this? It really doesn't put me in the best light."

"I don't care if it doesn't make you look good. I just want to help you if I can."

"You're sweet, but you can't help me. My sister kept something from me—well, I felt like it was a betrayal. She doesn't seem to think so. What I learned yesterday has changed everything for me. Now my up is down and left is right. Up until yesterday my life made sense to me, now I'm questioning everything and everybody." I took a deep breath. "I'm still hurt by what she did." I paused. "I told you I was divorced, right?"

"Yeah, I think you did, but you didn't go into any details."

"I've been divorced about a year. My ex's . . . his name is Jake."

"So what happened to Jake?"

"He's still around. We were together yesterday at the doctor's with his mother."

"Oh, you're still cordial with his mother? You must be okay with him considering you were with him yesterday."

"Well, there is nothing like a good old-fashioned crisis to bring people together. In our case the crisis is his mother. We hadn't talked in a long time because of Jake not wanting us to. Anyway, we hadn't talked in a long time. Jake's an only child, so what are you going to do?" I shrugged. "To be honest, I was okay with us not talking. Don't get me wrong: it hurt, but despite your best attempts there are causalities in war. I needed to do what was best for me, so I back away from the relationship as gracefully as I could and didn't look back."

"What did you and Linda—it's Linda, right? What did you argue about that has you rethinking your relationship with your sister?"

"Here's the Reader's Digest version. My husband continued to date after we got married, so I divorced him."

"A lot of men feel that monogamy isn't realistic for a man."

I took a sip of wine as my eyes narrowed. "I've heard it all in my profession . . . *I don't belong to you and you don't belong to me. It goes against a man's nature to have one woman. We're not property or possessions—oh, and the free will one which is my personal favorite.* My response is why get married? If a man feels they don't want to go against his law of nature then don't enter into the law of the land. Marriage."

"Okay, Alex, I said a lot of men, not me."

"I'm sorry," I winced. "I'm just an angry black woman right now. I should have warned you I've played that role longer than I care to remember."

Easton patted me on the leg. "So keep telling me what happened."

"Taylor, in the role of the mistress and part of the reason, though not the whole reason, Jake and I ultimately went our separate ways. Now Linda, my sister, was with my friend Sanford and saw Jake out with Taylor, but didn't tell me."

Easton asked, "So why didn't she tell you?"

"Because if she told me she was there, she would've told me why and who she was meeting with, which—I guess was a secret that is until now." I took another drink. "Oh God, does this sound as convoluted and juvenile to you as it does to me?"

"No, I'm following it so far. So, what can't she tell you?"

"I don't know—crazy, right? She still won't tell me. I have to ask Sanford when I see him."

"She's with Sanford—now, who is Sanford to you again?"

"Nobody—just a friend."

Easton grabbed my hand, gently caressing the top. "Your hands are soft."

"I'm glad you did this for me." I removed my hand from under his. "I'm starting to think this is more than just lunch."

"What if it is?"

"If you're interested in me after that high school without the musical story I just told you, then you must really like me."

"Hey, I'm definitely not one to let a few unfortunate events define me for the rest of my life. The events surrounding your marriage aren't going to scare me away. I like you, and I want to get to know you better."

I rolled over on my side to face him. "Okay."

"Okay, what?"

"Okay—let's get to know each other."

He smiled. "You've made me a happy man. Whenever you need me, I'm there."

"You didn't seem like you had a sense of humor, but you got jokes. Isn't that a line from something?"

"I'm not joking. I'm enjoying all of you, even though you have been talking about your ex-husband and his woman most of the time." He chuckled when he saw my face. "Okay, go on, tell me the rest."

I smiled. "There's no rest, that's it. Linda told me she wasn't going on our trip to visit Sanford and that was it—the end."

"You hung up on her."

"More like logged off . . . we were on video conference then at my house."

"You'll patch things up. You have to talk to your sister," he said.

I frowned at him. "No. I don't."

"You feel that way now, but you'll work this out with her."

"One day, but for right now we aren't talking and I can keep it that way. Trust is huge for me. I have to know I can trust the people around me."

He shook his head. "I don't know . . . this doesn't sound like a trust issue to me."

I threw up my hands. "I don't know."

"You don't see you and your ex ever getting back together?"

I felt a sudden chill as the sun began to set behind the trees—or maybe it was the chilling thought of Jake and me under the same roof again. Either way I was cold.

"Do you mind if we take this picnic somewhere else?"

"Not at all. What do you have in mind?"

"I live alone, so we have two options … we can go back to my place or someplace where we can get a cup of coffee to warm up."

"How about we do both. Let me help you up, and I'll get the blanket. Can you throw away the trash?"

"I think I can handle that," I said.

We got our clothes straightened out from lying on the blanket. Easton's jacket was extremely wrinkled when I handed it back to him. I gathered the trash and he rolled up the blanket before we both headed to the car. I hadn't done anything like this in a long time. It felt good. He didn't seem to mind I was a little on the sloppy emotional side either.

Easton opened my door. I took a deep breath of that new-car smell and snuggled back down into the seat. I opened the door for him on the inside. I don't think I missed a beat making my hand's way over to the door handle before he reached his from the outside.

"Thank you for that."

"Not a problem. You see chivalry for us ladies isn't dead."

Easton hopped in the car, started the engine and cut the heat on. *I could see me with Easton.* "Okay, I love heat, but I have to say most men wouldn't have turned the heat on."

"Yes they would have. You look like you're freezing. I can't have you freezing on me."

"I thank God you don't want me freezing on you. I'm cold, but willing to shake and shiver before I asked you to turn on the heat."

"You don't have to do that, Alex, I'm glad to do whatever you want me to." *Okay, there is that whatever you want me to again. I should make that his ring tone. I love the sound of it!*

"Don't think I didn't notice you haven't responded to my question," he said softly.

I snapped back into the present. "I'm sorry—what question?"

"First, tell me where I'm headed."

"Do you like coffee? I'm addicted, but I try not to influence others, so you let me know."

"I'll take you to get some. Just point me in the right direction."

"Okay, well we're on the Westside, so there should be one here somewhere. Just head back toward downtown there is definitely a shop, I think up this street near the hospital."

Easton pulled out of the park onto the street headed toward the main artery. I turned the heat down because I couldn't quite tell but I thought I saw little sweat beads starting to form on his cleanly shaven head.

"All right, now you can answer the question."

I was genuinely bemused. "I'm not trying to be evasive, but what question?"

"Do you think you and Jake will ever get back together?"

I shook my head. "No, I don't see that happening, nor do I want it to happen. That ship has sailed. What about you? Do you see yourself getting back with your wife, because technically you're still married?"

"Not technically: we are actually still married. I don't know what's going to happen with us. It's not like I don't love her, because I do. I just don't know if I want to be married to her."

"So how exactly does that work? You wake up one day and no longer want to be married?"

"Well, that's the overly simplified version, but more or less it's just a realization the person you're living with is more of a roommate than a wife. We got the kids and all, which we're raising together, but that's it. We would have the same relationship with each other and the kids even if we weren't in the same house."

I wasn't buying it. "You seriously don't think anything would change if you weren't living in the same house? There has to be more going on than this."

"No, seriously, there's nothing else going on. I'm not beating her, she's not beating me." We laughed. "I just don't want to be married anymore, and it's not just to her. I don't want to be married to anybody."

Okay, Alex, why are your feelings hurt by him saying he doesn't want to be anybody's husband? He's not your husband, but what if you wanted him to be?

"Anybody?" I asked.

"I mean—never say never. Anything can change. Meeting you, for example—I didn't expect that."

"I understand if that's how you feel—I'm always conscious of absolutes and you seem so firm. Most women like commitments."

"I know, but that's how I feel. I can't help how I feel, can I?"

I shrugged. "You can change how you feel. It doesn't seem real fair to her, you deciding not to be married anymore."

"It's not like I put her out or nothing—I just told her I needed some time to think things through. And she agreed. This isn't news for us: we've been having a rough patch for a while now. That one patch has turned into a quilt. We're both on the same page—take a break."

"I guess you don't need a reason to get divorced other than you don't want to be married." I sighed. "I took the 'until death do us part' literally. I guess for some people it's just a recommendation."

"But you divorced your husband."

"No, correction—my ex asked me to get married, and he asked me to get divorced when he cheated. I accepted both proposals."

He smiled. "All right, I hear you. This is your coffee shop on the right, isn't it?"

"Oh, yeah, now you're talking my language."

I asked Easton to grab us two chairs by the window where we could sit and talk relatively undisturbed. I grabbed our order and met him there. Easton was rubbing the mahogany leather chairs. "I like these chairs," he said.

It was about six o'clock and I realized I hadn't heard from anybody today. No clients, Karen, Tobey—*didn't want to hear from Linda*—nobody. *I feel like I'm in an alternate universe or something. I have actually gotten away, taking time for myself without any distractions. Unbelievable.*

I handed Easton his coffee, which gave me another opportunity to look at him head to toe. *If Easton and I were to have kids, our children would be gorgeous. Hopefully his height, since he's taller than me—but everybody's taller than me.*

"Do you have a picture of your kids?"

"Of course."

Easton reached into his back pocket, pulling out his wallet. He unfolded it, fumbled through a few credit cards, pulled out a picture of his kids, and handed it to me. *Oh, and his wife is in the picture too. How lovely . . . a family photo.*

"Oh okay, cute kids." I tried to act like I didn't even see her. She was pretty and tall. "How tall is your wife?"

"We're the same height—five-eleven."

I raised my eyebrows. "How did you meet her?"

"In college—law school."

"How did you two wind up together?"

"We were in the same classes, so it wasn't hard to notice each other. I invited her to our study group and she came. We talked, realized we had a lot in common, and then started dating. I asked her to marry me right after we graduated."

"That doesn't sound too bad."

"No. Not bad at all. I got to tell you, Alex, if you're looking for a smoking gun in my marriage you're not going to find one. There is nothing wrong with her or me."

"I'm sorry, Easton. I don't think it's so much I am looking for a reason you shouldn't be with your wife. It's more of me looking for a reason why I should be here—with you. Considering you are technically or actually married. I did mention my husband cheated on me, right?"

I felt the sleeve of my coffee cup. It cooled down enough for us to drink.

"This is good," he commented.

"I knew if you liked caramel and coffee, this would be the drink for you. Caramel and coffee go together well."

"Why, thank you, Dr. Nichols."

"You're welcome, Mr.—um, I don't know your last name."

"It's Mitchell."

"Easton Mitchell."

We continued to talk for another hour before heading to retrieve my car, and then to my house. It was getting late. Easton had to get up in the morning, and so did I. I couldn't run away forever, no matter how much I wanted to. He walked me to my door, hugged me, and then kissed me goodnight on the back of my hand. I couldn't really tell if he was a good kisser from the hand kiss, but it was soft, gentle, and made me curious to know what *more* would feel like. He embraced me, pulling my body into his, wrapping both his arms fully around my waist. I felt the strength of his arms and chest . . . his cologne smelled really good. He let me go just in enough time for my sniffing his body to not get weird.

I opened my door, turned and thanked him. From the living room window I watched Easton's tail lights fade further and further up Main Street until they were out of sight.

Chapter Twenty-Two

Funny thing about a story—it can be manipulated and twisted in all sorts of ways to make you either the villain or the heroine. But one thing always remains the same: There's a villain in every story.

I had a good time with Easton and I wanted—no, I *needed* the euphoria to last as long as possible. I even started rethinking my trip to see Sanford. Recurring thoughts of our lunch date helped to get me through the day.

My feelings of disloyalty, valid or not, were very real to me and I wasn't feeling benevolent, which is uncharacteristic of me. It'd been a few days since my difference of opinion with Linda and a couple from when I saw Easton. Easton and I were talking every chance we got. He was easy on me. I didn't feel the intensity or paranoia I felt when I was with Jake. Generally, I always have it together, but when we went out to lunch I clearly didn't, and he was fine—even helpful.

I told him Linda and I was getting together to talk about what happened so we could put it behind us. Both Karen and Tobey were leaning toward Linda's side of things. Easton didn't care what any of them thought. He just wanted to make sure I was okay. After several phone calls I finally convinced him I was. Linda wanted to have the meeting someplace we could talk freely without interruption excluding my office.

I vetoed that quickly. "I have to work and I am not leaving my office," I said. She conceded and the meeting location was changed to my office at six o'clock.

Karen let Linda in then left for the evening. Instead of sitting in my normal spot behind the desk, I decided I would sit on the couch with her. With work and in life Linda is always poker-faced, rarely if ever showing emotion. For the first time in our lives my sister was visibly shaken.

She put her things on the opposite couch and sat down beside me. "Alex, you must know I never meant to hurt you. I made the wrong decision. I should have told you I saw Jake with Taylor—there is no excuse only an explanation−"

I raised my hand. "Look—if you didn't tell me it must be for a good reason."

"Believe me, it—"

"Don't misunderstand—I can't think of why you wouldn't, but I have to believe whatever you and Sanford were talking about it must have been important enough for you not to betray him, and choose to be disloyal to me."

"I made a mistake. I should have told you what we were talking about when you asked, but if you want—I'm willing to tell you now."

"Nope, you said it didn't matter—"

"*Probably* didn't matter."

"Either way, I don't want to know, but if there is a next time—which I pray there isn't you better say something." I reached out for Linda's hand. "We're sisters—I would've told you in a heartbeat."

Linda wiped away a tear. "You know what—hindsight is twenty-twenty. I stuck my nose somewhere I shouldn't have. Then saw something I wished I hadn't." Linda pulled me in for a hug. "I couldn't tell you one secret without telling you the other. And, one of them I thought wasn't my place to tell—the other my responsibility to tell."

We released our embrace and faced one another. "I get it now, but next time—choose me, silly rabbit."

"I will—I promise. Are you sure there isn't more to the Taylor story you're not telling me." We stood up to gather our things.

I took a deep breath. "No, there's nothing more. Well, I got the ticket for D.C. Still not changing your mind?"

"No, you need to go. Talk to Sanford—finish out this chapter of your life."

I locked the outer door. "Sanford and me—the final chapter in the longest novel in history."

Linda walked toward the door. "You know . . . there's no reason why you should still keep protecting Jake. I sense something more happened. Don't know what, but more."

"Let's just say it was the same game out of a different playbook," I sighed. "When I actually sat down and figured out all the time I spent trying to hold on to Jake versus living my own life." I stood up and walked over to Linda. "I couldn't change Jake and make him into the man I needed him to be, and the more I tried to *fix* him, the harder he fought to keep things the way they were. I had to let him go, and that was a hard place—emotionally to get to. Unfortunately for me, in true Jake fashion, he helped to provide a visual aide to push me along."

"You're right." She smiled. "I don't need to know any more than I do now. I'm glad you're moving on. This trip will be good for you."

"I'm hoping so."

Chapter Twenty-Three

I arrived at the Baltimore/Washington International Thurgood Marshall Airport at approximately two o'clock where Sanford was waiting for me.

A week filled with lows, then highs, and then lows managed to bottom out on a high. I hadn't talked with Linda much after our heart-to-heart, but we were good again. I'd never disagreed with Linda, even though I'd packed a lunch for the long haul: it was good for it to be over. Not speaking to Sanford was one thing, but my sister—I'm not going to be in a position where I'm not talking to my sister.

I texted Sanford as soon as the plane landed and told him to meet me in baggage claim. No sooner had I grabbed the handle of my luggage than I caught a glimpse of Sanford standing behind me. In this short time his locks were gone and he was sporting a medium-length Afro. The mustache, beard, and black horn-rimmed glasses were still there, but trimmed up, and he'd lost a little more weight.

He grabbed me, lifting me off the floor. "I missed you!"

"I missed you, too! Look at me: I can't stop smiling. You look so good!" I ran my fingers through his curls.

"You always look good." He put me down. "You are so short without those heels."

We continued to stare as if we never saw each other before. Finally I said, "Okay, okay. Grab this bag for me."

Sanford and I headed out of the baggage claim area toward a black truck. I didn't expect someone to be with him, but in the passenger seat was a woman. I fell back behind Sanford to trail him. "We're right over here," he said. I already figured that part out once the woman got out of the truck to greet me. I immediately tensed up. This girl, whoever she was to him, was strikingly gorgeous. I was praying to God she was just a friend or a sister I didn't know about. Everything was running through my head. *Oh my goodness, this woman cannot be with him.*

"Alex, this is Simone." Sanford was beaming. I couldn't tell if he was happy about me meeting her or her meeting me. Sanford is six-five, this girl had to be six feet tall herself. Her skin looked like a dark chocolate Hershey bar. *I'm so confused. I don't know if I want to smack her or lick her.* That heart-shaped face with the deepest dimples I'd ever seen. You could put a couple of cherries in her face and they would hold. Her waist was tiny—she had to be a size four, with the most perfectly shaped boobs. And I know this because I could see them through her shear top. *Are you kidding me!* I could see very clearly she was cold—perhaps a jacket is in order. *I really don't like this girl.* I looked her up and down again. *Yes, I really, really, really don't like this girl!*

175

"Nice to meet you." I repeated in my head: *smile . . . don't forget to smile.*

"Hello?"

Oh, for real. She's English! Why am I here?

Simone was still standing there just smiling. I was quite sure—or at least I thought I was sure—English was the language in Great Britain. *Why is she staring at me? I'm so short standing here next to them maybe she finds me fascinating. Either way her staring is starting to creep me out. I thought the look of annoyance was universal—maybe she's a little slow.*

Sanford put the bags in the back, came around on the passenger side, and opened Simone's door and mine. We both hopped in, her in the front with me in the back. Simone was still periodically turning around and smiling. I was looking back at her nodding my head each time. *It sure would be nice to know who this girl is. But since it's only the first five minutes and Sanford has just got back in the car I think I'm being a little anxious.*

Sanford pulled away toward the expressway and his house. When we arrived, I was pleasantly surprised at how nice the exterior of the house was. He had a couple of roommates if I remembered right. It turned out it was his friend and sister. They must be doing pretty well . . . it's a two-story house near the park. And everyone knows how much I love the park.

"This is nice, Sanford," I acknowledged.

Simone beamed, apparently agreeing how nice the house was. I was truly curious as to who Simone was to Sanford. I couldn't wait until we got in the house, so I texted Linda and asked her what was up with Simone. Linda took a minute to text me back. We were inside the house when I got it.

The outside of the house was nothing compared to the interior. Sanford gave me the tour while Simone, who seemed quite at home, stayed in the family room watching the biggest flat-screen television known to man. *I guess he's into television now, and tech.* This house was definitely state of the art, with dark hardwood floors, beautiful cabinetry and glass backsplashes in the kitchen. The whole house looked like Pottery Barn came in and threw up. The bedrooms and bathrooms were gorgeous, too.

I really liked this house.

"Where are your roommates?"

"Oh, they'll be here later. They went to the grocery store to pick up something for dinner."

"Whose house is this?"

We stopped in a bedroom that clearly looked like it was Sanford's. He put my things down and we sat on the bed to talk for a minute. I was surprised my nutty professor's room was actually clutter-free, except for his books, papers and computers. For Sanford this was clean.

"Mason and his sister Nikki."

"The house is gorgeous." *It was killing me.* "Who is Simone?"

"Oh, she's been staying here off and on, she's a model working in New York, so—oh, let me back up, she's Nikki's best friend. But yeah, she's here for the weekend too."

"Oh, okay, that's cool."

"Why? Who did you think she was?"

"Hey, I didn't know. Kind of seemed like something may have been going on."

He grinned. "Ah, you were jealous."

"I was not jealous. I was curious."

"No, you were jealous. You thought she had taken yo' man away from you," he moaned, grinning.

"You know what? I'm not going there with you. Anyway, where am I sleeping?"

"Right here."

"What do you mean, right here? Right here, right here?"

"Is there any other meaning to right here?"

"Ah no—I guess there isn't."

"So, right here."

Sanford was looking right into my eyes with a straight face. Then he started to laugh. "I'm joking. This is where you're sleeping. It's not where I'm sleeping."

I breathed a sigh to release the confusion. "Oh, you had me going for a minute there. I thought you were—"

"I was what? Trying to push up on you? If I remember correctly, you made yourself clear before I left. There is no you and me . . . remember."

What was I supposed to say to that? "I changed my mind . . . then changed it back" really didn't seem appropriate. Luckily I didn't have to say anything. Simone, perky boobs and all, appeared at the door informing us that Mason and Nikki had returned with groceries and take-out. Sanford stood up and followed her out of the bedroom downstairs.

I told Sanford I would be down in a minute, which gave me time to check my phone. I didn't think I needed to anymore. Sanford told me she was Nikki's best friend and I wanted to believe him, but I checked anyway. Linda texted back she didn't know who she was. I put the phone down and looked around the room, dazed and mystified. I texted Linda back and told her Sanford said Simone was Nikki's best friend, but I had a feeling he's not being completely truthful. I went to the bathroom—*amazing, by the way*—and read her response, "If he said so, then she *is* Nikki's best friend."

I texted Linda, "I don't know. You'd think with all the training I received from Jake I could spot a lie."

She hit back, "What are you saying Alex? Didn't you tell him you wanted to put everything on hold?"

I texted, "Yes."

She replied, "Well, I think he may have taken that in the literal sense of the word." As I read Linda's message I heard my name being called with an English accent. I was being summoned downstairs. I typed back to Linda, "Yup, I think you might be right. Just didn't expect it to happen so quickly."

After we finished talking, eating and getting to know one another it was late. We all turned in. The plan for the next day was sightseeing: Union Station, and the Museum of American and Natural History. I love the Library of Congress, so Sanford made sure we spent some time there along with the other attractions.

At first I thought Simone was going to join us. I was glad to see she didn't. I hadn't talked to her much, but I already made up in my mind I didn't want to. My rational mind knew that utterly dismissing her was wrong on so many levels. I really didn't care. If I got to know her and discovered on top of all that European gorgeousness that she was a rocket scientist and a model . . . I'd have to kill her or worse. *Myself.*

For dinner, I wanted to go someplace nice. Sanford told me about a steak place not far from where we were. I didn't eat red meat, but he said they had seafood I would like. He hadn't been there, so we made reservations and headed out for the evening in Georgetown. The hotel was absolutely amazing! Everything sparkled. After Sanford and I finished gobbling down our food, I decided that before dessert I would ask about Simone again. It was bothering me.

"I talked to Linda last night," I said.

"Oh yeah, I haven't talked to her in a while. How is she doing?"

"She's good."

"How about Mitch and the kids?"

"They're good too. Everybody's fine."

He smiled. "What about Tobey, what she been up to?"

"Tobey's still dating Hunter—we don't see much of her anymore."

"Good for them."

"I know—we're happy for them too. Switching subjects, how is work going?"

"Work is great. I'm considering staying here longer if U of M will approve it."

"Oh, why would you do that?"

Sanford played with his beard. "Well, my project wouldn't be completely wrapped up by the time my contract ends, because we got a late start. That will bump me into spring classes. I have committed to teach, so if I don't get back I could jeopardize my job, which—obviously I don't want to do."

"Well, that's a problem."

"Yeah, but I'll work it out. It will be all right."

I took a deep breath. "Okay, so what's up with you and Simone?"

"What you mean?"

"You know what I mean," I said.

The server came back to our table to take our dessert order. I decided to skip dessert, ordering a drink instead. Sanford did the same. We stopped talking to give the server a chance to clear away our dishes, then started back up where we'd left off.

"What you talking about, Alex? What do you think is up?"

"I think she's your girlfriend."

"She's not."

"That's not what it feels like."

"Is she my girlfriend? No. Are we dating—yes."

"Wow, that was fast."

Sanford's posture stiffened. "What do mean, that was fast?"

"I don't know—it seems like you jumped right into something. If you're able to do that, maybe I misinterpreted what started between us."

He pointed at me. "You misinterpreted something?"

"Yeah, obviously, I must have."

"You're playing victim again. Alex, you told me—and I repeat 'we should put this on hold,' remember that?"

I sat up straight, folding my arms. "Yes, of course I remember."

"Let's play grownup for a minute . . . what did I say to you?"

"I don't recall what you said only the sentiment—you wanted to stay together."

"And you didn't."

The server came back with our drinks, something strong for him and wine for me. I watched Sanford take a sip. His face looked distressed. I'd managed to bring something out of him I had never seen before: anger.

"Look, I—"

Sanford leaned in toward me. "Do you really want to talk about this?"

"That's a good question. I talked to Linda. She told me she was with you at Rio's when you saw Jake."

"Did you stop talking to her, too?"

"I was upset—but no, I didn't. She said she would've told me, but if she had, it would have betrayed a promise she'd made to you."

Sanford nodded his head before taking another drink. "That's true. Did she tell you why we met?"

"No, are you going to?"

"Tell me why you wanted to break up before I left."

I didn't expect this question, and my reaction reflected that. "I told you—even you have to admit, six months is a long time, and now you're talking about extending it."

"Well then, I guess you were right. We should've separated."

"Extending your time isn't the reason I was right. Simone is. You did exactly what I thought would happen."

"Now we're getting somewhere . . . what's that Alex?"

"Met somebody else—moved on. Come on, you've been with me through all the breakups—I don't have a real good track record when it comes to men being faithful." For a split second I thought of the ramifications of being this honest, but I was here now with no foreseeable consequences for withholding how I felt. "It was better to end it then—before you cheated on me, while we can still be friends."

"You put me through hell, because you thought I was going to cheat on you?"

"Hell? Sanford, what hell could you possibly be in? You look like you're in heaven to me."

"This is not about Simone. It's about you never being where I am. Feeling what I felt and knowing what I knew from the moment I asked you to dance in college." Sanford slid his chair closer to me. Reaching for my hands, he looked in my eyes. Calmer now, he whispered, "So, I waited—I'd been waiting and trusting, with Linda's reassurance, you would eventually snap out of it, get rid of the last failure in a string of disappointments and see this is more than friendship."

Sanford leaned back in his chair, swapping my hands for what remained in his glass. He returned his glass to the table, but his hands didn't reconnect with mine. "It's getting late— we should head back." He stood up, dropped money on the table to settle our tab and walked toward the door.

Sanford wasn't waiting for me anymore. Even though my state of mind was struggling to find some emotional footing, I stood from my seat and walked toward the door where Sanford waited for me.

The car ride back to the house was quiet. Simone in all her English glory was standing in the door when we pulled up. The music from the house infested the stillness of the night. Cars lined both sides of the street. As we pulled into the driveway, Sanford informed me that Mason and Nikki had invited a few friends over for a little dinner and spirits for my last night in D.C. We continued to sit there and finally Sanford said, "Do you remember before you got married, Tobey and I took you over to that girl's house where Jake was?"

I continued to stare out the window. "Yeah, I remember."

"I said to myself if you take him back after this . . . that was it. We could only be friends. You want a real man, whatever happened to being a real woman."

He opened the door and got out of the car. Leaving me inside.

Well damn, there it was. I felt gutted. Our conversation had drained me. I wasn't up for company, but at the risk of appearing ungrateful, I put on a brave face and got out of the car.

I looked on as Sanford reached out his arm, failing to grab Simone's hand. She danced into his arms, drawing his lips to hers and kissed him. I observed from behind what was transpiring—the undercurrent of my decision. Free from her embrace, they walked into the party: together, hand in hand.

The next morning, quietly, I packed, then dressed and locked the door headed for the cab awaiting me in the driveway. I left a generic note thanking everyone for their hospitality pinned to the refrigerator. To wake Sanford up would mean I'd need to find him and if I did, the sight of him in bed with Simone would take me over the edge. *I think I'll pass.*

It wasn't until I boarded the plane I received a message from Sanford. It read, "I would've taken you to the airport," which didn't seem to warrant a response. I sent his message to the little white trash can on my phone, and then prepared myself for departure.

Sanford was officially black history.

Chapter Twenty-Four

The sun was leaving the day behind when I arrived at Metro Airport. During my trip, Easton had texted me off and on, nothing of significance, just brief abbreviated conversations here and there. I anxiously awaited the buzz in my purse that would take me away from my disenchanting conversation with Sanford. I settled for the illusion of something than the reality of nothing. Easton's message gave me the assurance something was possible.

Easton's message gave me assurance of something—a blank page. He was a story yet to be written: I needed that.

Like any emotional deserter, I wanted to move on to something new as opposed to fixing what I left behind.

After I put my bags down, I sat on the couch to catch my breath and my phone buzzed. It was Easton. He wanted to see me. I didn't feel like seeing or being seen by anyone. It'd been a long disappointing weekend. I always have a plan of how I think things are going to turn out—then, wham, I get sideswiped. I really need to learn how to manage my expectations.

I'd rather cut my losses and curl up into bed with some cookies and a pint of ice cream for company.

Never debate a lawyer. All my reasoning and rationalizing didn't add up to a night of goodies in bed alone. Easton's last message read, "I'm on my way." In D.C., Easton had asked again if anything happened between Sanford and me. He texted this question right before we ate dinner. Afterwards, I assured him there wasn't. Unlike before, this time I was certain. And, consequently, he believed me.

Easton arrived within the hour of us texting our last message. Granted I'd only seen him a few times, but Easton was well manicured each time I saw him. My outfit matched my mood: flannel pajamas. I couldn't think of a good reason to change, and that included him. The nights were getting cooler. He wore jeans, a dress shirt with loafers and, for the third time, no wedding ring. Logic dictated he either never wore his ring—hence no ring tan— or he was telling the truth about his marriage. My lie detector wasn't working. *The truth always finds a way and I have no doubt this situation won't be any different.*

When he arrived I was ready to eat. We settled on having a piglet day: eating whatever we wanted and watching movies, all of it from the comfort of my bed. Snuggled under the covers after he confiscated the remote he asked, "What do you want to eat?"

Leaning over him, reaching for the remote, I said, "I don't know—how about Chinese?"

Easton moved it out of my reach. "I had that yesterday—I want some fried chicken."

"Look, if I eat that, you will be watching these movies by yourself. I'll be asleep."

"You invited me over here to go to sleep?"

I gave up on regaining control of the television. "Well, if we're going to be real about it—" I cut him a look. "You invited yourself."

He laughed. "You got a menu?"

I reached over and pulled the local soul food restaurant's menu out of my nightstand. Easton looked on in astonishment. "I thought you were going downstairs." He laughed. "Why do you have menus in your nightstand?"

I laughed with him. "Look, don't judge me—I work late nights. It's convenient to have them here."

We decided what to eat, called the order in, and then I waited for Easton to return with our dinner. I knew soul food would be a bad idea. I got the catfish dinner, Easton the chicken. We loaded up on sides: yams, macaroni and cheese, greens, and black-eyed peas. For dessert we shared peach cobbler and banana pudding. This was just what I needed. Our food and drinks were in place, hot sauce in hand, and Gandalf arrived at Uncle Bilbo's birthday party—heaven.

By the time Frodo and Sam arrived at Mordor, we were knocked out. I slept through everything, and so did Easton. I told him soul food would knock us out and it did. I was tired, both emotionally and physically. We didn't get a chance to talk much this time, which was fine with me: I was all talked out from Sanford. I needed easy and that's just what Easton delivered: a stress-free evening.

I asked Easton if he would like to spend the night. It was around eleven o'clock when we both woke up to the movie credits. I assured him I wouldn't take advantage of him. Despite his disappointment, he stayed anyway.

I took a quick shower while he ran home to get clean clothes for the next day. By the time he returned in sweats and a t-shirt, I was ready for bed—for real this time. We cleaned up our mess from my bedroom and turned in. Easton rested behind me with one arm above our heads and the other wrapped around me.

He managed to bring out the sun, even in this cloudy head.

Chapter Twenty-Five

After piglet night, Easton and I were seeing each other regularly.

It'd been a few months since we'd met and still hadn't slept together. Tonight the girls and I'd made plans for dinner to catch up with one another. Unlike what I'd done with past relationships, I managed to keep the majority of my personal life to myself. The biggest news for tonight's discussion would be Tobey and Hunter moving in together.

At our age there aren't a lot of firsts for us to experience anymore, and this is Tobey's first true love. I get that, but it's soon, and I worry she's moving too fast. Ultimately they have to figure out what makes sense for them, but that's not going to stop us for putting our two cents in.

At work, Karen and I finished earlier than we'd expected, giving us time to take my car home and I hop in with her. We met at a seafood restaurant downtown. Karen and I arrived first, then Tobey—with Hunter. Linda walked in still negotiating business on her cell. Our disappointment at the sight of Hunter didn't go unnoticed.

Tobey's disapproving finger pointed at each of us. "Fix your faces—he just dropped me off."

Karen responded, "Oh, I wondered what was happening here."

Tobey shook her head. "He's going to the mall to wait on me."

We sat in the lobby ten minutes before our table was ready. After receiving our drink order, we ordered food and immediately began catching each other up on what's been happening. There wasn't anything new to report from Linda and Karen. Their biggest adventure was what their kids were wearing for Halloween.

Tobey's information (considerably more interesting than costumes) filled us in on what we already suspected. The move. I knew this was a shark-infested pool to be jumping into, but what the hell . . . I went first. "So what's up with you and Hunter? Are you moving in together?"

Tobey giggled. "All right, I knew that's what you brought me here for. Yes, we're moving in together. And yes, I know it's soon, but I don't care what any of you say, so let me get that out right now before you get started."

"Well, damn, Tobey, can we object before you put us in our place? Nobody said it was too soon—we were thinking it, but we didn't say it," Linda laughed.

Tobey was ready for her. "I'm just saying, none of that: I don't want you second-guessing my decision. It's been made by the two people who should be making it. So, be happy for me."

Linda, Karen, and I exchanged glances, wondering where the defensiveness was coming from. We hadn't said anything yet. I broke in with my two cents. "Look: you're happy, so are we." I glanced at Karen and Linda. "Yes, I think our first thought was its soon to be moving in with him, but as long as you know what you're doing we're supporting you."

Linda cut me a look.

"I'm not eighteen—it's not too soon," Tobey said.

We met each other's eyes again, but didn't say a disapproving word. Karen noted there were tons of people who dated their whole life and never make a commitment to one another. At least Tobey and Hunter were trying to be together.

Linda asked, "So are you thinking about getting married? Or just living together?"

"Living together for now—marriage isn't off the table, but it's too soon to talk about it," Tobey responded.

I didn't understand that logic. I had to ask, "Other than having the piece of paper, isn't it basically the same thing as living together?"

Karen jumped in. "I don't think so," she barked.

I looked at her, amazed. "Why not? It's the same to me."

Linda, taking a drink of her coffee said, "I think it is."

Tobey appeared disappointed with Linda's and my viewpoint. Her tendency to jump into things before thinking them through justified our hesitation. From my perspective, we had a healthy degree of concern, but I don't think that came across to Tobey. All she heard was "it's too soon."

Disappointed but appreciative, Tobey said, "Look, you, I know I haven't always made the right decisions, neither have y'all I might add, but I'm in a good place. Hunter is the best man I've ever met. He wants to be with me, and I with him. So we're taking a leap of faith, but I can't do this without my girls' blessing. So, give me your blessing, and let's move on to

191

Alex who thinks we don't know she's messing around with a married man."

I almost choked. "Karen, you have a really big mouth," I laughed.

"What did I do?" Karen replied, making a face.

"Tobey, we're not going help you move—but we're here when you need us," Linda said.

"Didn't nobody ask you to help us move. Hunter hired movers." Tobey rolled her eyes, grinning.

"I'm liking Hunter already," Linda confessed.

Just as our entrées arrived we put the subject of Tobey moving to rest, which meant I would be next in the hot seat. They were just pretending not to hear Tobey's revelation. I needed some liquid courage and, after a couple of sips, I felt no pain. I was ready for 'em.

Tobey got the ball rolling, so it was not more than fair for her to pick it back up. Before moving on to something new, she opened with something old.

"We never talked about you sleeping with Sanford."

Karen lifted her head up from her chicken salad. Her eyes slowly widened. "What? You slept with Sanford?" The news stopped her from eating entirely.

"I thought I told you. I *did* tell you."

Karen's face looked riddled with confusion. "You sure?"

Linda, who continued to eat, said, "She told you."

"No, I would've remembered that," Karen said.

I raised my hands. "Okay, I slept with Sanford, but it was a long time ago now." I turned to Karen. "I thought I told you. Sorry, I got so caught up and completely forgot."

"Is that why Sanford left town? Did something happen between y'all?"

Karen seemed nervous, surprised, and upset at the same time. She'd finally continued eating her salad.

"It didn't go the way Alex wanted it to go, that's for sure," Linda reported. As much as I was enjoying my pasta, Karen was still wrapped up in hearing the Sanford and I slept together story. I needed to explain myself.

"No, he didn't leave because of me or anything I did—"

"That's not true." Linda interjected.

"It's true. He got the grant—nothing to do with me."

Tobey blurted, "Tell her the rest."

"What rest?" I asked.

"The rest—do you want me to start you off?"

"You're just happy 'cause it's my turn," I said, chuckling.

"Yes, actually, now that you mention it, I am."

I looked back over at Karen who returned to her frozen position with Linda dipping her fork into Karen's plate. "Girl, eat your food," I shrieked.

"Oh." Karen snapped out of it in time to hit Linda's fork with her own. "Get out of my plate."

Linda laughed. "Oh, I thought you were done. What's the name of that salad?"

"I don't know—just a grilled chicken salad—don't change the subject, what happened with Sanford? You didn't like him? Sometimes friends don't make good lovers."

I shook my head. "That wasn't it. Just the opposite—I liked him a lot. I couldn't have been more wrong about dating friends," I admitted.

"You were all in before he left," Tobey said.

I sighed, "Yeah, well it didn't work out."

"Tell her why," Tobey added.

Linda, still intimately engaged with her food, managing to occasionally eat some of ours, too, said, "It's not all Alex's fault."

"Thank you." I said feeling a small sense of vindication. "Help me out—tell them it wasn't me."

"That's as far as I go. Look, I am out of the house, no Mitch and no kids. I don't care what's going on. I am enjoying this for every minute I can."

"I guess I'm on my own. Can I at least finish my food first?" I asked.

In perfect pitch they said, "No."

I responded to Tobey. "Before he left I told him we should cool things off until he got back."

Karen's frown sunk lower. "Why would you say that?"

It was hard to explain what I didn't understand myself. "I don't know—fear— maybe? I know—I messed up big time. Some things can't be fixed—I remember telling Jake that— now Sanford should've said that to me."

Karen wants this for me. So much so she's not giving up. "It can't be that bad you went to see him."

"That . . . really . . . didn't go as planned either."

Linda and Tobey followed our conversation. "After you texted I didn't hear back from you. What happened?" Linda asked.

"Well I asked you about the girl—"

"Girl—what girl?" Tobey shouted.

"When I got there—the airport—Sanford had a girl with him. I thought she might be his girlfriend—"

"He's got a girlfriend that fast," Karen yelled.

"He said he's dating her—she's not his girlfriend. Besides, I broke things off with him. Sanford is my fault."

"He was in love with you for so long—you had to know Alex," Linda said.

"On some level—I guess I did. I honestly don't want to talk about this anymore. It doesn't matter now anyway." I sighed. "He's moved on and I'm starting to."

Tobey asked, "What did the girl look like?"

"Now there's the real story—she's a model from New York—oh, she's also English."

"Are you serious?" Karen replied.

"I wish I wasn't."

"Was she seriously pretty or oddly pretty?" Linda asked.

"No, she's really pretty with the whole super model look."

"Prettier than you? Oh wow, now that's funny," Tobey said.

"If you compare us—she's a greyhound and I'm a Yorkie—both beautiful, but for very different reasons."

Linda laughed. "Oh, honey." She laughed some more. "I hoped you'd get a chance to talk, but with her there—"

"He talked, I listened. The gist of it is this—he's not waiting for me anymore."

"Waiting for what? You?" Karen asked.

"A bus—of course me."

"Sorry—"

"And no, I didn't know how he felt—Linda did, but I had no clue."

Tobey and Karen's attention shifted in Linda's direction. Linda defensively raised her hand. "Sanford called me before Alex and Jake divorced, wanting to talk about his feelings for Alex. He said he was in love with her—always had been. He couldn't be the best friend anymore waiting and watching her with Jake. He considered moving away. That's when he told me he applied for grants to work at other schools outside of Michigan."

"That's when you saw Jake with Taylor?" I asked.

Linda turned to face me. "Of all the restaurants in the city, they walked into ours. Sanford was right about something. Then you got mad at him—everything went downhill from there."

"You didn't know," Tobey said facing me.

"What's so hard to believe about that—I didn't know."

"Tell them about Easton," Karen chimed in.

I turned and gave Karen a look. "In a minute," I said.

"Oh, sorry. Maybe I need to get me another drink."

"Maybe you should," I echoed.

"Tell the story," Linda said impatiently.

"Okay, so out of the blue Easton called me and asked me to lunch."

"Okay, keep going. I didn't know you gave him your number." The restaurant thinned out. It would close soon.

"I didn't—he got it on his own. It's all pretty innocent right now. He came over after I got back from D.C. and spent the night," I confessed. "But nothing happened," I added quickly.

"So what *is* the situation at home?" Linda asked.

"He's married." I raised my hand to shield my eyes from the glares. "—but separated."

"He getting a divorce?" asked Tobey.

Frowning I said, "I would assume so, don't know. I haven't asked."

Linda blurted, "You haven't asked?"

"So what's the plan, Alex?" Tobey asked. "Just keep sleeping with this woman's husband until he goes back to her?"

"Of course not," I cried. "First and foremost, we are not having sex," I clarified. "I already told you nothing happened."

"So what are you doing?" Linda questioned.

"Not a whole lot. We're getting to know each other. We're *dating*. I'm trying really hard not to overthink this."

"How can you *date* somebody that's married? Isn't that what Jake was doing with Taylor . . . dating?" Tobey's voice dripped sarcasm.

"No, it's cheating, when you're married," I said.

"Isn't Easton married? As long as we're clarifying," Linda said.

Karen's elbows hit the table while her hands held her heart shaped face.

She wasn't in support of my budding relationship. I looked away from the table. "Yes . . . yes he is."

Linda paid for dinner, which made all of us happy. Just as we were wrapping up, Tobey's ride came in. We congratulated Hunter and thanked him for keeping our girl healthy. Tobey, thirty pounds lighter, looked better than ever.

I walked Linda to her car while Karen pulled hers around closer to the entrance and near Linda. We said our goodbyes and hugged. I pulled back to face Linda and rubbed her stomach. "Something you want to tell me?" I said.

She smacked my hand.

Linda smiled. "Go home," she said.

Chapter Twenty-Six

The cocktails from the restaurant had wired me up. Buzzed and restless energy is not a good combination, not for someone like me. Normally, I would work or try to sleep it off, but no—not this time. I'm stepping outside myself— let go and let flow as it were. I text Easton and asked him if he was up. He texted back, saying he was. I told him I'd just got home from dinner with the girls and wanted some company.

He texted me back. "If the lady asks, she shall receive."

I texted, "The lady is asking."

His next note read. "I'm on my way."

Oh my God! I can't believe I did that . . . *now what? Okay, I need to get me something else to drink to keep my bravery going.* I went upstairs to take a shower. There was no way driving over here would take long. I hopped in and out, keeping my phone near just in case he called.

While dressing, I received a text. "You want something from the store?"

I messaged back, "More wine."

"Okay, be there in a few."

A short time later headlights reflected from outside in front of the house.

I looked in my closet, grabbed a robe and tied the belt around my waist. The silk caressed my naked skin. My body confessed what I didn't want to—Easton was summoned to do more than keep me company.

"Were you in the bed when I texted?" I asked.

"Yeah—I mean, no—lying down, but I wasn't asleep." He walked into the kitchen pulling the contents of his bag out on the kitchen table.

"That's not wine. You know how to make this?" I asked, pointing at the liquor mix.

"I think so. It should be mixed already." Easton grabbed a couple of glasses out of the cabinet, ice cubes from the freezer, and poured us both a drink. The moonlight beamed through the blinds, lighting the room and revealing Easton's silhouette. He was so beautiful to me.

I sat at the kitchen table. Easton joined me as we sipped our drinks—which weren't half-bad, considering they came from a mix. I noticed he brought an overnight bag, *so I guess I'll have a play date for tonight.*

"How was dinner with the girls?"

"Eventful is probably the best way to describe it," I said.

"Meaning?"

"Hopefully you'll get a chance to meet the crew, but whenever we have one of our dinners somebody is on the hot seat."

"Who was it this time?" he asked, sipping his drink.

"Well, it depends on who you ask. Tobey at first then it switched to me, and stayed on me."

He smiled. "What were they giving you a hard time about?"

"It wasn't a hard time, really. More like me filling in the blanks," I admitted. "Lots of blanks."

"I'm sure you handled it," he said, and put down his glass. "No flannel pajamas tonight?"

"No, not tonight," I said. "You got here before I finished getting dressed."

He narrowed his eyes. "So, what is it tonight?"

"Ah—no pajamas."

His faced lit up. "Okay—"

Observing the excitement in his face I interjected, "Before you say anything, I have to tell you—I've never done anything like this before."

"What? Make a booty call?"

"See—I knew you were going to say that. Technically this is not a booty call, and for the record, I *do not* like that term," I laughed.

"But that's what's it's called and this is what it is—don't be ashamed now." Easton laughed uncontrollably.

"You're having way too much fun with this."

"No, but seriously—I don't think you would have made this move without a little liquid motivation."

"You're here now—does it matter?"

He gave me a blank stare. "Yeah, a little—I would like to think you would've called me eventually anyway."

"I don't know—the liquor helped me make the call, but my desire for you is how you got here to begin with."

We stood up from our seats. Easton pulled my face into his massaging my temples with his thumbs softly placing his upper lip between mine: our first kiss. My heart raced as we continued caressing each other and intertwining our tongues. I wrapped my arms underneath his, massaging my fingertips up and down his spine to the lower part of his back in small rhythmic motions.

Easton slid his fingers inside my robe, pulling it down and revealing my nudity. He quickly disarmed himself of his clothes. The bedroom was too far: the kitchen table would have to do.

And it did.

Easton made love to me with the skill of a master chef. The genie was out of the bottle. I felt the thickness of his penis against my thigh. I lay my back on the cold kitchen table, robe open down to my forearms, and Easton's naked body between my legs. I pulled my legs inward, knees at my shoulders, allowing his tongue to reach inside of me. My eyes closed slipping into a sexual abyss.

One hand on his penis, the other stroking my breast, he gradually pressed himself inside me. Each thrust accompanied by masterful tongue sucking each breast, never out of rhythm or off-beat, engaging all of me. My body responded to him with passion and purpose as his thrusts quickened. I held my excitement, but his moan was more than I could take, all space and time no longer existed. We were no longer two people, climaxing in perfect harmony, an erotic interaction fusing sound and silence. Exhausted, Easton laid his head on my stomach. I lowered my legs beside his wet body, coming to the one inevitable realization: Jake was right—we should have bought this table.

Chapter Twenty-Seven

I turned to Easton. Feeling the wine from last night, I said, "You hungry?" I put my finger on the tip of his nose. "I'm going to make you some fish and grits."

"As tempted as I am to take you up on that you *do not* have time to make fish and grits. We both have to be at work in an hour," he replied.

"Naw—naw—naw, fish and grits, that's what you're going to get."

He laughed at me. "All right, I put it down—where's my food at?"

I laughed. "Oh, babe, I was playing, I can't make all that. But I can microwave you some waffles if you go to the store and get some."

Easton cupped my face with his enormous hands. "I put it down last night. I want my fish and grits."

"I was joking. Waffles are all I have time for and that's if you go buy some."

Fooling around with Easton, entertaining the idea of making—microwaving waffles, I hadn't looked at the time. The clock was inconspicuously hidden behind a lamp. We'd made it to the bed for our second round of lovemaking last night. Easton's warm body embraced mine, only moving his arm just enough for me to reach over and twist the alarm clock into view for the morning alarm.

I gasped. "It's eight o'clock!"

"That's why I moved the clock. I wanted to pretend like we had all day."

I pushed him away. "But we don't have all day, goofball. Get up."

Easton's muscular arm felt like lead on my waist. His pulling me back each time I attempted to get up didn't help. Resisting him wasn't getting me anywhere. I turned to face him, morning breath and all. Kissing his cheeks I stared at his closed eyelids. He didn't flinch. I kissed his cheek again, pulled back and continued my gaze. He didn't peek. I removed my hand from underneath the cover and popped him on the forehead. That got me a smile, but nothing else.

I whined, "Easton, come on, get up."

He replied, "Once is asking. Twice is begging."

"Okay, so I'm begging. My first appointment is at ten."

"Mine is at eleven, so what you going to give me if I move?"

I grinned. "Another kiss on the cheek?"

"Not with that hot breath," he said laughing.

"Oh, no, you didn't. You got jokes, okay—now you ain't gettin' nothing. Get up."

He grabbed me tighter, hugging me close enough to know exactly what he wanted. "Got something on your mind?" I asked.

"Me? Nope."

"You sure? I'm thinking other parts of your body would disagree with you."

"Oh, that? That's your present for having me over."

"My present . . . seriously, Easton, get up."

His voice was husky. "I can't have you thinking I'm a bad guest, so I got you something."

"A big something . . . "

"Very big." He laughed. "For you—I figured I'd go all-out."

I put my cheek next to his and nibbled on his earlobe, whispering, "You're a hot mess." I felt his hand rubbing between my legs. There was no way I was getting out of this bed without opening my present. I only hoped Karen would move my appointment back—I was going to be extremely late.

Finally out of the house, I called Tobey. She was home packing, which meant the move would be taking place a little sooner than any of us realized. I don't know why I thought it would be down the road some—made no sense based on the conversation last night.

Tobey answered. "Hello?"

"Hey," I said.

"What's up?"

"Guess what I did last night."

She giggled. "Went home and went to bed."

"Between you and Linda, I don't know who has the worst jokes. No, I asked Easton to come over."

"Uh-oh, Alex, look at you making a booty call!"

"That is not what it was. I just wanted to see him."

"Oh yeah, you wanted to see him, all right." I could tell she was still giggling about it. "So, Alex—did you see him?"

"He came over, of course I saw him."

"Stop playing! You know what I'm talking about. Did you *see* him?"

"Yes, I *saw* him—multiple times."

She gave a hoot. "Details, girl, details! How was it?"

"Girl, girl, girl, girl, girl it was an out-of-body experience—I felt like I could fly."

"Oh-oh, Alex giving away the sweet tea on the regular now. Was he better than Sanford?"

That was easy. "Not better—different."

"Like what? Different how?"

"Easton doesn't love me. Sanford, that's different, he's physically capable of expressing how he feels about me. If Easton's earth—Sanford is the universe and beyond."

"And you gave that up?"

"Exactly."

"So, okay. I hate to break up a moment you're having here—afterglow and all, but how does his wife play into all of this? He is still married, right?"

"Ayah, he's still married."

"I'm all for getting your groove on, but—"

"I know what I need to do before this gets any more complicated than it already has. Can you give me a minute?"

"Take all the time you need, but keep your options open, Alex. I mean it. Don't get so wrapped up into this guy that you're hurt if he winds up going back to his wife."

I said primly, "I don't foresee that happening."

"You don't know what's happening, which is part of the problem. Even if you don't want to know the answer, you need to know the questions. Isn't this the same shit Jake did to you?"

"It's not the same. I'm not going after this woman's husband."

Tobey paused. "Alex, is that the distinction you hanging your hat on?"

"Yes, it is. He's not in the house with her, and I am not chasing this man."

"Okay," Tobey replied.

"What do you mean, okay?"

"I mean okay. Alex, what do you want me to say? You know that's weak. It's the same thing. I know you don't want to hear this, honey, but now that you have slept with him, you are sleeping with someone else's husband."

"Look . . . I don't want an ethics lesson from you Tobey."

"If you don't want an ethics lesson from the book of morality . . . let's take a page from the book of *Bitch Damn* or *What the Fuck*. I'm not a perfect person, but I know a dead end when I see one," she said.

"I don't think I can do this right now," I sighed. "I need to get off the phone."

"Alex, don't be upset. Same team—remember? I'm looking out for you even when you're not."

"Same team, Tobey. I remember, but I'm still getting off the phone."

"Why?"

"Karen's calling me, I got to get this."

"Okay, call me back."

Honestly, I had no intention of calling Tobey back. I'm getting sensitive in my old age. She kind of hurt my feelings. Then Karen called, wondering where I was, and to tell me that Jake had stopped by questioning her as to my whereabouts. I'm always at work and on time.

Karen said she covered for me but I don't need covering: Jake and I are not married anymore. She also wanted to know how soon I was arriving because Jake was grabbing a cup of coffee and coming back. I needed to get into the office for his second visit.

I didn't park in front this time. I pulled around back, grabbed my briefcase, paperwork, and headed inside. I hadn't stopped off for coffee considering I was already running behind. I hoped Jake would slip into old habits and get me something to drink, too.

Coming in the back way has its advantages: one is sneaking past any waiting visitors in the lobby or anyone parked out front.

Jake returned with not one, but two cups of coffee from my happy place. He walked in my office straight from the pages of a Ralph Lauren catalog. *God he is gorgeous.*

"So to what do I owe the pleasure of this visit?" I asked as soon as I'd sipped my coffee.

"I wanted to give you an update on Mom."

I took another sip. "How is she?"

"About the same," he said. "There hasn't been much change. We're just trying to keep her healthy after a couple of close calls."

"What close calls?"

"Oh, she caught a cold."

Jake leaned back on the couch creating, just enough movement to fill my nose with his cologne. Too bad it couldn't have worked out between Jake and me. What we lacked in partnership, we made up for in physical perfection: we did look good together. Sadly, that was about it.

"How long has she been sick?" I asked.

"A couple of weeks since we saw you, nothing bacterial only viral—but even viral can be a problem for her if it develops into something."

"Oh, Jake, you need to call me and let me know stuff like that. I want to be there as much as I can without—you know, getting in the way."

"How could you be getting in the way?"

I sighed. "You know exactly what I'm talking about," I said.

"Taylor is a part of my life, yeah, but so are you. You make Mom happy, and that predates Taylor, so we all have to play grown-up."

"I choose who I play with, Jake. You don't get to decide anymore. I didn't want Taylor in my life then, and I don't now. I—"

"Alex," he interrupted. "I got to stop you. Taylor is not an issue for you. I know how you feel, but more importantly she knows how you feel. Taylor won't be around when you're around. She doesn't live with me. There shouldn't be an issue unless you make it one."

"I think the bigger issue is probably not so much Taylor—although she is an issue—it's what she represented. I've never in my life been hurt the way you hurt me." I sighed. "Look, I've had a long day already and it's not even eleven o'clock—you've moved on and I've moved on."

"You keep saying I've moved on—"

"No, I don't—"

"Yes, you have—you really didn't give me much of a choice."

I rolled my eyes and said, "Oh, God, here we go."

"No, no—you brought it up," he said.

I paused. "I didn't mean for it to go someplace—I was just talking."

"That's just it—you're talking—you decide."

"Has everybody lost their minds today? You're acting as if someone told me you were cheating—I saw you." I snapped. "With these eyes."

Karen, being a proactive trusted assistant, heard the conversation heading off a cliff, and immediately got up from her desk and closed my door. This conversation made my neck and shoulders ache. I rotated my head in a circular motion to ease the tension—but only putting Jake out of my office would remedy that. Everything about his body was at attention now. He moved from the couch to a chair directly in front of my desk. Pandoras box officially opened.

"Why are we talking about this? You didn't love me. It was always this woman or that woman in my face and you put them there. Taylor was the icing on the proverbial cake."

"You wanted the divorce, not me. I asked you to work it out and what did you say?"

"I said no."

He nodded. "Not me. At the end of the day you walked away."

"Correction, I didn't walk away. You left me mentally, spiritually and emotionally then you moved out, so don't even try it. And who cares—you know how long ago that was—I'm over it."

"No you're not, because you always bring up Taylor but our issues weren't all my fault. Taylor, yes, but not everything."

"No, but they were compounded by your bringing a third party into our marriage. I could've gotten over anything—anything but cheating. How would you have felt if I was getting it on with another man?"

"I would have felt the same way you did. I feel that way now just thinking about you moving on with somebody else."

I didn't know what to say to that comment.

"What do you want, Jake? It's too late to stay married."

"I don't know what I'm saying, but I know this . . . if I had to do all over again, I would have stayed and tried to work it out."

I shook my head. "See, that was always the problem. If you could do it all over again, why not start with *not* cheating in the first place."

"Come on, give me a break . . . you know what I mean."

"You can't work it out by yourself. There have to be two willing parties," I said.

"I think you would have tried."

I shook my head. "I don't know about that one, Jake."

"Okay, I get that, but what if I told you I wanted to try now?"

"Try what?"

"Try working on our relationship."

"What relationship?" I was confused. "What are you talking about?"

"Would you be open to working on being friends?"

"What does that mean exactly?"

"I know you said you would support me with Mom. I appreciate that more than you will ever know, but what if I wanted you to do more—like work on your relationship with me. Would you be willing to do that?"

"I need to think about it. What would be the purpose in that?"

"To strengthen our relationship, work through the pain so we could possibly get to some resolution and forgiveness. I want us to be friends. We started off as friends."

"No, we weren't."

He didn't seem to be listening. "You don't have to answer today. The other reason I stopped by is because Mom wanted to see you, so this Friday, if you're not busy, maybe you can stop by for dinner, just the three us."

"I don't have any plans so far, but that could change. As long as you're okay with that—I guess I can come."

"I don't want to tell Mom you're coming, and you don't."

I caved. "I'll come."

"Good, I'm happy. This could be a new beginning for us."

"Jake look— I'm not sure I understand what you're expecting, but—"

He raised his hands. "Forget I said it. I'm happy you're coming, let's leave it at that."

We stood up. Jake leaned in, brushing his cheek against mine and whispered, "I'm glad you're coming," then kissed my cheek. He pulled his head back to face me so close that I could feel the warmth from his breathing.

I thought he was going to kiss me when Karen opened the office door and walked in. She handed me a sticky note. It read *'You have a visitor'*—another unexpected visitor. I'm never going to get any work done today.

"Jake's leaving," I said as I guided him toward the door.

"Yes—I guess I am."

Karen continued to stand behind me. "I'll see you Friday, just text me what time and I'll be there."

"I'll tell Mom."

Jake cleared the door as I turned to Karen to ask who was in the lobby then I heard a voice say, "What's up, man?" Karen and I froze. *Please, God, you are not doing this to me.* The second voice was unmistakable . . . it was Easton. Karen and I quietly tiptoed closer to the door to hear what they were saying.

"What you doing here? Trying to get some help?"

They laughed like old friends. *How could Jake know Easton and I'd never heard of him? Well, there was a lot Jake was doing that I didn't know.*

Jake's voice. "I'm here to see Alex."

I overhead Easton say, "Oh, I didn't know you two knew each other."

"Yeah, that's my ex. You remember I told you I was married."

"No, I didn't recall that. So you were married to Alex?"

"About seven years—she's helping me out with my mom."

"Oh, all right," I overheard Easton say.

Karen and I continued listening at the door. I heard Jake ask Easton, "So, what are you doing here?" I whispered to myself, but loud enough to get Karen's attention, "please don't tell him the truth." Considering I just gave a mini-lecture on the virtues of marriage, having Easton disclose that I'm seeing him wouldn't go over well—not at all. *Tobey's right—the sooner I get this back into perspective the better.*

"Oh, Alex referred a case to me. I was in the neighborhood, thought I would come by and let her know how everything's going."

"Yeah, okay, that's what's up. How did you meet Alex?" Jake asked.

"Oh, one of my boys introduced us. She needed an attorney—"

"Not for her—"

"No, no—for somebody else. I had time available. It just worked out."

Then I heard Jake ask, "How's your wife and kids doing?"

Easton responded, "Everybody's good."

I missed a few things they said. I inched closer and heard Jake say, "All right, man, I got to run, it was good seeing you."

Easton said, "All right, good seeing you, too. We'll have to hook up sometime and have a drink."

"Yeah, I'll holler at you."

Overhearing what seemed like the end of their conversation, Karen walked back into the lobby. I rushed to my chair behind the desk. By the time Easton walked to my office I appeared to be working hard—not ear hustling. Easton, dressed in a twill grey suit, checkered blue shirt, and striped tie looked as if he stepped out from the pages of a magazine. What Jake was to Ralph Lauren, Easton was to Brooks Brothers.

"Hello, gorgeous," he said.

"Hello to you. This is a surprise."

"Can I borrow you for lunch?"

"We just left each other. I haven't gotten a lot done today, fooling around with you."

"A *quick* lunch?"

"All right—but it has to be real quick." Clearing my throat I asked him, "Did I hear you make a friend in the lobby?"

"Not a new friend. I've known Jake about ten years."

I leaned back in my chair. "You don't say?"

"Yes." He smiled. "I do say—now grab your stuff and let's get out of here."

I looked at the clock on my computer screen. "It's kind of early for lunch, isn't it?"

"Not for where we're going."

"Where are you taking me?"

"It's a surprise. Come on, get your purse—let's go."

I gave in and called out to Karen through the open door. "I'm going to an early lunch." Easton walked around my oversized desk and held my jacket for me.

"Are you going to tell me where we're going?" I asked.

"Nope."

"If I guess will you tell me?"

"You'll never guess."

I grabbed my purse as we headed out the front door. "You driving or me?"

"Ah, you think you slick. I'm driving."

"Okay." I smiled. "Keep your secret."

Easton parked right outside my office building main entrance. He opened my door, ensured I was firmly seated, then got in on his side. I leaned closer to him resting my arm on the leather console with my hand dangling. Easton reached over and grabbed it interlocking our fingers.

We drove up a main artery away from my office toward the freeway. I watched the passersby out the window. I still had no clue as to where we were going, but he drove toward the university.

Dark clouds moved in from the east and mist filled the windshield. We exited off the freeway heading toward another main street in the city. I still had no inkling of where we were going until we reached the Art Institute. Easton pulled into the shipping and receiving area. Silent, I glanced over and smiled. He was right, the Institute wasn't open, and I would have never guessed this. Easton released my hand, pulling me in kissing me softly on my forehead.

"I've been a faithful supporter of the Art Institute for over ten years," he said.

"A faithful supporter?" I echoed.

"Yes, faithful."

I laughed. "Is that what it says on the website for members? Faithful supporter?"

"Actually, it does, but that's not relevant."

"Okay, you got to stop saying that," I said.

"What's wrong? I *am* faithful."

"Okay, go on—because you're a faithful supporter—"

"Well, there's perks and one of them is we're going to see the Institutes latest exhibit before it opens."

"Oh, okay—are you serious?"

"Yes, I'm very serious—let's get out of the car."

"Okay, never done anything like this before."

"I knew you would like this. I asked one of the curators to give us a quick tour—we'll have lunch after."

"Okay."

I couldn't stop smiling. Lunch at the Institute was beyond cool. *Who knew Easton had this in him?* I'd never done anything remotely close to this before. The curator at the loading dock greeted and escorted us to the exhibition. He described each piece—and there were about thirty of them—in great detail. One painting in particular blew me away. It was magnificent, and I was thankful to have the opportunity to share this experience with Easton.

The curator asked if I knew anything about the picture and of course my only knowledge about the artist came from a movie. The movie, it turned out, was based upon a novel, because there is little known about the artist or his paintings. Most of the artist's works was at The Hague, and of course I didn't know that, either.

After our viewing the curator told Easton we could take a strolling tour of the other exhibits. We walked through the entire first floor and a little bit of the second—or what I thought was the majority of the second, since the museum was bigger than what I'd remembered.

Our final stop was Rose Court, my favorite part of the museum. I went through the entrance and in the middle of the court was a round table dressed in white linens with two chairs, adorned with candles and pink roses for two.

"This is—" I stuttered to get the words out. "—is this for us?"

"For *you*," he said.

I felt like I couldn't breathe. The private showing is one thing—but this, this was more than I'd ever expected. I don't know what came over me. I was overcome with emotion from viewing the surroundings and him—such a beautiful gift came from someone I barely knew. Obviously his connection to the Institute enabled him to pull this off, but his desire to even want to plan this out left me speechless. It became difficult to continue to capture the moment through my tears.

"Baby, don't cry."

I buried my head in his chest to stop him from looking at me. I didn't want to mess up his beautiful suit, but emotions prevailed. Easton rubbed my back until I came up for air. "I just felt so overwhelmed. This is one of the nicest things anyone has ever done for me. Thank you for this."

"I'm glad I could."

Regaining my composure, Easton reached for my hand and walked me over to our table. We both were seated. Catching my breath, I wanted to absorb everything I set eyes on everything to capture details of this moment. Beautifully decorated, with candelabras in three different sizes and shapes, silver tablemats and chargers, full place settings of white china with silver trim, cake dishes with red velvet cake. My favorite. The centerpiece was made of white tree bark covered with white and pale pink roses, large pink hydrangea, blush pink peonies, and sweet peas. How Easton pulled this off was remarkable. When did he have the time?

I touched the flowers to see if they were real. They were. "I am speechless. This is amazing!"

"I hoped you would like it. It took some scheming on my part to keep this a secret."

"How did you know this stuff? My favorite flower, the Rose Court—who helped you? I know it wasn't Linda."

"No, it wasn't Linda, and the person only helped with your favorite flower. I guessed the rest."

"What rest? Is there more to the surprise?"

He smiled. "This isn't enough?"

"Yes, more than enough. I don't think my heart can take much more."

"Karen helped with your schedule and flowers. We were scheming to keep your schedule free."

"Oh, so she knew you were coming today."

He nodded. "Yeah, she knew. She didn't tell you, did she?"

"No, she didn't tell me anything."

"I thought she might've blabbed a little. But you're not a good actress."

"Not that good of an actress? Man, I could have done a Meryl Streep on you and you wouldn't even know it."

"I would know if you were faking it."

"No, dear, I'm sure you wouldn't know, but it doesn't matter because I wasn't faking. I'm surprised. I truly am."

"I'm glad you are. I wanted you to be. So the chef has prepared us something to eat. I hope you like it. I made some assumptions about what I thought you would like."

"I trust everything is going to be wonderful." I pointed to the other end of the room. "What are those chairs over there for?"

He smiled. "Maybe I have one more surprise, after all."

A string quartet with instruments, sheets of music and stands entered the Court: two violins, a viola and a cello.

Easton took my hand. "Karen might have told me how much you really love the symphony. I pulled a few strings— no pun intended, and asked if we could have a performance during lunch. It's not the symphony, but its classical music all the same."

"What! Easton, I don't deserve all of this! We've only been dating a little while! This is so much." I was starting to feel overwhelmed by it all. It was so beautiful, the exhibit, tour, lunch and now a string quartet. I didn't even know what

PATRICIA WALKER CHATMAN

they were playing, but I felt the musical vibrations in my chest.

This is what I prayed for, always wanted—now it's here. Enjoy this, don't analyze it, overthink it, just relish in the moment. You deserve to have someone in your life that treats you better than the men in your dreams. Easton deserves my full attention—and a little something else for later.

Chapter Twenty-Eight

Needless to say, I didn't go back to work.

Easton changed me from a work-every-second-of-the-day girl to only when necessary. The Art Institute left me high on ambiance, music, food, and wine, and later—on Easton. This time around, we explored each other's erogenous zones more empathically than the last. Lying in bed, I tried to observe every lash, muscle, and wrinkle as his body slept by my side.

As with most, if not all girls, I flashed the moments of our day together in my mind. It was magical from the second we walked through the door. I knew this relationship wasn't ideal, but Easton wove his way into my heart. After today, there wasn't a doubt in my mind giving him up wouldn't be easy, and I honestly had no intention of letting him go. Married or not.

Easton stayed overnight again after our date, which was becoming a regular routine for us. I liked that he stayed with me from time to time. It was just mid-week, but I already knew he planned to spend time with his kids this weekend, so I would be on my own. I thought I'd have time to catch up on my paperwork and make some phone calls as long as I didn't have any unexpected distractions. The only deviation, if all went as planned, would be catching up with Linda and Tobey. Carving out time for that was right up there with finishing some work.

The next day when I returned, I filled Karen in on my date. I also took time to thank her for the part she played in making sure it was a special day for me. I'm never surprised, but I let her know they got me, and good.

Karen asked if I'd taken any pictures, which I didn't even think about. Relying on memory wouldn't capture everything I wanted them to see and share. If I was going to have any chance of convincing them this relationship is good for me, I needed to paint a fuller picture.

I wasn't thinking on my feet, too busy crying. I took about an hour before work to completely tell Karen everything from start to finish, special touches he threw in she didn't know about. There was also personal information about Easton and me I hadn't shared, namely the situation about Easton's marriage, the kids, and him not wanting to get married again. Unfortunately, her blessing would have to wait. She was on the same page with Linda and Tobey. Great date, but end it before I get hurt, which I had no intention of being. But whoever does?

My conversation with Karen was overdue and long. I valued her opinion, despite it being contrary to mine. One point she did raise was the need for me to find out Easton's endgame. Getting married wasn't relevant, but his plans on divorce were. I thought my relationship with Jake proved I was willing to ignore the elephant in the room a really long time.

I wasn't that girl anymore.

I promised Karen I would have the talk, but before any conversation took place I desperately needed to get my head back into the work game. I was behind and I'm *never* behind. So for the next few days this would be it work, and only work. Karen left me in the office alone for the remainder of the evening after locking up. I got into a rhythm, managing to complete a few plans and write out my notes from my last sessions, which seemed like centuries ago.

The week went by quickly. On Saturday my goal didn't change. I tried to focus on work and not "other stuff," no luck there. My mind wandered—reflecting not working. I wanted to get into something, but didn't have anything to get into. I sat my laptop beside me on the bed there was no sense in going through the motions. I wouldn't be getting much done. I pulled the pillows from the other side of the bed to prop my head on. Staring at the blank television screen, I wondered what Sanford was doing, whether he was still seeing that girl. For a split second I considered calling him, but no—I'd done enough damage with Sanford. He was doing what he was doing—our time had passed.

It's like that sometimes—once a door closes it can't be reopened. It's a shame it takes us too long to figure that out. I need to figure what's going on in my own life versus if Sanford would ever return to it. If push comes to shove and I was forced to choose between the two of them, I would go with the memories that don't hurt me, and right now that's Easton.

The worst thing about being single was not creating memories with anyone. I had nothing to recall, and now I did, but it was with someone who was married. *I want somebody in my life where I can say do you remember when this happened? Don't forget this? Or you remember when we did that the last time? I want Easton. This . . . us, this is what I want. Moments like at the park and the museum those are what I know I need to make it through a lifetime. I had this feeling before and after Jake, but not with Jake. I don't know if that makes any sense or what it says about my failed marriage. If I sit here and think about all these men in my life I have Jake, who . . . if I'm honest with myself, is trying to get back with me. Sanford, who loves me and isn't talking to me, and Easton, who likes me, maybe loves me, but is married to someone else. My love life is muddy. To be with Easton, I have thrown my moral compass out the window. I had to break it first then throw it out the window. I'm hiding from heaven. All too soon the day will come when I have to figure all this out. But that wasn't today. Today I'm going to lie in bed, work and daydream about my non-existent future with Easton. I may be dick sharing, but Easton is mine—for now, and I want to make it last as long as I can. Soon reality's ugly head is going to put all this to an end.*

Instead of just lying there, I decided to pick up my journal and write down some of my thoughts. My first line read, "I'm lying to myself. No matter how much I'm telling myself this is different, it's not all that different. No matter how much logic you bake into crazy, it still comes out crazy. Trying to make us different doesn't alter where I am in this relationship or what I've been doing. I've wrestled with being a causality of war from a broken marriage for so long. I empathize with Easton's wife. I know how it feels to be powerless in fighting a feeling."

I put my journal down after a few entries. I wasn't quite ready to be this open. I opted to watch a movie instead. No romantic dramas for me. I could write my own. I went through my movies to see what I had that was decent and wouldn't have me making late-night phone calls. I settled on something to take me out of reality. I put in the DVD and had just hopped back into bed when the phone rang. It was Linda.

"Hello."

"Hey, girl, what's up with 'cha?"

"Nothing, just watching *The Matrix*."

"Again, Alex? Why you watch the same movies over and over?"

"I identify with them, that's why. Plus it helps to shut my brain down. What are you doing? Where are the kids? I don't hear them screaming."

"It's Saturday, they're at the movies with their father."

"You don't go? Why are you at home?"

She laughed. "Getting some peace and quiet for a minute. Where is Easton?"

"Oh, he and his wife are taking the kids to some show—Sesame Street—something or another, so no Easton for me today."

She laughed. "Boy, I could go in so many different directions with that, but I'm going to let this one go."

"Please do, I'm struggling enough with my own thoughts—I don't need yours in my head, too."

"Okay, so guess what?"

"What?" I asked.

"I said guess." She sounded a little petulant.

I wasn't in the mood. "I don't want to guess."

"Girl, just guess."

"You're pregnant."

There was a stunned silence. "How did you guess?"

"For real, Linda—"

"I'm just saying, you got it on the first guess. It took Mama at least a few guesses. Did Tobey tell you?"

"No, Tobey didn't tell me, I haven't even talked to Tobey."

"Oh, well. So that's it. I'm pregnant with baby number four."

"Congratulations," I said.

There was a pause. "Why you sound so dry? What's wrong with you?"

"Nothing, just sitting here thinking too much. You know how it goes—a woman alone with her thoughts can either solve problems or create them, right? Ignore, I'm just in a mood. I'm happy for you. Is Mitch happy?"

"Mitch is happy with whatever, you know him. I could've told him we were having a puppy and he would be ecstatic."

I cut the volume down on the television. "Have you heard from Sanford?"

"Not since you got back from D.C.," she said. "Why? What's up?"

"Nothing," I said. "I just thought somebody should call him and make sure he's okay."

"I'm sure he is," she laughed. "He just doesn't want to be bothered with you."

"Oh, Linda, that's funny, real funny."

"It's the truth, ask Tobey. She talked to him."

I frowned. "She didn't tell me she talked to him."

"That's because he told her *not* to tell you he talked to her." It actually made sense the way Linda said it.

"Then why are you telling me?"

"He told her, dummy, not me."

"Oh, I guess that's true." I hesitated. "So what did he say?"

"Oh, I don't know, you have to ask Tobey."

"Okay, now you're just a bad comedy routine."

"I'm sorry, I don't know. For real, I didn't ask. Pregnant lady over here."

"You all with this don't tell Alex business is getting to be really annoying."

Linda sighed, "Well—yeah, that's what happens sometimes."

"I guess so, do you know how far along you are?"

"Only a few months. I found out this week, but I thought I was sick, a little more bitchy than normal."

"No, not you!" Two can be sarcastic, I thought.

"Real funny. Okay, I don't have anything else. Call Tobey and find out what he said."

"I'm working, I'll call her later."

"No, call her now, before you forget."

"Linda, I'll call her later. I'm not supposed to be talking to you. I'm trying to get some work done. I've been taking too many days off and I'm almost caught up."

"You said you were watching a movie. What you taking days off have to do with us? Go on and give her a call. I want to know what he said."

"Then *you* call her." I cut my volume back up.

"No, I got to get off this phone and clean up before they get back here."

"You know what—" I started to state my position, but decidedly didn't know what the point of that was. I wanted to call her. "Okay, I'll call her."

"Call me back and tell me what she said."

"Girl, get off my phone."

I didn't want to admit to Linda I wanted to call Sanford earlier, but chickened out. Her needing to convince me to call Sanford was an act. No one wanted to know what Sanford said to Tobey more than me. I cut down the volume again to call Tobey.

Tobey answered, "Yeah, girl, what's up?"

"Hey! Linda just told me she's pregnant."

"Oh, yeah, she told me. Where you at?" Tobey asked.

"At home. Why you whispering?"

"I'm at work."

"Oh, I thought you worked afternoons?"

"I do. I'm actually off today, but I picked up another shift since Hunter was working."

"He's teaching on a Sunday?"

"No, he had papers to grade, then a meeting at the college."

"Oh. Anyway, I'm actually calling to find out what Sanford said to you."

Her tone changed. "What do you mean?"

"Tobey, I know you talked to him. What did he say?"

"He said not to tell you."

"Girl, if you don't tell me what the man said—"

"He said he loves you, but things are getting serious with Simone, so he wanted my advice as to what he should do. That's all." She made it sound so simple.

"So, what did you tell him?" I demanded.

"I told him you're doing what you want to do and he should do the same."

"What kind of advice is that?"

"It's *my* advice, Alex, the operative word being *mine*. I know you don't want to hear this, but he cares about this girl and he deserves to be happy. You need to let this thing you have with Easton go."

"And be alone again? I don't think so."

"So, to not *be alone* means you'll settle for whatever? That's not you, Alex. Well, then again . . . maybe it is."

"I've changed. I'm not settling for a cheating man anymore."

"I was talking about being disrespected," she said.

"Easton's not disrespecting me. Give me your honest opinion—do you think it's too late for me and Sanford?"

"I don't know. When you left," she paused, "put it like this, you should have stayed. Then, yeah . . . maybe, but now . . . I don't know now."

"So it's too late?"

"I didn't say that. He waited for you to come around then you broke up with him, around the time he met her—I don't know—I think it might be. Especially if he found out you're kicking it with this guy."

I knew I was wrong, but I was committed to the crazy. "Point of clarification, Easton and I are friends who are enjoying each other's company. That's it."

"Alex, the point of clarification is this—if you want anything with or from Sanford you need to tell him before it's too late. Stop stringing this boy along. If not, tell him the truth so he can move on with his life with this Simone person."

"When is he coming home?"

"I don't think he's coming home. He's probably going to stay there."

I felt my stomach tighten. "Oh, wow, I didn't think he would stay there."

"Why would he come back here, Alex?"

"His family is here."

"Girl, you know the only reason he would come back here is for you. And you don't know what you want."

"You right—"

"I already know I'm right. So let him go so we can all move on."

"I will."

"Just do it," she said. She sounded like she wanted to wash her hands of the whole situation. "So what you and Easton got up for today?"

"Nothing, he's with his kids." My handset beeped. "Wait, speak of the devil, he's calling on the other line. Let me let you go."

"All right, hit me back after you talk to Sanford."

"Okay, 'bye." I switched over to the other line. "Hello?"

"Hello, beautiful," Easton said.

"Wow this is a surprise," I said, smiling. "I didn't expect to hear from you today."

"I know, but my mother has the boys right now, and I thought I could bring you breakfast."

"Oh—and coffee?"

"Of course."

"You're on the way? When can you get here?"

"Look outside."

I hopped out of bed, walked into the guest bedroom facing the street and there was Easton standing beside his truck with a brown bag in one hand and coffee in the other. I jumped up and down, dropping my cell phone on the bed. I rushed downstairs to open the door, forgetting all about my unsexy flannel cow pajamas. He'd seen them before. I opened the door and a brisk fall wind whipped inside. I grabbed the coffee first, then the breakfast.

"So what you get me? It smells so good!"

We walked into the kitchen and set the food on the counter. Easton took off his hat and coat. "I thought you were getting rid of this table."

I turned and looked at the kitchen table. I'd forgotten about that. "I didn't realize I said that out loud."

"I thought we talked about it. Maybe we didn't, and I was just reminiscing, thinking that you should," he said.

"Yeah," I smiled as I took a sip of coffee, "good times . . . good times."

He looked me up and down. "What's up with the cows?"

"Oh—well, I didn't know you were coming, so this is what I had on. Sorry, baby, I know it's not sexy."

Easton grabbed me from behind. "No—actually I'm digging it. You should wear flannel with farm animals more often."

"Yes, I think I can feel how excited you are, but that has to wait. I'm starving."

"I don't have time anyway," he said regretfully. "I have to head back."

I put my coffee down. "You're not staying?"

"Nope, I just came to bring you breakfast."

"Oh, my God, how sweet is that?"

"I know," he said, and winked. "You can thank me later. They'll be gone by six, so I'll swing back by."

"Okay, another sleepover?"

"Yeah, I'll bring my stuff."

"Oh, I'm happy now."

As quickly as he'd come, Easton was out, down the street and headed home. It was still fairly early I had plenty of time to finish working, call Sanford, and watch the Matrix.

I took the food out of the bag. *So much for getting rid of Easton.* An egg-white omelet and wheat toast.

It wasn't long before I'd finished all three Matrix movies and my work. I turned to look at the clock, it was just a little past three, and I was so sleepy I could barely keep my eyes open. I wanted to lie in my bed, but I promised to call Sanford or I wouldn't hear the end of it from both Linda and Tobey. I got out of my comfortable position in bed, put all my materials from work away, and disposed of my dishes from breakfast.

Downstairs I sat at the kitchen table slated for donation, trying to recall if I'd left a window open to call him again. *It's going to be awkward enough without him wondering why I'm calling. I said I'd call, so I am.* I went back upstairs, grabbed my phone, located him in my contacts and dialed. The phone rang and continued to ring this time. He didn't answer—which I was thankful for. I didn't want to talk or leave a message. All I wanted to do was lie down and get some sleep before Easton came back.

I must have been really tired. It was dark outside when I heard the doorbell. I felt crazy reaching for the lamp to turn on the lights. *Whew!* It had to be Easton. *What time is it?* I dragged my body out of bed with every ounce of energy I had remaining, navigating my way in the dark, down the hallway stairs, to the front door. I didn't look through the peephole. I assumed it was Easton and opened.

It wasn't. Jake stood there. Crying.

"What's going on?"

"It's Mom. She's not doing well. Can you come with me to the hospital?"

My stomach tightened with fear. "Yes. Just let me change real quick, it'll only take me a second. Come inside."

Jake walked into the foyer, wiping his eyes. He looked around the house. He hadn't been back since he moved out. I'd made minor changes. Everything else was just as he'd left it. "You changed things around."

I yelled from my upstairs closet. "A little—not much. Tell me what happened. I knew she caught a cold?"

I could hear Jake pacing in the foyer. "I don't know. She was fine, and then she started getting worse. Alex, I don't mean to rush you, but the EMS took her from the house. I have to meet them there."

"I'm sorry—here I come."

I turned around toward the staircase and ran down, skipping stairs as I went. My purse, coat, and tennis shoes were in the kitchen. Jake stood in the foyer watching my every move, still pacing. I put those on in the kitchen, headed back out when the doorbell rang.

Jake answered it, opening the door to Easton's less-than-thrilled face. If Jake had any lingering questions about my relationship with Easton, I guess that clearly confirmed we were more than work colleagues.

"Hey, man, what's up?"

They shook hands.

"Come on in."

Easton walked in and I stood in the kitchen. I didn't know if I should hug him or not. We hadn't discussed being open with our relationship, which I guessed we shouldn't do, since he was married. I didn't know what the rules were.

"Are you leaving?"

"Yeah, actually, I am. I'm sorry. I was going to call you on the way."

"What's going on?"

"Jake, can I meet you in the car? I'll be quick."

Jake nodded and headed out the door, closing it behind him. I walked to my office to grab a book. "I have to go to the hospital with Jake. His mother has cancer and she's not doing well."

"Oh, I didn't know. Is she going to be okay?"

I shrugged. "I really don't know. I'll know more once we get there. I'm sorry, but EMS took her and we are trying to get to the hospital before she does."

"Oh, no, I understand. Just give me a call when you get a minute."

"I will. I know this probably seems a little odd, but she's someone I care about, and Jake really doesn't have anyone else." Then I thought about Taylor.

"At least I don't think he does."

"No, I understand. Call me later."

I kissed Easton, and we walked out the front door. I ran to Jake's car and Easton returned to his.

The universe works in mysterious ways. Easton had naturally been put on hold, at least for now.

Chapter Twenty-Nine

In the car, Jake inundated me with questions about Easton. "How do you know him? When did you meet? How long have you been dating him? You know he's married, right? How can you accuse me of being an adulterer when you are too?"

I didn't have the energy to go back and forth with Jake. I was more concerned about his mother. I think I helped to take his mind off of her for a second, but not long enough for me.

I'd thought Tobey and Linda were bad. He asked me so many questions, firing one after another. Some of them I didn't have the answer to. I prayed we would get to the hospital soon. If he didn't shut up about Easton I was going to ball up my fist and dot him in the eye. *EMS would take her to the hospital the furthest away from my house.* To make a shift in the "Quiz Alex" program, I took out my book and pretended to read. It didn't work. Finally I said, "Jake, can we focus on what, and who I'm here for?"

Finding it hard to keep his eyes on the road, he said, "You need to tell me something, Alex."

"Jake, we're not going to have this conversation right now. Let's stay focused on your mother, getting her back on her feet and home. You can quiz me about Easton later."

The ability to have his questions answered later proved to be satisfactory. For now, he let it go. The EMS vehicle had arrived before we did. We drove around to find a spot to park. A very busy night at the hospital, which wasn't a good thing. It was taking too long. "Just pull over and go in, I'll find a spot," I said.

It took a minute, but I finally found something way on the other side of the hospital. I walked around to the emergency-room entrance. I could see Jake in the waiting area talking to a person who looked like a doctor. Jake was visibly upset by what he was hearing. I entered just as they concluded their conversation and the doctor headed back to the treatment area.

Jake reached out and pulled me into him. He wrapped his arms around me and whispered in my ear, "She's not doing well, Alex."

I pulled away and took a step back to look into Jake's eyes. "What did the doctor say?"

"He said her vital signs are weak. They're still assessing her. We can see her in a few minutes. They'll call us back."

I grabbed his hand. "Let's sit down."

Jake wasn't thinking clearly. It was hard for me to get information out of him. We found a spot in the corner with two seats that wasn't too crowded with other families. "So what does that mean, she's not doing well? What's wrong with her?"

"She has a bacterial infection. In a healthy person that's no big deal, but with her diagnosis, her body is having a hard time fighting it off."

I grabbed his hands. "Do they think she's going to recover? How serious is this?"

"It's pretty serious. They're trying to get her to respond to the antibiotics. I don't know, I guess we'll know in twenty-four hours. They're going to admit her."

"Can we go back and sit with her?"

"Yeah, remember—he said they'll call us."

"Okay." I released his hands and sat back in my seat. "Are you thirsty? I can get us some water or coffee."

"Yeah, would you? Some coffee would be good."

"Okay, let me ask where I can get some."

I got up and walked over to one of the emergency room desks. The woman said there was a coffee shop in the South Tower. On the walk over I called Easton. The phone rang a few times before he picked up.

"Hey, babe, how is Jake's mother doing?"

"Not good. She has a bacterial infection and according to the physician's assistant—"

"Is that the doctor?"

"No, it's like the doctor's assistant, I don't know, Easton. The man in a white coat that came out from the back said it doesn't look good. He could be my mailman, for all I know."

"Okay, I'm sorry. I know you're upset so I'm going to ignore that last part."

"God, I'm sorry—it was a long car ride," I said. "But that's what he said and Jake's having a hard time—it's his mother."

"Well, I know you have to be there for him, so when you get some time let's try and get together."

"Hey, thank you for being so understanding. It's not too many men who would be cool with their girl leaving with her ex-husband, no matter what the situation."

"Oh, are you my girl?"

"You know what?" I paused. "I don't know what I am. We have to talk about that eventually."

"I know. We do, but for right now, be there for Jake."

"Okay, I'll call later."

"All right, babe, talk to you soon."

Easton hung up right when I arrived at the coffee shop. While I waited for our drinks, I called Linda. She picked up on the first ring. I don't think that's ever happened before.

"Hey, everything okay?"

"No, it's not. I'm at the hospital with Jake."

"Is it his mother? What happened?"

"She's not doing good. The doctor said she has an infection, which is an issue—because of the Cancer . . . it's complicating everything."

"Oh, wow, I didn't know that. I haven't talked to Jake since he started talking back with you."

"Well, we both could use you now."

"Where is Jake at?"

"He's in the waiting room."

"Where are you?"

"Getting us coffee."

The staff person at the counter called out our drink order. I picked them up, and put them in a drink carrier while I continued to talk to Linda. "Hey, I'm going to have to get off the phone. I have it on my shoulder, and it's hard for me to carry the coffee and talk to you too."

"Okay, go ahead. Do you want me to come up there?"

I felt relieved. "Yeah, if you don't mind, that would be wonderful."

"Okay," she said. "Let me get myself together and tell Mitch. Which hospital?"

"St. Mary's. The emergency room."

I could almost see her checking her watch. "Okay, I'll be there in half an hour."

"Wait, do you know if Tobey is here?"

"No, but I can call her on the way."

"Would you? Thanks, Linda. See you in a few—be safe."

I walked back to the waiting area where I found Jake still sitting in the same spot I'd left him in. I handed him his coffee, but he didn't drink. He set it on the table, and went back to holding his head in his hands.

Jake looked like a broken man. In that moment, I would have done anything for him. The doctors hadn't come back out. So we continued to wait along with all the other families hoping to hear something—anything to bring hope to the hopeless. After ten minutes passed, Jake finally looked up at me. "Did you have far to go to get the coffee?"

"No, it was okay," I said. "I called Linda to let her know what was going on."

"Is Linda coming up?"

I nodded. "Yeah, she said she would be here soon."

"Good." He paused. "You talk to anybody else?"

I waited for a second before saying, "Just Easton."

He frowned. "Why did you call him?"

"I didn't, he called me. He wanted to find out if we knew anything."

He sighed. "Alex, you shouldn't be seeing Easton."

"Why not, Jake?"

He wasn't looking at me. He picked up his coffee and looked into it while he spoke. "Well, for starters, he's married, and his wife Grace is a nice lady."

I really didn't need this. "Grace and Easton were separated long before I came along, Jake."

"Yeah, but you may be the reason they're not getting back together."

"That's crazy. I'm not the reason."

He took a sip of coffee. "Then why aren't they back together?"

"I don't know," I said. "He doesn't discuss that kind of stuff with me."

"I know you think our situation is different, but this is worse, Alex. We didn't have kids, and you didn't give therapy a chance, but Grace is."

I stopped drinking. "What do you mean, Grace is?"

"Grace and Easton. They're in therapy—they've been doing it for months now," Jake said.

I suddenly felt cold. "How do you know that?"

"I still see her at the gym—Alex, I think you're the reason it's not working. He has feelings for you."

I stopped talking then. I didn't want Jake to know that Easton's marital therapy was news to me.

"What happens if they work things out?" he asked. "Where does that leave you?"

I shifted in my chair. This conversation made me uncomfortable. "Isn't that the purpose of therapy? To work it out."

"She doesn't know Easton is seeing someone."

I shook my head, "Jake, you don't know that."

He turned toward me, "Yes, I do know that. Alex, she has no clue—sound familiar?"

I turned back toward Jake. "I'm not the reason. Please don't insinuate that. It makes me uncomfortable."

He wasn't into playing games. He looked me squarely in the eye. "You may not be comfortable with it, but it's the truth. I wasn't comfortable with everything you said about me, but I know it was the truth."

"I shouldn't have said that stuff about you."

"What about the stuff you said about Taylor? You called her every name in the book, and now you're doing the same thing to someone else."

I had a sudden horrible image of myself. I took a deep breath. "It *is* the same, isn't it?"

"It's not exactly the same," he admitted. "In some ways it's better and in others it's worse."

I'd managed to come full circle and make it right back to where I'd begun in my horrid romantic story. A triangular romance where someone is married, but this time, I played the role of the other woman, the person I loathed the most.

"I know this is an odd time for us to be having this conversation, but how did it really go with you and Taylor?"

Jake stood up and reached out for my hand. "Let's go somewhere else to talk."

I followed him outside the waiting room to a bench down the corridor. We sat down with our backs against the wall. Jake said, "We were both to blame, but nobody was chasing anybody. Alex, we weren't happy, and hadn't been for a long time. Does that excuse what I did? No, it doesn't, but it doesn't give you the right to blame Taylor, either. Should Grace blame you?"

"I loved you more than life itself. I knew this girl, invited her in my home, and talked to her. I haven't done that—"

Jake started to interject something. I held up my hand.

"Let me finish—I know now I'm not blameless, but there was no malicious intent in dating Easton. They *are* separated. I don't know what agreements or understandings they have, but—" I rubbed my shoulders while adjusting my neck. "What do you want me to say? I don't have this all figured out."

"Look at it from Taylor's point of view. She felt like she made a mistake and got in too deep—but, unlike you, she ended it way before you and I even got divorced."

I looked up sharply. "What do you mean, she ended it?"

"Taylor and I stopped seeing each other romantically almost as soon as we started. We weren't in a relationship, Alex, we made a mistake."

"But I thought you were seeing her. Even your mother said something about you seeing her."

"Yes, I see her. We work together. I can't help seeing her."

Linda and the doctor appeared at the end of the hall. I stood up and waved my sister over. The doctor followed. Jake rose and reached out to hug Linda.

The doctor asked us to walk with him to a more private area to discuss Mom's diagnosis and course of treatment. We all walked down the hall to a private meeting room. It looked like the room in which doctors inform family that their loved one passed away.

Linda, forever the mother, grabbed my hand as we entered the small room. My eyes met hers and she mouthed *what's wrong?* Even she knew it was more than Jake's mother. I whispered back, "I'm fine, we'll talk later."

There wasn't much news, not really. Ms. Thomas would remain in the hospital—she was gravely ill, and the next twenty-four hours should tell the story. Linda and I stayed with Jake until Mom got set up in her room. She was pretty much out of it, her eyes were closed the entire time she was being positioned in the room.

After the nurse left, Jake decided to stay the night in the lounge chair by her bed. "Let me get you a pillow and blankets from the nurse's station."

"Thank you," he said.

When I returned, Jake and Linda were deep in conversation. They tailed it off when I entered. "I'll be back in the morning." I handed him the pillow and blankets.

"What time do you want me to come back?" Linda asked.

"Maybe about one o'clock, Jake what do you think?"

Jake said, "One is good."

I pulled a brush out of my purse and sat it down on the nightstand. "You'll need this in the morning." I moved his hair aside with my hand and kissed his forehead. "See you in the morning—call if you need anything. Here's a rubber band for your hair."

It was midnight by the time we walked out to our cars. "Will you call Tobey and Sanford and let them know about Jake's mom?"

"I called Tobey on the way here. Her shift is around two o'clock tomorrow, so she'll already be here in pediatrics."

"Okay, I'll still be here by then."

Linda hugged me, "take care, kiddo. I'll see you tomorrow afternoon."

"Thanks for coming out. I know it means a lot to Jake," I said.

"Feels like old times, don't it?"

"If this is what heartbreak feels like—then yeah, just like old times."

Chapter Thirty

Over the next five days Jake, Linda and I took turns at the hospital in eight-hour shifts. Tobey checked in throughout the time she was working to help out. Ms. Thomas, still unresponsive to the treatment, came in and out of consciousness with the medication in her system. We talked to her when we could, but mostly we received smiles.

Early Friday morning, I sat at her bedside reading a book, while Jake took a quick shower. "Alex is that you?" she asked.

I put my book on the floor. "Yes, Mom, it's me. How are you feeling?"

She whispered, "Tired, baby—" She turned her head toward the door. "Where is Jake?"

I reached for her hand and held it in mine. "He's in the shower—let me get him for you."

I hurried to the bathroom door and knocked. "Jake, Mom is awake." The water stopped. He yelled back, "Let me grab a towel."

I walked over and closed the main door to her room. The sight of Jake clothed was enough to put any woman into cardiac arrest. I wasn't confident I would be strong enough to resist the sight of him naked either. His clothes were in a chair next to the bathroom door. I grabbed them all up in my hands, and then knocked on the door. "Here are your clothes." Jake opened the door with the towel wrapped around his perfectly chiseled body and took them from my hand. I pulled the door closed and leaned against it to catch my breath. *Oh boy . . . oh boy . . . oh boy. I actually think I stopped breathing for a second there.*

I walked back over to Mom, picked my book up from the floor and sat down. Just as quickly as her eyes opened they were closed again. I assumed she drifted back off to sleep. The bathroom door opened, filling the room with steam from Jake's shower. He walked over to the bed where he found her fast asleep again. "When did she fall back to sleep?" he asked.

"Right after I gave you the clothes."

He sat down on the other side of her. "Did the doctor come in?"

"No, nobody since you went into the bathroom. He should be coming in soon. Do you want me to go to the nurse's station and check?"

"Do you mind?" he asked.

I stood up. "No, I'll go." The warmth from the shower still lingered at the door. It felt good on my skin perhaps a shower could do me some good too. Walking through the halls I stretched my back and shoulders to relieve the stiffness from sitting in the chair for hours on end.

To my surprise Easton was walking down the hall toward me.

As he grew nearer his smiled widened . . . and my bewilderment deepened. I didn't understand. He opened his arms and I stepped into his embrace. "What are you doing here?" I asked.

"Hello to you, too."

"I'm sorry—it's just that—this is not really a good time. Jake is in there with his mother. I only stepped out to get the doctor."

"I haven't seen or talked to you. I thought I would take a chance and come here."

I motioned for him to walk with me. "That's really sweet of you, but Jake is already not happy about us seeing each other. Right now—I don't want to be another source of frustration for him."

As we walked, I checked behind me to make sure Jake didn't step into the hallway to see what was taking so long. Easton said, "I'm not sure I understand what you mean."

"Look, I really can't go into too much detail right now, but Jake told me you and your wife are seeing a marriage counselor."

"Wow—he did. I would have liked to tell you that myself."

I checked back down the hall then turned to Easton. "Here's the thing—you had plenty of time to tell me what you were doing, but I blame myself. I should have asked."

We reached the nurse's station, and I made a final check behind me to see Jake standing in the hallway watching from a distance. Easton rubbed my head. "Maybe this isn't a good time. I want to explain all this to you."

I glanced back to see Jake moving toward the nurses station. "I think you better go. I promise I'll call later tonight when I get a chance." I turned around, nearly bumping into Jake. "I thought I would come see what's keeping you."

Easton answered back, "I was just about to leave."

He bent down, ignoring Jake's glare, and kissed me on the forehead. "I'll call later," I said gently, deliberately pushing him toward the elevator.

Easton opted to leave without uttering a word to Jake or asking about his mother. We looked on as he entered the elevator, presumably leaving the hospital. I turned to face Jake. He wasn't happy about Easton's unexpected appearance.

"Did you call him?" Jake asked.

"No, he just showed up." The nurses were busy ignoring us. In all the commotion, I didn't notice Tobey walking from the direction of Jake's mother's room. She got to us before Jake could say anything more.

"How are you guys holding up?" she asked.

We gave a unified response. "We're doing okay."

"Has the doctor been in this morning?"

"That's why we're down here, to see when he's coming in," I said.

"I can find out—go ahead. I'll be down in a minute."

Jake rubbed my arm, motioning for me to come with him. Down the hall a ways he said again, "I don't like that you're seeing him."

"I get that, Jake. What you don't get is it's not your decision to make."

We reached his mother's room. She remained silent and unchanged. Tobey and the doctor came into the room a few minutes later to confirm what we already knew. Her condition wasn't improving.

We were losing her.

I cried for all the time we had, and didn't have. Jake walked out with the doctor while I repositioned myself in the chair next to her bed. I placed her cold hand in mine, rubbing it against my cheek praying she would come back to us. God had other plans.

We'd checked her into the hospital on a Sunday and two weeks later to the day she died.

Chapter Thirty-One

Death was a blessing and a curse.

It took Ms. Thomas, but it gave birth to clarity. The insight I'd been avoiding for some time now. At about four o'clock we said our final goodbyes before his mother's body was removed from the room. We packed two weeks of clothing, books and blankets in a suitcase and departed the hospital for the last time. I needed to go by the office to check in before Jake took me home.

Jake pulled up to the back entrance where we both got out and entered the building. I heard Karen on the phone taking an appointment for the next week. Jake lay down on the couch in front of my desk, while I booted up my computer to take a look at my calendar. It wasn't until Karen entered that either one of us uttered a word. Karen approached Jake, her arms open. "What happens now?"

I answered. "Most of everything was preplanned, so—" I glanced over at Jake on the couch. He added, "Just planning the reprise, which—" he said at me, "if you don't mind, I wanted to have at our house."

"You mean my house?"

He smiled. "Your house."

Karen stepped out of the way avoiding the conversation. "Let me know if I can do anything," she said.

"You can help me with the obituary."

"Do you have a date yet?" she asked.

Jake responded. "Wednesday, next week."

"I'll have to move some stuff around."

I clicked the calendar icon on the desktop. It didn't look too bad. "There's only one appointment on Wednesday and it's late." I pointed to the date on my screen. "Can you explain what happened and possibly move this one up a day?" I asked.

"I can certainly try—oh, before I forget you got an invitation. I put it inside your desk."

"From whom?"

"I couldn't tell from the envelope." She pointed to my desk drawer. "It's in there." I glanced at the door, but didn't open it.

"Did anybody call Sanford?" she asked.

Jake sat up. "Why would she call Sanford?"

I was a little taken aback by his response. "Why wouldn't I? He's met your mother before." Jake lay back down without responding.

"Karen you don't have to stay here," I said. "I got it."

She took a step back. "Are you sure? It's only three-thirty."

"Yeah, I'll be here until four, nothing should happen between now and then."

"All right, if you don't need me—just don't forget that invitation."

I continued checking my appointments. "I won't."

Karen yelled bye from the other room while Jake continued to doze off on the couch. Skimming my appointments, I noticed there was nothing on the calendar for Mr. Johnson. I started to yell Karen's name when I remembered I told her she could go for the night. The next thought that entered my mind was the invitation. Maybe that's why I haven't heard from him. I opened the desk drawer and pulled out the large envelope. It looked like a wedding invitation. I pushed my finger through the edge of the envelope to open it. *Mystery solved. He's getting married. At least somebody's love life is working out okay.*

As I read the wedding details my cell phone rang. I put the invite back in my desk, got up and retrieved the phone from my purse. Jake, still sound asleep, didn't appear to hear anything going on in the room. I looked at the screen. It was Easton. I answered, "Hold on, let me move to the other room." I glanced back at Jake then walked into the receptionist area and took a seat behind Karen's desk.

"Hey," I said. "What' going on?"

"It's been a few days. How are you, babe?"

"I'm fine, just tired. It's been a long week."

"How is Jake holding up?"

"Ah—as well as to be expected."

"What do you mean—as well as to be expected?"

"Oh God, I'm sorry—Jake's mom passed this morning. I haven't had a chance to call anybody. We literally left the hospital and came here."

"Where is here?" he asked.

"My office."

"Can I help in any way?"

"You've already been wonderful just by being patient with me."

"Anything for you. You know that," he said. "Don't give me too much credit, I've been missing you like crazy. I wanted to come back and snatch you away one day."

I took a deep breath then exhaled. "I want to talk to you when things settle down a bit."

There was profound silence on the other end. His words seemed weighed from my request. "Oh, that can't be good."

"No, it's not like that. We just need to talk."

"Can you tell me what's it's about?"

"Well—sitting in the hospital gave me a lot of time to think—about us."

"What about us?" He paused. "We're having fun—right?"

"That's just it—I think I'm looking for something more than *fun*."

"That may have been a bad choice of words," he said.

"Yeah," I said. "Maybe, which is why I think we should sit down and talk about this."

"Can I come by later today?"

"Maybe not today, but look—I'm going to get out of here. Can we talk later?"

"How long do you think that will be?" he asked.

"I don't know. A few days, maybe."

"Okay, then, in a few days."

I hung up the phone and walked back to find Jake awake. I stopped short at the door and put my phone in my sweater pocket.

"Who was that?" he asked.

I walked back behind my desk. "I think you already know who it was." I began shutting down my computer system and gathering my things to take home.

"What did he want?"

I looked around the monitor on my desk. "Nothing—I told him about your mom. He's checking in."

"So, what are you going to do about him?"

"Jake!" I put my hand up. "I'm not talking about Easton with you. So just stop . . . please."

He stood up, stretched and fished his keys out of his pocket. "Fine. You ready?"

"Yeah." I turned off the computer and walked around the desk to get my purse. "Let's go."

Jake and I exited the same way we'd arrived. In silence. On the ride home, I rested my elbow on the window and looked out at everyone whose day didn't appear to be going as unpleasantly as ours. I whispered to myself, "this too shall pass." Jake overheard. "What did you say?"

I shook my head. "Nothing—talking to myself."

He let it go and a few minutes later I was back inside my house. It was only five-thirty and pitch black outside. I dropped everything on the kitchen table and cut on the lights. For a split second, and it may have been shorter than that, I contemplated calling Easton, but elected against it. The only person I wanted to talk to was the one I couldn't. I decided to give what was left of the day to the night and went to bed.

Chapter Thirty-Two

"Can feelings that change so dramatically in a week's time ever have been real?"

"Do you want an answer to that or you thinking out loud?" Tobey asked. Linda and Karen walked into the kitchen from the living room.

"I don't think so," Linda said as she retrieved more plates for the buffet table we'd set up in the living room for the guests.

Karen, leaning against the doorframe said, "Why do you ask?"

I stopped arranging flowers to respond. "Because a couple of weeks ago Easton was the only person I wanted to do or see and now I'm dreading talking to the man."

Tobey walked across the kitchen and handed me her finished vase of flowers. "This is pretty," I said. I walked into the living room with the vase and Karen followed me.

"This is what I think," Linda added. "You had broken it off with Sanford, and Easton took your mind off of that. No love jones—just a distraction."

Karen said, "I agree. I never thought you and Easton would be anything more than friends."

"Especially with him being married!" Tobey yelled from the kitchen.

I sat down on the couch and examined the room to determine our preparedness for the reprise service. "I think we're done ladies," I said.

Tobey walked in with the last vase of flowers. "Where do you want these?" She stood holding the final bouquet of roses. "I guess we can put those on the kitchen table. What do you think?" I turned to Linda for a decision.

"Is this the same table?" she asked.

"Yes, I am ashamed to say, I haven't gotten rid of it."

"Hopefully you're not keeping it to remember him by," she said.

"What happened on that table?" Tobey asked.

I stood up. "Never mind," I said, taking the flowers from Tobey's hands. "I'll put them on the kitchen counter."

"What do you mean, never mind? I've eaten at that table."

I looked back at Tobey. "Real funny." I put the flowers on the island in the kitchen.

Everything looks beautiful. Jake will be happy. "I think Linda's right. It couldn't have been real, because I am so over it already. To think he was going to counseling and didn't tell me." I strolled over to the refrigerator and took out a bottle of wine. I held it up as I walked into the living room.

"Anybody game?" Karen stood up. "You can count me in. I'll get the glasses."

"Obviously I'm not," Linda said. "Why are you drinking your guests' liquor?"

Karen returned to the room with three glasses. "It's not liquor," I said. "It's wine, and I'm in the mood."

Tobey agreed, holding up her glass. "Me too."

I poured a glass of wine for all non-expectant mothers in the room. Linda and Karen were hanging out on the couch. Tobey lay across the floor on pillows in front of the fireplace. "Did anybody tell Sanford?" I asked.

"I texted him that Friday," Linda responded.

"What did he say?"

"Give Jake his condolences."

"That's it?"

"Yeah, pretty much. What were you thinking he would say?"

"That he's still in love with Alex," Tobey offered.

Karen rose up and poured herself another glass of wine. "Is that why you're done with Easton all of a sudden?"

"Of course not, I just asked if one of you told him— that's all."

"Don't even try it," Tobey interjected. "You still have feelings for Constantine."

Linda burst into laughter. "Oh my God—that is his name. I forgot about that."

I set my glass down on the floor and sat up. "What if I do still have feelings for Sanford? It wouldn't be the worst thing in the world—would it?"

"Maybe you should have figured that out before you broke up with him," Linda snapped. "Sorry," she added, rolling her eyes. "I may be too sober for this conversation."

"I think you are." I motioned toward the kitchen. "Go get some water or something and let the less rational people talk it through."

Linda stood up, laughing. "Not a problem," she said.

"Tobey, I asked you before if you thought it was too late. What did you say?"

"Are you kidding? I don't remember what I said to you. Look, when I am having profound moments—you really should pay attention," she laughed.

"If he shows up for the funeral, I think I'm going to tell him how I feel."

"Don't do that," Karen said. "For one, it's bad timing and two, he's probably still with that girl."

"No," Tobey said. "I do know he's not with her anymore."

Linda walked back into the room returning to her seat. "He's not?"

"I wonder why he didn't call me?"

"Oh, I think I know the answer to that one—because unlike you, he wasn't dating Simone to forget about somebody. He gave up waiting for you—the irony of it all. This is college all over again in reverse."

"This side of it sucks big time," I said.

"Lying there getting tipsy before your ex-husband's mother's funeral isn't helping anything." Linda held up her bottle of water. "Again—sober."

"You're right, it isn't helping." I grabbed the bottle. "But it sure isn't hurting." I turned to each of them. "Another round, ladies?"

"Not for me," Karen said. "It's getting late. I better turn in before Keith sends out a search party."

"Tell Keith he needs to relax," Linda advised.

"I'll tell Keith if you tell Mitch," she said getting her coat from the hall closet

"Touché," Linda said. "I better hit the road too." Linda joined Karen in the foyer, while Tobey picked up the newly added mess to the living room. I looked on as both of them put on their coats and retrieved purses.

"Thank you for helping me out." Sandwiched in the middle, I hugged them both. "See you in the morning."

"Yes, ten o'clock on the nose," Linda said.

I opened the door and watched them to their cars. Tobey took the glasses into the kitchen and began loading the dishwasher. "Maybe I should call and check on Jake," I said to Tobey. I picked up my cell from the kitchen counter, hitting it against my chin, contemplating. "Naw, the morning will be here soon enough."

Tobey started the washer and said, "In all seriousness—tell Sanford, don't tell him either way—I think my consistent advice is you have to stop being this afraid of love and make a decision one way or the other."

"Relationships shouldn't be this hard."

"I don't think they are. You were never this indecisive before. Do you know where this is coming from?"

I sat down at the kitchen table. Tobey shot me a look. "Oh sit down," I exclaimed. "The table's clean. You've eaten at it fifty times since then."

She pulled out a chair. "Is that true?" she asked, sitting down.

"No—not really," I laughed. "But thanks for sitting.

"You're welcome."

Over the noise of the dishwasher I said, "Sanford is the longest relationship I've had with a man—if I lose him—"

"You're not going to lose him."

"Haven't you been paying attention?" I said. "I've all but lost him now."

"I've never been the girl who doesn't get the guy. Rejection in my twenties—yeah, maybe, but forties? From a guy I blew off in college? I don't know if I can ever be that brave."

"Guys get rejected all the time—how do you think they feel? Or better yet, how Sanford felt when you did it to him countless times."

I patted my hands on the table. "Hello, remember, I didn't know Sanford was secretly in love with me? I found that out after I broke up with him. No, I take that back—because I said we should cool things off until he gets back."

"Well, now's your chance—he's back, call him."

I slid my chair back from the table. "You're joking—he's not back here."

"Why would I lie about that?" she asked.

I narrowed my eyes, pulling the chair back to the table. "Why didn't you tell me before tonight?"

"It didn't come up before tonight. Remember, dying mother-in-law?"

"So," I moved my hands rapidly in a circular motion. "Details, how long has he been back?"

"He literally got back the same night Jake's mother was rushed to the hospital."

"Wow, Linda didn't even know he was here when she texted him."

"No, I don't think so. Hunter told me he would be moving back, and then I got a text from him. He was back."

I leaned in placing my elbows on the table cupping my head in my hands. "I guess happy endings just don't happen, do they?"

"No, dear—I'm afraid not. If you want a happy ending you're going to have to make it happen. The cowardly lion is going to have to find some courage."

I leaned back in my chair. "Without a wizard—this relationship is screwed."

Chapter Thirty-Three

The dark clouds opened up and it started to rain.

"Even the angels are crying," Linda announced. I looked out the limousine window while Jake rested his head on my shoulder. "I think they are," I said as I patted Jake's leg. The funeral and burial were over. We were en route back to the house for the reprise. Karen, already there, received the guests who awaited our arrival. Jake wanted a few more minutes at the gravesite.

I kept watch at the church, but no Taylor or Sanford appeared. After all we'd been through it always came back to Jake and me. The thought occurred to me as I watched the raindrops find each other, then connect to form one seamless stream on the car window, that perhaps we were each other's silver lining.

Karen had things well under control in the house. Jake settled in with family, listening to stories about his mother as I listened in from the doorway. There was so much chatter behind me that I didn't notice anyone entering or exiting until I felt a gentle tap on my shoulder.

I turned to my right and there he was—Sanford. My heart pulsated through my blouse. I wrapped my arms around him burying my head in his chest and said, "I'm so glad you're here."

"So am I," he said.

I pulled away and wiped a runaway tear from my face while he smoothed my hair back into my tightly woven bun. I grabbed his hand. "Let's go upstairs for a second. It should be a little quieter up there." From my peripheral vision I could see the girls gathering in the kitchen. I didn't acknowledge their stares. Sanford and I sat down on the dressing room chairs. I looked around. "I used to hate this room," I said.

"Why is that?"

"This is where I caught Jake and Taylor."

"Is that why it's a big closet now?"

I laughed, "Yes, that's exactly why."

He rubbed his hands against his pants. "So, how are you? Besides the obvious."

I sighed. "I'm good—work is fine."

"What about the guy you were seeing? How's that going?"

Surprised, I asked, "How did you know about that?"

"How do we learn anything about each other these days?"

"Oh, right—the usual suspects." I smiled wryly. "Things have slowed down. What about you?"

"The same—we were just having fun. Nothing serious."

I nodded. I understood for the first time what it really means when a guy talks about having fun. "Same for me."

Sanford dropped his head then placed his hands on his thighs as he stood up. "I think I'm going to take off."

"But you just got here," I said.

"No, I was here for a second talking to the ladies before I said anything to you."

Unable to hide my disappointment, I said, "Oh, okay—well, if you have to go." *Ask him to stay, silly*. Sanford walked out the room and I followed behind him with the word "stay" still inside my mouth.

Karen awaited us at the bottom of the stairs. He walked into the living room where Jake moved through family and friends to greet him. They exchanged a few words, a laugh, and then Sanford turned around to hug more family, then walked back toward the door.

I felt like I was watching a movie, and the audience was commenting, "She is so stupid." Except, this is real, and it's me. He finally reached the door where Linda and Tobey were waiting to see him off. I continued to stand still, poorly pretending not to care. He touched my shoulder as he passed by, which sadly, meant the world to me. I turned only slightly to catch a glimpse of him walking out the door.

After five more hours, to my relief, everyone was gone except for Jake. He said goodbye to the last guest as I picked up the final remaining cups and napkins from the living room. Jake closed the front door and came into the room with me.

"Need any help?"

"You feel up to washing some dishes?"

"Yeah, it'll take my mind off things."

"Well, your mind should be occupied for a while, there's a nice pile in there." Jake went into the kitchen. He yelled back seemingly surprised by how many dishes there were. "I thought Karen and Tobey were on dish duty."

"They were," I said picking up the last napkin before walking into the kitchen. "But Tobey had to work—remember? She left about three hours ago."

"What time is it?"

"It's nine o'clock, Jake." He was standing in front of the sink, staring at the dishes. I handed him the trash bag. "Staring at them isn't going to make them go away. Never mind, I'll do it."

He gladly exchanged jobs and took the trash outside. "Are you sure?"

"I'm positive. I'll wash—you dry." I emptied the sink, then ran the dishwater. Jake walked past me taking off his suit jacket, hanging it on the back of the kitchen chair.

"This is familiar," he said.

I started washing and piling the clean dishes in the empty sink for him to rinse. "So does that mean you're going to bail halfway through? Then it'll really feel familiar to me too," I said with a hint of sarcasm as I laughed.

"Why do you always have to remember the bad stuff?"

"You didn't think that was funny?" I continued to laugh.

"No," he said splashing water at me. "I didn't."

I shrugged. "Huh, I didn't when it was happening to me, either."

We carried on, me washing, him drying, and then he said, "I talked to Sanford."

"Yes, I saw you."

"He was cool."

"Why wouldn't he be?"

"Ah, I never told you he checked on me after seeing me out with—you know who."

"You can say her name," I glanced at him. "Where was she, by the way?"

"I have no clue."

I gathered more dishes and put them in the sink. "Sure you don't."

"Why didn't Easton show up?"

"No clue either." I stopped washing dishes with my hands still in the water. "Wow, I forgot about him. What does that say about the state of the union?"

"Your relationship resembles the real one—dysfunction," he said and grinned.

"Okay, you get two snaps for that one," I pointed at the dishes still awaiting his touch in the sink. "Finish drying those—you're slowing down. I realize this is usually the point where you bail."

"Lucky for you I have absolutely nowhere to go."

"Finish telling me what Sanford said to you."

"Sanford was lucky I didn't kick his ass for what he said to me."

"You? White boys can't fight," I laughed. "Or is it jump?"

"It's jump," he said emphatically.

I was beyond curious, but would have no chance of getting it out of Jake if I appeared the slightest bit more interested than that. "You're right—it's jump. Okay, seriously, what got you so mad?"

"It doesn't matter. That was a long time ago."

I finished the last dish and put it in the sink. Jake continued his end of the deal as I began putting the dried dishes away. "I'm being nosey—what did he say?"

Jake stopped drying the dishes. "He had feelings for you when we were married. Did you know that?"

I turned around to face him to see he'd stopped working. "Oh, no," I pointed again to the dishes. "Rinse-dry-talk."

He turned on the water to rinse the last of it. "You didn't answer."

"No, I didn't."

"Is that the truth?"

"Of course it is. In the famous words of Tobey—why would I lie?"

Jake sat the last of the dishes on the counter. I started putting them away while he dried his hands then took a seat at the kitchen table. He rubbed his hands across the top. "I always liked this table." I bent down to put the pots in the lower cabinet. I couldn't help but snicker a little before standing back up. "It's a nice table," I said.

"Hey, thanks for everything today. I really appreciate it. I know Mom would've been happy with how things turned out."

I approached the edge of the counter nearest the table. "You think so?"

"I'm positive."

"Are you going to be okay tonight? You're welcome to crash over here on the couch."

"What happened to the guest room?"

I smiled. "I turned it into a closet."

He tilted his head. "Seriously?"

"Again—"

"I know-why would you lie. Thanks for the offer, but I'm going to head home." He stood up and put his suit jacket back on. I hugged him from behind laying my head against his ponytail.

"We turned out all right—didn't we?" Jake pulled my hand from around his waist and kissed the back of it. "Amazingly enough—we did."

"Trouble doesn't last always."

He raised his head toward the ceiling. "No, Mom, I guess it doesn't."

I watched him drive away through the blinds from the kitchen window. The house was back in order, but I had to go to work in the morning. Getting prepared for bed it hit me again, I hadn't heard from Easton, nor had I thought about him. Talking to him now seemed a little ridiculous. We haven't talked and tomorrow it will be a week. I was planning on telling him I wanted to stop seeing him, but I think he's stopped seeing me. Laughing at that took the final ounce of energy I had, casting me off to sleep.

Chapter Thirty-Four

Three weeks passed with no word from Sanford or Easton.

I was pretty clear on why Sanford and I weren't talking, but Easton—well, that one was a mystery. All I said was we needed to talk, which we did. I'd thought I had avoidance issues.

The wind woke me up from a sound sleep. I got out of bed and looked out the window. *It will be a cold Thanksgiving this year if this keeps up.* I got back into bed and cut on the television to check the weather to figure out how to dress for this wedding. The traffic was on—no news there. Weather on the twos, I think that's the promotion. He started talking about the weather in California—*nobody really cares about what's happening where they're not at.* The weatherman didn't seem to care what I thought, either. Finally Michigan, a high of fifty-four degrees—I might not freeze in a dress.

Either way, I had my information.

I reached over to my nightstand and grabbed the invitation, opened it and began reading to make sure I had the time correct. *All right Mr. Johnson, one o'clock it is.* I snuggled back under the covers. I could afford to lie here a few more minutes before getting the day rolling.

I felt so comfortable I dozed off. When the doorbell vibrated throughout the house I didn't want to move. I stared at the ceiling hoping whoever it was would go away. They didn't. The bell rang—then it did again, until I was forced to get up.

"Who is it?" I yelled from the top of the stairs, praying I wouldn't be compelled to go all the way down.

I heard a faint voice say, "It's me, Tobey."

Why is she here so early? I hopped down the stairs and answered the door. A strong wind pushed her inside. "Why are you here so early?" I asked.

"It's not early, it's eleven o'clock."

My eyes widened. "I only dozed off for a second," I said as she took her coat and laid it across the couch. "Are you kidding me?"

"No, I'm not—were you in bed?"

I ran back up the stairs with Tobey following behind me. "I don't even know what I'm wearing." Inside my room I went straight for the closet. "It's only eleven, slow down," she advised.

I walked into the other room and sat down in one of the dressing-room chairs with Tobey in the adjacent one. "You look really pretty," I said.

"Thank you. I can finally fit in a size ten again!"

"Why do you have on black? I thought black was bad luck."

"At a wedding? I never heard that before."

"If it's not, then I'm wearing my black tube dress with some pearls and call it a day."

I left Tobey in the dressing room, grabbed the dress and went into my room to take a shower. Afterward, I blew out my hair to wear it straight then met Tobey downstairs in the kitchen with almost a full hour to spare. She made coffee, which I was thankful for. "Will you know anybody besides Mr. Johnson at this thing?" she asked.

I took a sip from my cup. "I don't think so."

"Okay, well, we better get on the road if we want to beat the traffic."

"What traffic? It's Saturday."

She poured her remaining coffee out in the sink. "I don't know—*the* traffic. It's a long way."

I poured mine out too. "Girl, come on." We put on our coats and walked outside on the front porch. "Where is your car?" I asked.

"I didn't drive. Hunter dropped me off."

"I would've warmed up the car if I'd known that."

We both stood there on the front porch staring at one another. "Stop it," she laughed. "You can be so lazy. I'm going to this thing for you remember."

"Me? Lazy? Who keeps getting dropped off everywhere? Ever since you got a man you can't drive."

Inside the car felt colder than it did outside. We waited, allowing time for it to warm up for a few minutes, then headed toward the church. "Have you heard from Jake?"

"Yeah, earlier this week."

"How's he doing? Did he get his mother's stuff squared away?"

"For the most part—I went over Tuesday night and helped him pack some of it. The rest he was donating."

Tobey held her hands in front of the vents. "Do you think you and Jake could ever get back together?"

I took my eyes off the road for a split second to give her a well-deserved glare. "Are you joking?"

"It seemed like you two were getting along," She raised her hands to surrender. "I'm just asking."

"No. Getting along and back together is too very different things. We're friends, Tobey. That's it."

"Maybe you think that's it."

"Jake has a girlfriend, so I'm not the only one who thinks that's it."

"Oh wow, didn't know that."

"Neither did I, until I met her."

"He moves fast," she commented, shaking her head.

I laughed. "Jake is Jake."

We drove up a winding dirt road that ended on a hilltop. The church looked like a converted barn. There didn't seem to be a clear parking lot. Cars were everywhere. "Is this it?" Tobey asked. She looked around at the guests. "I think so. The barn must be the church."

"Yeah—this is the address."

"Where is the reception at? In a farm house?"

"Girl!" I pretended to smack her hand. "Stop it and get out. I think I see everybody following that gravel path."

The entire room was done up in holiday décor with the scent of pine, cinnamon and rosemary. We were seated at our table in sufficient time to take it all in. "I really like this," Tobey said admiring the view. "Maybe me and Hunter should get married someplace like this."

"I know—it's probably even prettier when it snows." We got up to walk around before the ceremony started, out the back doors down a wooden bridge to the cathedral. Outside,

I heard water streaming in the distance. Tobey pointed at another barn a little further off than we were. "Are those horses?"

Squinting, I tried to focus on what I thought I saw. "Yes, I think so. That over there looks like a sleigh."

"Oh, Hunter and I have to come back up here. This is so pretty."

"It wasn't that far. What would you say? About an hour to get here?"

"Or a little less." Tobey's voice trailed off. Something else drew her attention.

"What's wrong?" I asked, trying to find the distraction.

She pointed at a couple in the distance. I followed her finger. "Look at that man," she said. "I know I haven't seen him in a while—but, I could swear that's Easton."

My stomach took a turn inside out. "You're right—it's him."

"Who's the woman with him?" she asked.

"I don't know—his wife—maybe?"

"He's headed this way, so we won't have to guess for long."

Easton kissed his date on the cheek before she veered off into the church. He continued walking toward us. "Maybe I should give you a minute," Tobey said, as he got closer.

"Not necessary—you can stay."

She reached for my hand gently squeezing it and whispered, "No thank you. I think I'm going to sit this one out. See you inside."

Tobey and Easton exchanged pleasantries as they passed one another. "I didn't expect to see you here," he said.

"I could say the same for you."

He pointed to the left then the right. "So, which is it—bride or groom?"

"Groom."

He pointed at himself. "The bride."

I smiled. "Looks like we're on the opposite side of each other, counselor."

"It wouldn't be the first time," he pointed out.

"No, I guess it wouldn't."

"So, what happened to my three-day phone call?" He placed his hands in his suit pants pockets. "I waited."

"The phone works both ways." I nodded in the direction of the church. "Doesn't appear you waited long."

"Everything is not always what it seems," he said moving closer to me.

I put up my hand to block his approach. "Yeah, but then again, sometimes it is." I leaned in to kiss his cheek and whispered in his ear. "You take care." I walked back toward the church to give Easton time to be alone with his thoughts.

After the ceremony everyone seemed to be enjoying themselves, including us sipping wine. Easton and his date left shortly after the ceremony, which led to me getting fifty million (a slight exaggeration) text messages and a few phone calls. None of which I responded to which seemingly disturbed Tobey just as much as it must have annoyed Easton.

"That buzzing is driving me nuts—give it here." In search of Mr. Johnson I handed her the phone. Arnie, Mr. Johnson and his wife Donna, re-entered the church just as the reception got under way.

I tapped Tobey. "I'm going to go say hello and meet his wife." I left her at the table deep in the texted conversation Easton was having with himself. When I returned, I asked, "So, what did you learn, Scooby-Doo?"

She exhaled. "That Easton's an idiot," she said, "oh, and that was his wife."

I rolled my eyes. "I figured as much."

"That he's an idiot?"

I laughed. "No, the wife part."

She handed me back my phone. "You aren't the least bit curious?" I opened my phone and held my finger on his first message until I prompted to delete or save. I hit delete all messages.

"I guess not," she said. "He wants to be your man, girl."

"I already have a man—he just doesn't know he's my man yet."

"Uh oh, are you ready to check out of Heartbreak Hotel?"

"Yup, I gave up my standing reservation."

Tobey stood up and drank the rest of her wine. "That's my girl."

Chapter Thirty-Five

So the LORD God caused a deep sleep to fall upon the man, and he slept, then he took one of his ribs and closed up the flesh at that place. The LORD God fashioned into a woman the rib, which he had taken from the man, and brought her to the man. The man said, "This is now bone of my bones, and flesh of my flesh. She shall be called Woman, because she was taken out of man."

Genesis 2:22

Easton continued texting and calling throughout the following week. He went as far as to stop by once, but to no avail. I was out on an appointment. His inability to comprehend the truth wasn't my issue. I stated my position on the phone, then again via text. What we did—or didn't—have was over. He's in the friend zone, and I don't have sex with my friends. I was in love, and no longer scared about the likelihood of getting my heart broken. I needed Sanford to know what was in my spirit and in my heart, and if by some small miracle he still felt the same way, I planned to never leave his side.

My angels of mercy, Linda and Tobey, gave me a hint as to where Sanford would be for the evening. Ironically, it was the same place he'd brought me for the poetry reading. He sat alone at the far end of the bar doing the one thing nobody does at a bar—reading, with a sip of red wine remaining in his glass.

I sat down at one of the tables far from his line of sight, took off my coat and settled in. The server approached the table and took my order. I ordered myself a glass of wine and asked the server to send another of whatever Sanford was drinking over to him. I watched in the shadows as the bartender refilled Sanford's glass. They exchanged a few words, then the server turned and pointed in my direction. I waved my hand and mouthed "Hello." Sanford did the same accompanied with a smile. *Encouraging.* He picked up his book bag, slung it with his coat behind his back, grabbed his wine, book and headed to my table. I pulled out the chair for him.

"This is a nice surprise," he said, putting his things on the next table.

"Is it?" I asked. The server returned with my drink.

"Of course." He looked confused, pushing his chair back to look at me. "Why wouldn't it be?"

"I don't know." I stopped to gather my thoughts. "It seems like we haven't been on the same page for almost two years now."

"I think it's been a lot longer than that," he said before taking a drink.

I smiled. "This is what I'm talking about—I say two years, you say more. Don't you think we need to talk about this?" I hesitated. "I feel like you're angry with me."

"I'm always open to talking. And—" he looked directly into my eyes "—I'm not angry. I've just given up trying to convince you of anything."

That made me nervous, but I fortified my resolve with another swallow of wine. "I know you may not believe me, but I didn't know you cared about me the way you did."

He looked down into his glass. "That's not true, Alex." He looked back up at me. "Let's take a little virtual trip down memory lane—do you remember in your dorm room you were crying about some guy—what was his name?"

"I cried about some guy every other month," I admitted. "I don't remember his name."

Sanford snapped his fingers. "Larry—that's his name."

I wagged my finger, taking another hit of my drink. "Yup, Larry the loser."

"Yeah," he laughed. "Larry the loser. Well, after I dried the tears out of your hair and questioned your taste in men for the hundredth time I told you something. Do you remember what that was?"

My lies had become my truth. I knew how Sanford felt about me for all these years yet I'd continued to lie about it. *No more denying or lying allowed.* I took a deep breath, held it and exhaled the words, "You loved me."

"No," he said, "I confessed I was *in* love with you. And what did you say?"

I closed my eyes, wishing I'd said something other than the truth. "I didn't feel the same way."

The server returned to the table. Sanford raised his eyebrows, pointing to my glass. "Yes, I'll have another," I said.

"Two," Sanford informed the waiter. When he cleared the table Sanford continued. "And even though my manhood hung by a thread, I asked you, if there was any way you thought you could ever be with me, and you said—"

"No, we're friends."

"Just friends."

"Sanford, I was eighteen years old. I'm shocked you got *anything* thought provoking out of me. Those weren't exactly my wonder years."

"I knew that, which is why I decided the timing wasn't right. Figured you weren't ready for all this." He pointed at his head. "Now you know why I get upset when you say you didn't know—because I know that you did. You may not have been ready to hear it, but you knew."

"I did know—and you're right, I didn't want you to love me. What we had was something better. Friendship." I swallowed more wine. "I don't know if you've been paying much attention, but the men I love don't last very long."

"I'll grant you that, so fast-forward to last year, we hook up. It's good—at least I think it is—"

"I felt so, too."

"You couldn't have—because you broke it off a month after we got started."

I took in a deep breath. "In my head—"

"What?"

"Don't interrupt, hear me out," I said. "This is probably the most honest I've been with anyone, including myself, in a long time. Our relationship would have been ill fated if we'd stayed together. I felt that in my heart, and nothing could have convinced me otherwise."

Calmly he asked, "What are you basing this assumption off of?" He sat straight up in his chair. "Indulge me for a minute, I'm really curious, because it couldn't have been from me—you have no experience with me. All I did was love you, care about you, and worship the ground you walked on, so it couldn't have been me. Was it Larry? Jake, maybe? Oh," he snapped his fingers, "how about this married guy you're seeing? What's his name—Easton?" My mouth dropped open. "What about him? Tell me which one of these trick bags did you lump me into?"

I cursed each tear that welled up in my eyes, betraying every emotion I wanted to keep hidden. "Maybe we should stop talking about this."

"Be clear. This door will not be reopened without some work on your end," He leaned toward me. "I am not meeting you halfway. I came *all* the way to get you. You shut the door in my face." I started to say something when he raised his finger, shutting me down. "And it wasn't the first time. You came here for a reason—right? You still committed to getting what you want?"

"I am," I said, and then took another sip of wine.

"Then okay, Popeye, stay strong to finish without the liquid spinach."

I smiled. "I haven't heard you say that in a long time."

Firmly, he said, "Answer the question. Where do I fit into this melodrama you got going on?"

I inhaled all the oxygen in the room and blew it back out. "That's just it—you didn't fit. You're not familiar to me. Wait—maybe that's the wrong choice of words. What I mean to say is what I felt wasn't familiar to me."

"The word you're looking for is called *love*."

"I didn't care what it's called, only how it felt." I shivered. "Foreign and unfamiliar."

"Running away from love is taking you further away from me—"

"You need to understand that what I felt with Jake and Easton—it was familiar. I knew who to be and how to be. Familiarity made my life work, wife, victim, other woman, alone. I know these roles—heck, I wrote the script. Pain—I can do pain, avoidance, denial—I got all of that in my cookie jar. Happy? I haven't played that part before."

"So where does that leave me? Because happy—baby, that's all I got."

"That's all I need," I said simply. "I've spent more time worrying about being loved than building my ability to love someone else. You're all I need," I said again, reaching out for his hand. "I am so sorry it took me so long to get over my fear, but I'm a lot stronger now, and I'm not afraid of loving you, but more importantly . . . I'm the woman *I* needed to be, to love a man like you."

He signaled the server for the tab.

"I wasn't the only one who started seeing someone," I said.

The server put the bill on the table. "Yes, you were," said Sanford.

I snorted. "I didn't imagine the amazon from the modeling jungle."

"You didn't imagine Simone," he agreed, "just me being in a relationship with her." He put his money on top of the bill and held it up for the server to retrieve.

I didn't let go. "So what was that kiss, her leaping into your arms and all that about, then?"

"All for show," he said and shrugged. "I was and still am in love with you. Real love doesn't go away that easily. I've loved you my entire adult life. You think I'm going to forget you in a few months?"

"I feel silly now, but yeah, I did." The waiter came back to the table and took the money.

"Well—you were wrong." Sanford stood up. "Keep the change," he told the server.

I didn't know what to say or do. I felt like an open sore. I'd never been this desperate in my life to hold on to anyone or anything. I couldn't image life without Sanford in it. He was the only person who had always made sense. I stood up, sensing that our conversation was over and I'd failed to accomplish what I'd come here for.

Sanford put his own coat on before helping me with mine. We gathered our things in silence and headed out the door toward my car. "That you?" he pointed down the street.

I could feel it coming on. "Yeah, that's me." We continued walking until we reached my car. I nervously fumbled for my keys to open the door and popped the locks. I turned to Sanford. "Okay, then."

He pointed. "I'm parked right there." I looked down the street and saw his car.

"All right then," I said again, opening the door and threw my purse and myself inside. He stood there for a second, and then walked away. *Just in time.* I put the key in the ignition, started the car, then turned up the radio and sobbed. It hurt—I couldn't find the words to get him to forgive me. I draped my arms around my steering wheel and hugged it for dear life. I tasted tears and snot running down my face into my open mouth. I didn't care. I screamed I'm sorry—I'm so sorry—between choking down body fluids as quickly as I produced them.

I felt sick to my stomach. All the wine, tears and snot soured in me—it was coming up. I frantically pulled on the door handle. Locked. There wasn't enough time. I threw up in the only thing I had, my purse, which made me cry even more. My expensive parting gift from the divorce—ruined.

Just like my marriage, Sanford and me. I wailed some more, wiping my nose and face on my sleeve. The car windows were completely fogged up, preventing me from seeing anything or anyone outside. I only heard a single tap at the window. I cut down the music. My voice cracked, "Yes."

"Are you going to open the door?"

Jesus, you are not doing this to me. I quickly dried my face with my hands and wiped it on my pants leg. "Who is it?"

"Open the door," he said.

I reluctantly popped the locks. He opened the door immediately. He jumped right in and looked at my cracked, torn-up face. "Oh God, what happened to you?"

I started crying again. "You're what happened to me."

He looked around the car, puzzled in search of what was making his eyes burn. "What is that smell?" He held his hand up to his mouth. "Did you get sick in here?"

"A little," I said, tears streaming down my face.

Coughing he said, "Okay, let's get you outta here and into my car."

"What about my purse?"

He turned his head from side to side searching for it. "Is that where the vomit is?"

I nodded. "Yes."

"I pulled up behind you. Lock your car. I'm going inside to get a trash bag for the purse." I did as instructed and awaited Sanford in his car while watching him put the purse in a big black plastic bag then tie it. He wiped down my steering wheel, closed the driver's side door, and locked it before returning to his car and me. He pulled out more tissue from his pocket and dried my face then placed a tissue up to my nose. "You're on your own with this one," he laughed. I smiled and took the tissue from his hand to blow my nose. "All better?" he asked.

"Much," I confessed.

He continued to look at me through those dark frames. "I'm not trying to upset you—I hope you know that."

"I believe you're not, but you *are* hurting me."

He leaned back in the driver's seat then reached his enormous hand over and placed it on my chest. "I always thought the biggest wall blocking me from your heart was betrayal, but it turned out to be fear. Leaving made me realize I can't break down walls you've built, Alex. Only you can get rid of them and let me inside—you don't need protection from me."

I opened his jacket and put my hands underneath his shirt. I could feel his heart beating in between my fingers. "I love you more than life itself," I said. "You are the one person I don't need to safeguard my heart from and I know I've hurt you in the past, but if it takes the rest of my life showing you how deep, far and wide what I feel for you is— I'm willing to do that, because what scares me now isn't letting you in—it's you wanting to get out."

He pulled my hand from under his shirt and softly kissed the back of it. "Love never leaves," he said. "It's going to take more than a snotty nose and purse filled with vomit to get me away from you."

I smiled. "Good to know. So how does this end?"

"Well," he said. "Your happily-ever-after ends with you brushing your teeth." He was grinning. "Then making love to your forever man for the first time. How's that?"

I leaned toward him as we pulled off. "Yeah," I said and squeezed his arm a little tighter. "You in my life . . . for the rest of my life is all I'll ever want or need."

"That's good . . . because *happy* is all I got."

A List of Sources Consulted

Water Theory(Yu). (2014). *Hapkido philosophy.* Retrieved from http://www.internationalhapkido.co.uk/hapkido-philosophy.html